"WHO THE HELL ARE YOU?" PARKHILL DEMANDED. "TURN THAT MAN LOOSE BEFORE YOU GET HURT."

Ross covered the big man with his revolver, looking right over the sights. "Send an unarmed man for the doctor."

"If you don't stop givin' orders, *you're* gonna need the goddamn doctor!"

Ross watched his pistol sights float to the high ridge of Parkhill's cavalry cap. He squeezed his trigger, felt the satisfying recoil, saw Parkhill standing wide-eyed and hatless.

"Frank," said Parkhill. "Take your guns off and fetch a doc."

BY MIKE BLAKELY FROM
TOM DOHERTY ASSOCIATES

Comanche Dawn

Come Sundown

Dead Reckoning

Forever Texas

The Last Chance

Moon Medicine

Shortgrass Song

The Snowy Range Gang

Spanish Blood

Summer of Pearls

Too Long at the Dance

Vendetta Gold

— THE —
LAST CHANCE

Mike
Blakely

A TOM DOHERTY ASSOCIATES BOOK
NEW YORK

THE LAST CHANCE

Cover art by Dave Henderson

A Forge Book
Published by Tom Doherty Associates, LLC
175 Fifth Avenue
New York, NY 10010

www.tor-forge.com

Forge® is a registered trademark of Tom Doherty Associates, LLC.

ISBN-13: 978-0-8125-3027-8
ISBN-10: 0-8125-3027-6

First Edition: July 1995

Printed in the United States of America

0 9 8 7 6 5

ACKNOWLEDGMENTS

Thanks to my editor, Bob Gleason, a literary survivor out of the old rock.

A special thanks to Joe Vallely of the Flaming Star for riding points on the long trail.

ONE

THEY CALLED HER Chug. Ross wondered why, but he didn't ask. You kept your mouth shut in this man's army. You followed your orders and you didn't bother anybody with questions. When your sergeant said, "Private, you'll ride Ol' Chug today," you saddled Ol' Chug and awaited your order to mount.

She was the smoothest-riding horse Ross Caldwell had straddled since taking the Union oath. The other troopers bounced all around him on swaybacked nags, but he rode at a glide on Chug. He had covered hundreds of miles on stiff-legged cavalry cobs rough enough to split you in two from the crotch up, but this big gray mare could waltz.

You and your rump ought to be grateful, he thought. But he was not. Good fortune in the cavalry service tended to rouse Ross's suspicions. There was something wrong with all this. The other troopers should be grousing more. They should be coveting this mare. Ross hardly knew this Sergeant Parkhill, or any of the other men in this detachment. Why had he been given the privilege of riding Chug today?

And why "Chug"? It wasn't unusual that a horse like this should have a name. She stood out—a hand taller than any other mount in the string, sleek, well muscled, alert. He had heard that she came from the regimental band at Fort Laramie. But why "Ol' Chug"?

He pulled the brim of his campaign hat down low over his brow and squinted through the dust and the glare of summer sun on the dry plains. The valley of the North Platte fell away to his right, but his eyes kept drifting away to the left, where the Laramie Mountains rose. There were trees up on that near ridge. He could see rows of them sticking up like hackles on a dog's back. Trees meant shade. No shade down here.

Damn, these blue coats were hot. The grays had never seemed this stifling. Not even in Georgia. No cause to complain, though. This was still freedom, after all. Open territory as far as a man could see. A chance to start over in a young country. A chance to be with Julia. Sure, it was dusty. Hot, too. Cold last winter. Hard under the hailstones and lightning and sheets of pounding rain. But any common hell beat that prisoner of war camp in Chicago.

The telegraph wire stretched ahead of the riders, sagging between crooked posts as if it would melt in the sunshine. They had strung this section tight last winter, Ross recalled, after the blizzard winds had flattened four miles of it, snapping posts like toothpicks. Now the line drooped like strings of taffy in the heat.

It was broken somewhere west, and Ross had been riding with Sergeant Parkhill's detachment since dawn, looking for the break, wondering what had caused it this time. Probably Indians again. Ross fully expected to fight Indians today. If there were fewer than fifty, the detachment could hold them off. If there were more, he hoped Ol' Chug could run. Up to now, he hadn't let her go faster than a trot.

"The missus could ride her," a voice said to his right.

Ross looked, recognized the face, but couldn't place a name with it. "Pardon?" he said. The plains had murmured with Southern drawls since they rode out this morning, but this was the first to speak to him.

"Ain't she your wife? The laundry gal?"

"Yeah."

The corporal grinned. "Shore is nice to have a lady to talk to now and then. She's a fine lady. Your name's Caldwell, ain't it?"

Ross nodded. He saw Sergeant Parkhill look back at him, the dark pupil hard against the corner of the eye, the stubbled cheek bulging with tobacco.

"My name's Gene Dillon." The corporal thrust a tattered leather glove over the fork of his McClellan saddle.

Ross shook it. "Pleasure," he said. This Corporal Dillon had about six teeth missing from his smile. He had seen that gapped smile a time or two at

Fort Laramie. Several times at Camp Douglas, Chicago. And even that day in Ohio. The day of the battle at Buffington Island. Two years ago. The day he threw down his weapons and became a prisoner of war.

"How'd you end up in this outfit?" Dillon said.

"Been down with the grippe. My squad rode to Platte Bridge without me and I got reassigned."

"Lucky for us you got sick," said a high-pitched voice. A blond-haired private reined his horse closer.

"What do you mean?" Ross said.

"I reckon your wife would have gone to Platte Bridge with you."

Ross nodded. "I reckon you're right."

"That would have left us shy of women around camp."

Ross smirked down at the private. The first sergeant at Camp Marshall kept a Cheyenne wife. One of the civilian scouts lived with a Sioux woman whose sister also stayed with them. A couple of privates and the camp sutler had also taken Indian wives. "There's half a dozen women there yet," he said.

Dillon and the yellow-haired private laughed at Ross from both sides.

"I ain't talkin' about no half-assed squaw brevet-wife," the girlish voice said. "I mean the genuine thing—a Southern white gal. We ain't got but one of them."

Ross didn't like the way he said "we," but he let it go. In a way, Julia did belong to everybody in K Company, 11th Ohio Cavalry. She was its inspiration. A heroine to every man in uniform. In that way, Ross knew he had to share her. "Maybe when the new captain gets to camp, he'll bring a wife with him," Ross suggested.

"Wouldn't be a Southern gal," the blond-haired private said. "Better not be, anyway. No damned Yankee captain better not marry a Southern gal while I'm still a Rebel."

Sergeant Parkhill tightened his reins and let his mount fall back between Chug and the mount of the blond-haired private. "He ain't married, anyway," Parkhill said.

"Who?" Dillon asked.

"The new company commander we're fixin' to get. Captain Jasper Jones. Now, ain't that a name for a Yankee greenhorn?" He drilled Ross with a squint, craned his neck, spit on his mount's rump, adding to the brown streak that trickled down the horse's leg, collecting dust.

For a bunch of soldiers in Union fatigues, these men sure threw that term "Yankee" around freely enough, Ross thought. Every man in this detachment, though a former Rebel, wore Yankee blue now. Galvanized Yankees, as the newspapers called them, although Ross couldn't figure why. To galvanize meant to coat with zinc—at least that's what it had meant back in his father's hardware store in Georgia. He couldn't see that he had been galvanized. A Georgia Rebel-turned-Yankee coated with zinc? What kind of sense did that make?

"I said, ain't that a name for a Yankee greenhorn?" Sergeant Parkhill growled. He rode a shorter horse, but his own height made up for it, and he looked square at Ross.

"Sounds like it," Ross said. This big sergeant seemed to be testing him for something. Ross didn't really know Parkhill, but remembered him wearing the tattered rags of a prisoner in Camp Douglas, Chicago. It was still strange to see him wearing blue, though he wore it with no great pride—his jacket and shirt both missing buttons, revealing a patch of chest hair under his sweaty civilian bandanna.

"How do you know this Jasper ain't married, Park?" Corporal Dillon asked.

"I've studied up on him. They kicked him out of West Point for sneakin' out to meet girls. Went through some academy for his commission. Only fought one battle before the war ended. Kennesaw Mountain. Got his arm shot off. Don't know a damn thing about Indians. He'll get us all killed if we give him a chance." The dark pupil drilled Ross again. "Of course, we won't give him a chance, will we, Private?"

Ross squirmed in the saddle. He couldn't tell if Parkhill was joking, or what. "I don't guess that would do us much good," he said.

"Riders comin' back!" a voice shouted.

Ross saw the two plumes of dust slanting against the sky, like twin whirlwinds. Behind them, something he hadn't noticed before. A haze in the air, hanging low—a reddish blur under the crisp blue of the big sky.

Parkhill spurred ahead to meet the advance patrol. As the riders reported, the big sergeant sat hunched in his saddle, turning once to splatter tobacco juice on the rump of his horse. He was an intimidating specimen, Ross thought. Shoulders like a bull, legs like whiskey kegs, a trim waist, a jaw like a block of granite and fists to match. Crafty, too. The only Galvanized Yankee Ross knew of who had managed to climb to the rank of sergeant. He hated Yankees, yet could get whatever he wanted from them. The upper echelon considered him a model soldier.

When the detachment caught up to its sergeant and scouts, Parkhill was drawing his Colt revolver from his cavalry holster. "Get ready, boys," he said. "They're over the next divide."

"Who?" Dillon asked.

"The bastards that busted our telegraph wire. Hundreds of 'em."

"Hundreds!" the yellow-haired private said. "Then let's turn tail and git!"

"You do and I'll shoot you in the back, Lloyd. No coward deserves any better than that."

Ross glanced at the other faces, felt the familiar throb of sick fear in his stomach. Time after time he had held it down and charged into ridiculous dangers. He had never taken worse than a scratch from bullet or bayonet, but this looked like the final charge. Hundreds of Indians over the divide and a sergeant crazy for battle.

"Park, there ain't but seventeen of us," Dillon argued. "Why the hell should we go attackin' 'em?"

"They ain't carryin' no guns. Just pointy things to stick you with. We'll stampede 'em before they figure out what the hell hit 'em. Form a skirmish line and draw your weapons!"

Ross groped at the flap of his holster. Were they really going to do this? Outnumbered—what—ten to one? Twenty to one?

As they trotted toward the divide, he began to figure out why he was riding Ol' Chug. His head stuck up higher than any other—a tempting target. And which horse would the Indians want most? He could already feel their arrowheads and spear points. He remembered the bodies of horribly tortured settlers he had come across on the plains. Staked to the ground, burned, slashed, scalped, butchered.

He felt the initials, *RWC*, that he had carved into his pistol butt, slipped his hand around the wooden grip, and drew the Remington from his holster.

The war was over. Everybody else had gone home. But Ross Caldwell had switched armies, found new enemies. Oh, how could this be happening? Why now? Why here? What would become of Julia?

Two

———◆———

HE SENSED SOMETHING in the air besides dust. A hum, like voices at a crowded ball, but different. It came from over the divide, through the rattle of the detachment. Ross thought he heard a cough, a moan, maybe the collective chaw of a great herd grazing.

He glanced down the line, saw Parkhill grinning around the quid in his cheek. This army life galled a reasonable man. He could not fathom why maniacs so readily made rank.

They approached the telegraph pole planted at the top of the divide, the cursed wire dragging the ground under it. A spiderweb stood a better chance of lasting in this hostile wilderness. Ross reckoned a million splices must have been made by now between Missouri and California—all so the newspapers could spread rumor and the army

could issue its ridiculous orders. Might as well dig
a ditch and fill it with the blood of soldiers and Indians who had killed each other along this route.
Send messages down that. They said the railroad
would follow the telegraph line. The railroad was
a damn fool if it did.

He held his Remington revolver at his shoulder.
Chug smelled something, her nostrils flaring, ears
angling forward. She wanted to lope, but Ross
held her back. Maybe his luck would hold. It had
to be hard to aim those bows. He wondered what
an arrow felt like piercing one's skin, slicing
through muscle, slamming into bone.

One thing for sure. The moment Sergeant
Parkhill gave up his scalp, Ross was going to turn
tail and see how fast Ol' Chug could run.

Riding a head taller on the big mare, he saw
first over the rise—a sight he could scarcely
gather. The sallow plains had grown dark and rip-
pled now like windblown waters. Sunlight struggled through the haze of dust overhead and
glinted against curves of black horns. Something
twitching violently a quarter mile away caught
his eye. A telegraph pole: a scratching post for a
woolly buffalo bull. It cracked and fell across the
back of a cow, sending a shock wave through the
herd as a stone tossed into a pond.

"God A'mighty!" Dillon said under his breath,
wheezing with relieved laughter. "It's buffler!"

"You expect Indians?" Parkhill said. "You think
I'd risk my ass for a damn piece of Yankee wire?"

"No, but I 'spected you might risk mine."

The herd found the riders on the divide and
started moving away.

"They're fixin' to git," Lloyd said, pressing his hat down tight over his blond hair.

"And we're fixin' to git after 'em," Parkhill said, speaking loudly. "Give 'em a Rebel yell, boys, and lay 'em low!"

Ross gouged with his spurs as the voices rattled and whooped like a whole battalion. His fear lifted like a bank of steam, and joy rushed into his heart. Ol' Chug surged ahead, and he gave rein. Within two leaps she had the lead. Yes, Ol' Chug could run!

The muzzle of his carbine slipped out of the socket on the saddle ring and began to bounce on his right thigh, so he held it down with his elbow. If it went to flailing just right on the strap slung across his shoulder, it would raise knots all over him.

He saw heels and bristly tails appear through the dust ahead. He heard—no, *felt* a rumble that must be shaking Georgia now. He spotted a hump higher than the others—a big bull. He cocked his revolver as he faintly heard Gene Dillon's voice:

"Hold on, Ross!"

He couldn't find his gun sights for the dust and the rollicking gallop, but he aimed by instinct, pointing his weapon at the bull. He almost had to hit something in the mass of woolly flesh ahead of him.

His pistol bucked and he rode instantly through the pungent black smoke. All at once he saw the buffalo butt the ground and roll, heard a concerted volley behind him, and felt Chug leap forward under him.

He cocked his feet outward to keep his toes in the stirrups, felt the cantle rising hard against his rear. The mare hadn't even begun to use her steam! Ross groped for leather, managed to pull himself back into the seat. His heels found the stirrups. Now he leaned back on the reins, but Chug charged headlong among the galloping buffalo. She had taken the bridle bit in her teeth. Ross jerked. The bit was lodged! Like trying to rein in a locomotive or a riverboat chugging downstream.

Didn't they call her Ol' Chug?

Ross saw a tongue lolling out against his right knee, an eye rolling back in a mass of dark curls, a blunt black horn crusted with dried mud and hair. He heard another volley, and Chug angled in front of the bison, bumping it aside as she streaked deeper into the herd, gun-shy and cold-jawed.

He jerked the reins, felt them jerk back as Chug stretched her neck through the stampeding bison. He smelled a hundred cuds. His carbine bounced off his knee, whirled on its swivel, slammed its barrel against his shoulder, came down on his thigh, sprang up to his cheek. It beat him like a living nightmare on a tether until he managed to knock it down and pin it with his elbow.

He felt for his holster with his pistol barrel and glanced back, as if help might be coming. He saw galloping bison, three rows deep, billows of dust rising behind them. He had to make Chug stop, or they would tell stories about how he disappeared in the stampede, never again to be seen.

He pulled the right rein, hard and wide. Chug ran cockeyed, head sideways, but veered a little to the right. He wrapped the rein once around his hand and pulled wide again, looking over his right shoulder. He saw an opening behind him—a gap in the stampede.

His shoulder muscles were burning with the strain when he saw the hooves of the cavalry mounts cutting the dust behind him. A corridor had appeared in the buffalo herd, but it wouldn't last long. He took a wrap with the left rein, pulled with everything he had as he flung the leather from his right. Swinging his right leg over the cantle, he jumped clear, taking up slack on the rein as he sailed through acres of dust.

The rein jerked tight, stretching him out to bounce hard on the ground. Chug bowed her head, touched her nose to the dirt, and somersaulted as Ross burrowed into dirt, slid, hit a clump of grass, rolled.

He saw the belly of a horse pass over him, then dirt clogged his eyes. His ears rang. The ground quivered under him.

"You all right?" Dillon's voice said.

Ross wheezed, choking on lingering clouds of soil, but he nodded at the trooper.

"Knocked his wind out," Dillon said.

Ross heard the yellow-haired private laughing over him.

"Bet you wondered how come us let you ride Ol' Chug!"

"Stand back!" Parkhill said, casting his shadow on Ross's face. He put his palms on his knees and peered down, the bulge in his cheek like a grotesque goiter in silhouette. "You're all right. Give me your hand."

Ross reached upward, felt the sergeant's big hand grasp his like a vise. Parkhill lifted him to his feet, but as he rose, he felt something in the grip of the sergeant—two deliberate points of pressure, alternating, from the little finger to the index finger. Ross belonged to the brotherhood. He knew a secret grip when he felt one. But this was not the Masonic grip. It was something else. Parkhill was testing him out. Did he belong? Belong to what? He stared at the sergeant, coughed, squinted dust from his eyes.

Parkhill released his grip. He wrenched his thick neck to spit over his right shoulder, a dismounted private dodging to avoid the brown stream. The sergeant shook his head. "I don't know about you, Caldwell. I just don't know."

Ross took a sudden idea. He squeezed one eye shut and looked sideways, at just the left side of Parkhill's face. Yes, now he remembered. The huge bulge of tobacco had been throwing him off. There had been no tobacco inside Camp Douglas. That was where he knew the sergeant from. They had spent a year behind the walls of the same prisoner of war camp in Chicago.

Gene Dillon's tooth-shy smile and Lloyd's pale yellow hair came together now, too. They had always been a trio—Parkhill their leader. The memories he had forced aside were surfacing again. This big Union sergeant had commissioned himself a Confederate captain in Camp Douglas, created a secret troop of Rebel cavalry. They had all looked different then—half-starved and sickly—but it was them. The Knights of the Golden Circle. And now he knew their secret grip.

"Mount up!" Parkhill shouted. "Take the humps and tongues, then we'll have to go back to camp for more wire and poles."

Ross caught Chug, backed her up to test the bridle bit. She was fine now: a model of equestrian discipline. He mounted and began checking his gear as he rode toward the nearest kill. He seemed engaged with his equipage, but his mind was drifting back, trying to remember how he had landed so far west with this bunch of Confederates in Union dress.

THREE

ROSS HAD WANTED no part of the Rebellion when it began. He had never owned slaves. He wasn't mad at any Yankees. He had friends in the North, in fact, and did business with them through his father's hardware store in Athens. And he had just married Julia Lynn Porter, daughter of a town councilman. This was no time for running off to get shot at.

The conscription law gave him no choice. He donned the gray, kissed his bride good-bye, left Athens. He owned a horse, so he wound up in the cavalry under General John Morgan. He learned to mask his fear in a Rebel yell. He did his duty. He was, he thought, neither hero nor coward.

Then one day he and another trooper, looking for forage, spotted a cornfield and crossed a creek to get to it. As they came out of the creek bed, a squadron of Union infantry opened fire on them from the rail fence across the field.

Ross's partner took a rifle ball in the chest and gouged his mount with his spurs as he fell back. The horse bolted, carrying the wounded rider into the center of the cornfield, dropping him there, as Ross managed to rein his horse back into the creek bed for cover.

He could have ridden back to his company. He knew his partner only well enough to know that he didn't like the man very much. He didn't even know if the man was still alive, but he lay alone out there in that cornfield between Ross and a squadron of enemy foot soldiers.

Thinking about it took only a fragment of a moment, then Ross was off his horse, tying the reins to a switch. He knew the Union boys would detect his approach through the field. He had plowed across only three furrows when the fusillade began.

What had only been an idea a second before was happening now. He was charging a superior force to rescue a man that might well be already dead. Between the rifle reports, he heard bullets clipping the broad leaves of the green corn plants. An ear exploded beside his head. He kept running, following the path the horse had half trampled into the field.

When he got there, he found the man heaving strangely for breath, blood spurting from his wound. The Union men were shouting, rattling ramrods down their barrels. The soldier looked up and smiled as Ross reached for him.

Bullets cut the corn like sickles again as Ross struggled to run under the weight of his fellow

Rebel. When he reached the creek, he had a dead man on his back, and the Union boys were cheering him—cheering as if he were General William Tecumseh Sherman.

He mounted and rode up the creek bed, never telling anyone what he had done, not understanding it himself. Was he fool or hero? He couldn't say. But the image of that smiling Rebel stayed with him in glory.

He did not, of course, tell Julia. She would have felt more rage than pride. He wrote letters to her daily, telling her about camp life, the boredom, how he missed her cooking, her embrace. He did not mention the casualties. That would only have upset her. He knew she wrote back every day, but her replies only occasionally found him in camp.

Then came Indiana, Ohio, invasion of the North. Total defeat at Buffington Island, he and hundreds of his fellow Rebels swarmed under by bluecoats. A hard march to Chicago. Camp Douglas—a greater hell than battle.

He found walking corpses there. The men were sick, dirty, ragged, covered with fleas and lice. Some of them could only wallow in their own filth along the latrine ditches, too weak with dysentery to crawl back and forth to the barracks. The dead left daily, wrapped in blankets.

Ross stopped to help a fellow prisoner one day, the man delirious with fever, writhing on the ground, cursing. "Let the son of a bitches take me!" he said. "God, let 'em have me!" His shredded clothes were alive with fleas. His skin hung across his bones like soiled white linen. Ross rolled the man over to help him up and found maggots crawling in open sores on his knees.

"Oh, they've got me!" he screamed. "They're all over me!"

One morning, his third month there, he walked to the edge of camp, stopped at the line of lime wash on the ground—the dead line, the guards called it. The plank wall of the prison camp stood fifty feet away. He looked up at the sentry house, the guard looking back at him, the rifle barrel jutting over the wooden rail. He could step over and end it. Wasn't it better to die trying to escape than to rot by degrees?

But what if the war ended tomorrow? What if Julia came next week?

He turned away from the line while he could still walk. When he came crawling, consumed by vermin and maggots, he would cross it.

He stole scraps of paper, hid his stub of a pencil, begged the Union clerks to mail his letters. A single page from Julia found him, lifting him higher than the prison walls. He saw Georgia that day. The page said she was trying to borrow money to get to Chicago.

He was shivering in his blanket one day, sitting on the floor of the barracks, methodically picking lice from his hair, pinching them between his fingernails.

"You Rebels get up!" a guard shouted, bursting in. "It's your turn in the house."

As he shuffled across the frozen yard on bare feet, Ross mulled over the rumors he had heard. Some called it an interrogation. Others said it was an interview, a survey. A wild-eyed man from another barracks had said it was a way out. He was a big man who called himself Captain Parkhill, though he wore a sergeant's stripes. This Parkhill was always whispering and plotting with a clutch of hardened men. Two in particular seemed always at hand. One with a bunch of teeth missing, the other yellow-haired.

"It ain't treason if you don't mean it," Parkhill had said. "An oath can't change allegiance. The idea is to get out of here and finish the Rebellion."

Ross waited, shivering, outside the guardhouse until the prisoner before him had left. Then he entered to find a one-armed lieutenant sitting behind a desk, the empty left sleeve folded up and pinned short.

The young officer glanced at Ross's bare feet, his hatless head. "Sit down," he said.

"I'd rather stand at the stove," Ross replied.

"Very well. State your rank, name, and native state."

He saw a pen in the lieutenant's hand, a large ledger book open in front of him. "Private Rossiter Caldwell, Georgia."

"What is your age?"

"Twenty-three."

The lieutenant made an entry in the book, dipped the pen in his inkwell. "I have a few questions to ask you, Private Caldwell. They are all hypothetical and independent of one another. Do you understand?"

Ross rubbed his hands above the stove. He nodded. His whole body suddenly convulsed with a short-lived shiver.

With the heel of his one hand, the lieutenant adjusted a leaf of paper over his book and read from it. "Given the opportunity, would you desire to go South as a prisoner of war for exchange?"

Ross's eyes widened. "Yes, sir," he said. He watched as the one-armed officer made a mark in the book.

The little finger of the clean white hand moved down the page to point to the next question. "Given the opportunity, would you desire to take the oath of allegiance to the United States of America, and be paroled from this camp, under penalty of death if found in the South before the end of the war?"

His eyes shifted, and he took a moment to interpret the language. "Yes," he answered, coming now to the chair the officer had offered. Yes, to get out of this prison, he would speak a damned oath.

"Given the same opportunities and penalties, would you desire to be sent North to construct public works?"

Ross sank to the hardwood surface of the chair. "What kind of public works? Forts? Breastworks?"

The officer tapped the page of questions with the point of his pen, leaving an ink spot. "I'm not sure," he said.

"Then neither am I, sir." He sniffed, rubbed a tattered sleeve under his nose.

The officer scrawled a note in his book. "Given the same opportunities and penalties, would you take up arms against the Southern Rebels?"

Ross sneered at the book. "I believe I am a Southern Rebel."

"What is your answer?"

"Of course not."

The one-armed lieutenant put a mark in its column, then looked up from the book, into the sunken eyes of the prisoner. "If given the opportunity, would you take the oath of allegiance to the Union and enlist in the Army of the U.S. to be sent to the western territories?"

Ross stared at the officer for several seconds. This was the real question. He could sense it. The officer had committed the words to memory and was looking back at him to judge his response.

"For what purpose?" Ross said.

The lieutenant lay his pen aside and fell back in his chair. He shrugged, causing the empty sleeve to flap. "I would presume to protect travelers and settlers from hostile Indians."

He's only a couple of years older than me, Ross thought. I could have been an officer. This one's brass buttons are tarnished, his hair unkempt, jacket wrinkled. I guess it's hard to press a jacket with just one arm, though. How will I look in Union blue?

"What is your answer, Private?"

"Well, sir. West ain't South, and West ain't North. Yes, I'd take the oath and go West. I'd rather fight Indians than tribes of vermin."

Several weeks passed before Ross heard his name on a muster roll for the 1st U.S. Volunteer Infantry. He was allowed outside the walls of Camp Douglas, given a uniform, fed decent rations.

The regimental surgeon interviewed him one

day in a hospital tent. "Have you ever been sick?" he asked.

"No, sir," Ross answered, lying straight-faced. He only thought the words he wanted to say: Yes, sir. Sick of your lousy Camp Douglas.

"Have you ever had fits?"

"No, sir." But I expect I might have if I hadn't gotten out of Camp Douglas.

"Ever received an injury or wound upon the head? A fracture, dislocation, or sprain?"

"No, sir." What if I have? There's a war going on, you damned fool.

"Are you in the habit of drinking?"

"No, sir." Except when I'm thirsty.

"Have you ever had the horrors?"

"No, sir." Except for Camp Douglas.

"Are you subject to piles?"

"No, sir." Except for those piles of unthinkables I was subject to inside.

"Do you have any difficulty urinating?"

"No, sir." Would you like a demonstration?

A dozen desertions occurred after word came that they would travel west to Fort Laramie, in the Dakota Territory. Ross feared the army would send all the converted Rebels back behind the prison walls, but nothing of the kind happened.

The day before they were to board the train west, he still hadn't heard from Julia. He had to wonder if he would ever see her again. He had tried to explain in his letters why he had joined the Yankee army. For all he knew, she considered him a traitor. He might go back to Georgia after the war to find a lynch rope waiting for him, Julia ready to fix it around his neck.

It was the self-commissioned Captain Parkhill
who provided him with a patriotic argument.
Parkhill was a Union corporal now, having already convinced the company commander to pro-
mote him from private.

"Hey, soldier," he said, catching Ross alone in a
four-man tent the last day in Chicago. "Have you
heard there's a meeting of the Golden Circle tonight?"

"The what?" Ross said.

"The Knights of the Golden Circle. Ain't you
ever heard of 'em?"

"No."

"Are you true to the South?"

"I'm from Georgia!" Ross said, lifting his chin.

Parkhill glanced both ways down the row of
tents. "The Knights mean to carry the war west.
There's a secret meeting tonight in the woodlot,
after taps."

Ross caught Parkhill looking at the letter he
was writing to Julia and put his forearm across
the fresh ink. "Are you a member?"

"I'm just tellin' you what I've heard, soldier."
And he withdrew from the tent, his shoulders almost pulling it down as he left.

Ross turned back to the letter, picked up his
pen.

. . . You must understand, my dearest Julia,
that even in this, the army of my recent enemy,
I cause no harm to my beloved Georgia. Perhaps I may even serve the South in the Army of
the Potomac, or serve the causes of Southerners
in the West. I take not lightly my allegiance to

the Confederacy, but how shall I serve her rotting to death in prison?

Oh, Julia, that this war might end, and I might enfold my trembling arms again about you. I fear neither battle nor death, only life without you . . .

FOUR

THE DRY WIND blew hot across her hands, cupped as they were around the hewn points of the timbers at the top of the watch tower. Another minute here and her hands would dry, crack, bleed. It was better to go back down the ladder and plunge them into the laundry barrel again, into the harsh lye soap and wads of dirty woolen uniforms.

Behind her, and below the guard tower on which she stood, Camp Marshall writhed with rare energy. The new company commander, Captain Jasper Jones, had arrived, and every soldier was making his first impression count. The sentry on duty beside her stood at attention on his post, glaring across the valley, trying hard not to blink.

Julia lifted the chestnut hair from the back of her neck, the hot wind cooling her sweat there, feeling good. She put the other hand on the small of her back, arched the kinks out of her spine, twisting her hips. She caught herself and snapped to attention, her hands falling on the points of the timbers again. It wasn't wise to provoke all these men with too much bodily undulation. A woman had to remember her military bearing here.

East of camp, La Bonte Creek twined through the valley like a long spangled snake lazily taking in sunshine on its way to the North Platte. Greenery only feathered its flanks, hard-pressed by shortgrass and sage-covered slopes. Ross had looked magnificent riding up them this morning on the big gray mare, his crisp, clean uniform sitting ramrod-straight in the saddle.

Julia was bone-weary of war and Indian campaigns. She longed for days of peaceful civilian pursuits. But she still admired the way her husband looked in his cavalry outfit—the dark blue blouse over the azure britches, the shine of polished black leather from knee boots and the rifle strap slung across one shoulder, the hat cocked forward on Ross's head. He had the legs of a horseman, the dash of a cavalry soldier, and she would always remember him that way, even after he traded his uniform for a store clerk's apron and went back to hawking hardware.

He had looked as well in the Confederate grays she had tailored for him before he left her in Georgia. She had watched him ride away in them, too. She was a silly young bride then, weeping because she figured she was supposed to. Now she knew a cry was not a thing to waste; now she had wept genuine tears and somehow cherished every one as a pearl.

She had had her first real cry when she learned

the truth about Camp Douglas, Chicago. News of
Ross's capture had actually relieved her until
then. She had assumed he would be safe there, removed from combat. But a letter from another
Camp Douglas inmate, to his wife in Athens,
found its way to her, and the horror occurred to
her all at once. In his one letter that had gotten
through, Ross had said nothing of the sickness,
the filth, the death. But he was like that, never
one to worry another with his own trials.

Julia knew she would have to go to Chicago, but
there was no money, no reliable transportation.
When she received his letter saying—almost apologetically—that he would rather take the Union
oath and go west than endure another year in
prison, she left Athens on foot with food for only
two days. She would never see him again if she
didn't. He would not come back to Georgia after
wearing Union blue.

She slept in a barn the first night, under a
wagon the second. The third day north, she heard
distant gunfire. It lasted all day. At dusk she
reached the tents, soaked by the rains that
seemed to follow all big artillery battles. She
thought the soldiers might feed her.

As she spoke to one of the pickets, a soldier
staggered aimlessly by her, bleeding from a terrible wound that had taken one ear off. She steered
him back toward camp, asking for the hospital
tent. As she sat the man among other bloody,
moaning uniforms, a harsh voice called out:

"You, girl! Come here! I need you!"

Julia looked up to see a heavyset woman standing in the opening of the tent. The front of her

dress was covered with blood, and she held a pair of scissors in her hand.

"Well, come on! Hurry up!" The big woman turned back into the tent.

Julia saw two men staring at her, one with a ball of bloody bandages around the stump of a leg, the other with an empty sleeve dangling. She swallowed and went into the tent.

"Put these limbs out," the big woman said. "They're piling up."

Julia stood over the arms and legs, mounded randomly like branches on a beaver dam.

"Buck up, girl, and make us some room. Boys are dying!"

She picked up a leg, warm and limp, cut off above the knee. Carrying it outside, she found a patch of muddy ground to drop it on. She thought of running, but a soldier inside was screaming, and she did not care to think herself a coward.

She stacked the limbs like cordwood. They were cold and stiff on the bottom of the pile. "What do you need now?" she asked the woman.

The big bloody matron glanced at her pale face, looked closely at her for the first time. "You can't be more than nineteen. How long have you been a nurse?"

"I'm not a nurse," Julia said.

"Then who are you?"

"Just a wayfarer," she said, her Southern voice smoothing the edges from the words. "My husband's been taken prisoner and sent north."

"When was the last time you ate?"

"Yesterday, but I'm not hungry now."

A surgeon was calling for a saw.

"Go out and find the ones we can save," the

nurse said, turning to the table. It was a common kitchen table, strewn with bloody cutting instruments. "Get the worst ones first, but if they're dying, let them lie in peace."

Two days later, Julia rode a supply wagon north, the horrors of the hospital tent lingering, oozing among her thoughts. She felt a lasting pity for the dead and wounded, but none had disgusted her, no matter how terrible the wound, how mangled the flesh. She surprised herself in this, and set her jaw as she rode north. Things would turn out all right. The West could be no worse than that battlefield.

She came out of the green grass to a field of mud—a vast mire stamped by thousands of marching feet. Over the sagging canvas ridges of the troop tents she saw the plank walls of Camp Douglas. She smelled beans cooking, heard the swearing Southern voices. The four men at the first tent sprang as if to attention when she approached.

"I'm looking for my husband," she said. "His name is Ross Caldwell."

The men looked at each other.

"I don't know him, ma'am," said one.

"You can find the lieutenant and check the roll," said another, "but some of the boys are changin' their names. Don't want their real names to go down on Union rolls."

"Where is the lieutenant?"

"The big tent up the row," a private said, pointing.

Julia quickened her step. Oh, for a bath. But she had freshened up some at the creek a few

miles back, crushed some wild rose petals for perfume.

She rapped on the tent post, saw the surprise in
the lieutenant's eyes as he looked out through the
open flaps. "I'm looking for my husband. His
name is Ross Caldwell." She glanced at the men
standing all around, staring at her, but none was
Ross.

The officer sprang from his stool. "Please, come
in. I'll check the rolls."

"I'll wait out here," she said, searching a new
face among the tents.

The lieutenant came out with the muster roll.
"Rossiter Caldwell?"

Her heart vaulted into her throat. "Yes."

"He's assigned to Company B right now. Tented
on the next row over, at the end. If you wish, I can
send someone . . ."

Julia had already turned. Her foot slipped as
she mounted a trot. She sprang over a guy rope,
reached the next row of tents. Toward the end,
she slowed her pace, peered into a couple of
tents, catching one soldier shirtless. She turned
her eyes quickly, pursed her lips in frustration.
He was here. Ross was right here. She couldn't
stand this.

"Ross!" Her own voice surprised her, squeaking
down the row, silencing the low voices of men.
"Ross Caldwell!" She turned, saw heads poking
out of tents. "It's Julia, Ross! Where are you?" She
came around, full circle, found him standing four
tents down, paper in one hand, pen in the other.
Thin, drawn, nearly beaten, but it was him.

He dropped the letter on the mud as she ran toward him. He lifted her from her feet, pressed his

stubbled face against her neck as three other men poured from the tiny tent.

"God forgive me, Julia," he murmured, his voice breaking.

"Hush, Ross."

A Galvanized Yankee looked at the sky and nudged one of his comrades. "No rain tonight, boys. We'd best quarter outside."

FIVE

THEY WERE HURTING now—all those places that had taken blows from the flailing carbine and the trembling ground. But Camp Marshall was in sight and Ross was thinking more of Julia. Soon he would be alone with her inside their little log cubicle, and he could forget about his bruises, Sergeant Parkhill, and the Knights of the Golden Circle.

Suddenly she appeared in the guard tower, her faded print dress setting her apart from the uniforms on sentry duty. He saw her hand raise and wave, and he waved back, unable to keep his face from grinning.

"Look at him, Gene," said the yellow-haired private named Lloyd. "Looks like a damn possum."

"Hell, I'd grin, too, if I was him," Gene replied.

Ross paid them little heed. He was squinting ahead, the grin melting from his face. Julia was saying something. Her signs were subtle, but he knew her every move. She was like a signalman to him. She stood at attention, then looked purposefully down into the fort.

Ross saw Sergeant Parkhill's mount turn. The big man twisted in the saddle, spit on the horse's rump, and drilled Ross with a glare. "She tryin' to tell you somethin', Caldwell?"

The sergeant might as well have stepped between them in a dance. He had no business intruding like that, and it galled Ross more than his bruises, more than the fatigue of the hard day's ride.

It alarmed him, too. This Parkhill missed nothing. Not even signals sent unspoken between a wife and husband. Yet, Ross enjoyed his leverage. Only he could interpret Julia this way. He knew what was going on in the fort. He might have gloated over it, and kept the intelligence to himself, but he wanted to make a good first impression. He would stand out on Chug. Better to warn the whole party.

"I think the new captain's here," Ross said, glancing up at Julia's faraway outline against the graying sky.

"Oh, hell," Parkhill grumbled, slumping for a moment in the saddle, glowering at Ross as if it were his fault. "All right, shape up, you sorry-lookin' sacks of shit. Dust yourself off, Caldwell. You look like hell."

The moment the column rode into Camp Marshall, Ross found Julia near the laundry tubs. He winked, then looked toward the officers' quarters.

He spotted the new commander, recognizing him almost instantly. It was the one-armed lieutenant from Camp Douglas, now wearing twin bars of silver.

Captain Jasper Jones was leaning against a post on the porch of his quarters, pulling at the collar of his rather disheveled uniform. The empty sleeve was bunched haphazardly below the stump of his left arm. There was little dash about the man, but Ross remembered him well for germinating his release from the prisoner of war camp. It made sense now, the interest this officer had shown in sending captured Confederates west. It was probably his project, his idea. Now he was here to make it work.

"Sergeant!" Captain Jones said, stepping down from the porch. "Report!"

Parkhill sniffed, raised his hand to stop the detachment. He jumped down in front of the captain and cocked his thick arm in a salute. "Sergeant Parkhill reporting as ordered, sir."

Jones returned the salute as if swatting at a fly. "The wire, Sergeant, the wire."

"Busted. Over the mountains in the Platte Valley. Big herd of buffalo took out a stretch almost a half mile long. We'll take a wagon load of poles and wire tomorrow and fix it."

Jones squinted at the big sergeant. "You from Mississippi, Parkhill?"

"Before the war, sir."

"Northeastern Mississippi, I'd say."

Parkhill's eyes widened. "Yes, sir."

"I thought I recognized that strain in your dialect. Did I interview you at Camp Douglas?"

"Yes, sir."

"You've made good rank." The captain frowned as he looked over the men, his eyes finally landing on Ross, perched high atop the big gray. "What happened to you, Private?"

His answer was ready. "The buffalo stampeded me, sir."

Jones snickered. "Get any meat?"

"As much as we could pack, sir."

"Georgia, right?"

"Yes, sir."

"Make sure you clean every speck of dirt out of those weapons tonight."

"Yes, sir."

"Sergeant, you've got two minutes to care for your animals and get your men in formation. Lieutenant Deihl! Any more detachments out?"

"No, sir," the lieutenant said.

"Then call a general assembly. I want three sides of a hollow square around the flagpole."

The post flew into instant pandemonium as all troops save those on sentry duty rushed to find their places, the lieutenant screaming, sergeants cussing. The wire detachment was the last to fall in, after hastily stripping mounts at the corral.

As the last boot shuffled into position, Captain Jones cleared his throat and looked over his new command. "My name is Captain Jasper G. Jones," he began, his sharp tenor voice easily reaching the back rows. "The first man who considers that name amusing will find himself on the sorriest duty this camp has to offer for the duration of his enlistment." He paced in front of one prong of the formation, stopping to glare at a corporal who refused to make eye contact with him.

"Those of you who are former secessionists will remember me from Camp Douglas. It was my idea to have you rot here instead of there, so you can thank me if you want to—I really don't care either way. Don't expect me to thank you back, though, because you've all but ruined my military career. I put my trust in the idea that a Southern man could serve the Union as well as a Northern man, and that has been my undoing."

Jones turned the corner of the hollow square and strode in front of the second row of troops. "Your primary mission here, gentlemen, in this garden spot of civilization, is to keep the telegraph line intact between Platte Bridge and Bridger's Ferry. One damned skinny piece of wire, and all you have to do is keep it spliced together. So far, you have failed miserably."

He stopped in front of Sergeant Parkhill, stood facing the big man, inches away, staring at the missing buttons on his blouse. "Like most of you, I don't give a *damn* whether or not some Californian can wire Washington, D.C., or New York City. I don't give a *damn* whether or not the United States Army can telegraph its orders across the continent—most of them contradict each other, anyway. What I give a damn about is *this*!"

He whipped a folded sheet of ink-smeared newsprint from his pocket and waved it in the air. He turned away from Parkhill and walked to the middle of the square. "Sergeant Parkhill, what is this?"

"It's a newspaper, sir."

The captain rolled his eyes. "Not just a newspaper, Sergeant, a *western* newspaper. No self-respecting eastern rag could fold up in a man's breast pocket without making a bulge! This is a copy of the San Francisco *Daily Alta California.* Allow me to quote from one of its editorial columns."

He shook the paper open with a flourish, struggling to arrange a page with his one hand. Clearing his throat, he began.

" 'The telegraph wire was cut by Indians between Platte Bridge and Bridger's Ferry again, and as such we have no news from the East. Repairs are commencing with the usual dedication to lethargy and disinterestedness along that section. We have recently learned the reason for this weak link in the transcontinental telegraph system. Several companies of Galvanized Yankees are stationed in that region. We must not expect any finer level of service from captured secessionists and defeated Rebels.' "

The captain threw the newspaper to the ground and let it blow away on an evening breeze that plastered it against a private's shin.

"If I ever want to wear an oak-leaf cluster," Jones continued, "I must make liars of the editors of the *Daily Alta California.* I must keep telegraph communications open from the Atlantic to the Pacific with a mixed force of Southern and Northern men. I must repair promptly all breaks. To rescue my military career, I must prove what I still suspect to be true: that former enemies can put aside their old differences and splice a nation back together. I ask you to do nothing I am unwilling to do myself. I buried my left arm at Kennesaw Mountain!"

He paused to let his echo resound across the parade ground. "But I buried my bitterness and enmity with it." Captain Jones began slowly to approach Sergeant Parkhill, moving like a stalking wolf.

"The war is over, gentlemen, but the states are still divided. Their only common ground lies here, in the West. The reparation of a nation begins with us, men. And it starts with a piece of wire."

He stopped in front of Parkhill, looking the big sergeant in the eye. "From this moment forward, no wire inspection detail will take the field without a supply wagon loaded with the materials needed to repair one mile of line.

"Sergeant Parkhill! You will mount your detachment on fresh horses, harness a buckboard, load it with posts and wire, and leave immediately to repair the break you found to the west today. I want communications restored by dawn. The rest of you men report to your lieutenants for inventory duty. We will count every post, every foot of wire, every peg, clamp, insulator, posthole digger, and pliers before breakfast.

"Dismissed!"

Ross felt the company surge against him as the sergeants barked. He groaned, looking for Julia. She was there, shrugging at him from her laundry barrels. He took a step toward her, felt a hand clamp his shoulder.

"Where the hell do you think you're goin', Caldwell? The corral's that way!" It was Parkhill, fuming like a mad dog. He shoved Ross toward the horses and went to rant at another private.

Ross gestured helplessly to his wife. She put her cracked fingers to her lips and blew him a kiss.

Six

———◆———

THE INVITATION CAME as a complete surprise, and almost terrified Ross. Dinner with the captain in his quarters? That kind of fraternization was against regulations, wasn't it? But Ross had learned in the three weeks since Jones had arrived that the camp commander abhorred regulations. The man had a knack for getting things done on his own terms, regulations be damned.

Ross shined his boots as Julia buttoned herself into her finest gown. They stood at the door and inspected each other in the lantern light before they left.

"You're beautiful," Ross said.

"Oh, hush," she answered. "And stop worrying. It's just dinner."

They felt the eyes on them as they walked across the parade ground to the captain's quarters. When Jones opened the door, he was wearing an apron over civilian garb, holding the handle of a large wooden spoon between his teeth.

He took the spoon in his hand and kicked the door shut behind his guests. "Welcome, Mrs. Caldwell, Private Caldwell. Hope you like antelope stew. It's almost ready, and I've made enough to feed the regiment."

Julia inhaled the aromas as she entered, and let Ross take her shawl from her shoulders. "Are you baking bread?" she asked.

Captain Jones was on his way back to the kitchen. "Sourdough biscuits," he shouted. "I'll give you a starter if you'll use it."

"Thank you, I will," she answered, standing uncertainly in the dining room. She gestured at Ross. "Say something," she whispered.

"What?"

"Anything."

Ross frowned. "Beg your pardon, sir, but you do your own cookin'?"

"Always have," the captain answered, clacking his spoon against the rim of his stewpot. "Learned from my mother. She runs the best boardinghouse kitchen in Boston. Simple fare, but it sticks to your ribs." He jutted his head from the kitchen. "Set the table, Private. Silver's in that drawer. Mrs. Caldwell, you're not to lift a finger."

When it was ready, the captain banged the pot of stew on the table and whipped the lid away with a flourish. "The only way to cook this wild game is to boil the devil out of it! Do the two of you indulge?" He raised a bottle.

Ross looked at Julia. "Whenever we can get it, sir. If it's affordable."

The captain put the bottle between his knees and pulled the cork stopper. "It's just some porter I borrowed from the surgeon," he said, filling three glasses. "Not much spirit to it, but I've got plenty. Sit down."

The captain blessed the meal and attacked it, sopping his biscuits, slurping broth from his spoon. He was still wearing his apron and used the tail of it as his napkin. "Private Caldwell," he said, "I'm told that Mrs. Caldwell is an inspiration to the entire regiment. What has she done? Killed an Indian or something?"

Ross laughed, feeling more at ease after a few glasses of porter and a feed of hot stew. "No, sir." He beamed at his wife. "She just does what has to be done, that's all."

"That so?"

"Yes, sir. When I was in the infantry, 1st U.S. Volunteers, she marched with the regiment all the way from Leavenworth to Laramie, step for step."

"Did she?"

"Yes, sir. Then we got reassigned to the 11th Ohio for some reason . . ."

"A mysterious quirk of military logic," the captain injected.

"Yes, sir. And even then she wouldn't ride a wagon when we dismounted to lead our horses. She'd jump off the wagon and walk with the men."

Julia put her hand against her throat and felt herself blushing.

"Mrs. Caldwell," Jones said, raising his glass, "you are of more value to this company than my entire corps of officers. No general can command inspiration."

Ross lifted his porter and clinked it against Julia's.

"I'm told we nearly lost the two of you to Platte Bridge recently."

"Yes, sir. I was sick when my squad rode out. Just before you took command."

"How did you come to be reassigned to Sergeant Parkhill's squad?"

Ross shrugged. "Mysterious quirk of army logic, I guess."

"There's something mysterious about that squad, all right," Jones said, wringing his hand in a wad of his apron tail. "I've been studying the muster rolls, and there are supposed to be quite a few Northern men in that unit, but they all speak with a Southern drawl. How do you explain that?"

Ross's chair squeaked like a new saddle as he squirmed in it.

"If I may, sir," Julia said. "Some of the men are reluctant to use their real names and their home states on the muster rolls. Afraid they may suffer some bad treatment when they return to their homes in the South if it was discovered that they served the Union Army."

"They've lied about their native states?"

"They've chosen new homes in the North," Julia said.

"Yes, though they don't intend ever living there," Jones said. "And the false names?"

Julia turned her glass between her toughened fingers. "General Grant changed his name when he entered West Point."

Jasper Jones smiled, chuckled. "So he did. *Noms de guerre.* Perhaps I should have chosen one." He looked at Ross. "What am I to think of Sergeant Parkhill?"

Ross raised his eyebrows and glanced about the room. "He's tough. Not afraid of anything. Smart."

"How smart?"

"Sir?"

The captain sighed as he refilled his glass with porter. "Private, I'm going to put you in a very delicate position. I'm going to ask you to watch and listen for signs of unrest in your squad. I've looked into Sergeant Parkhill's background and found that he's managed to keep the same clutch of men with him since he was active in the Confederate cavalry. They're apparently quite loyal to him, and perhaps to the Confederacy. If you overhear anything, I want you to inform me through Mrs. Caldwell. Have her deliver a note in the pocket of my uniform when she does my laundry."

Ross looked at Julia, found her face showing a mixture of pride and surprise. "Why me, sir? I'm just a private."

"I wired your former lieutenant at Platte Bridge. Asked him to recommend an enlisted man at Camp Marshall I could trust. He suggested you. I tend to agree with him now. Any man who could convince a woman like Mrs. Caldwell to follow him out to this ten acres of perdition must be worthy of trust."

Ross was beginning to suspect Captain Jones's flattery. "What is it you expect me to find out about Sergeant Parkhill?"

"Nothing that isn't there. Hopefully nothing at all. But I fear he may be planning either a mass desertion or a mutiny. As you said, he fears nothing, and he has a rumored history of involvement in groups like the Knights of the Golden Circle and the so-called Sons of Liberty. If you hear anything, report to me through the laundry. For obvious reasons I won't invite you back to my quarters."

Ross pushed his half-full glass of porter away.

"I trust I'm not asking too much."

Ross looked at Julia. "No, sir. Not of me."

"Mrs. Caldwell?"

"No, sir," Julia said, concealing her excitement. *I am a spy*, she was thinking.

The captain rose and his guests sensed it was time for them to go.

"Private, tell your squad that I am the most high-handed, obnoxious, arrogant personage you have ever had the misfortune of dining with. I'll invite the other married couples at the post to dinner in the future so no one will suspect our arrangement.

"Yes, sir," Ross said, draping Julia's shawl over her shoulders.

Jones opened the door, then grasped his chin and studied the young couple. "The two of you come from the same hometown, don't you?"

Ross nodded.

"East of Atlanta, I would guess. Maybe near Monroe or Athens or Jackson."

"Yes," Julia said, quite surprised. "Athens."

The captain's eyes glittered. "Dialects fascinate me. I remember you from Camp Douglas, Private Caldwell. You were the one who said you would rather fight Indians than tribes of vermin."

Ross smiled, this time surely impressed. "Yes, sir. But here you have to fight both. I think we're winnin' against the vermin, but the Indians haven't showed us their strength yet."

"Indeed they haven't, Private. Good night, Mrs. Caldwell. Thank you both for coming."

Later, alone in their little room, curled together on the narrow bed, Ross whispered to Julia about Sergeant Parkhill and the Knights of the Golden Circle.

"Why haven't you told me before?" she asked.

"I didn't want to worry you. This is dangerous business."

"Oh, hush," she said, dragging her rough hands across his skin. "I'll show you dangerous business."

SEVEN

SWEAT RAN FROM him like a river. It was ninety-five degrees to begin with, and Ross was making wagon tires red-hot in a big bank of coals. He could grasp his shirt, unbuttoned down the front, and pump some air across his sweaty skin for a moment of coolness, but he longed to douse himself with the bucket of creek water he knew Julia would have waiting for him.

The post's blacksmith grunted at him, and Ross put his tongs on the iron wheel rim in the coals, lifting one side as the smithy raised the other. Wordlessly, they moved the smoking iron ring to the wagon wheel mounted horizontally near the fire, tapping it down around the perimeter of the wheel where it would cool and draw tight. It was between taps of the smithy's hammer that Ross heard the first shot.

"Indians!" a sentry shouted. "Damn! A hundred of 'em!"

Captain Jones burst out of his quarters as if they were on fire, and the crackle of distant gunshots reached into the fort. "Saddle thirty mounts!" he shouted as he scrambled up a ladder to look over the rim of the sentry box.

Ross looked toward Julia's laundry barrels, relieved to find her there. She might have been trapped at the creek. He ducked under a corral rail and caught a horse as other soldiers grabbed blankets and saddles.

"They got the horses!" the sentry shouted as the captain sprang to the platform beside him. "Three men pinned down."

Jones leaned over the hewn points of the timbers, squinting at the struggle taking place almost a mile up the creek to the south. The three herders had shot their horses to use as cover and were fighting back a circling ring of Cheyenne warriors.

Jones all but grinned at the beauty of the sight, the men staggering their fire to keep the enemy at bay. Since taking command, he had refused to let the entire herd out to graze at one time, though it meant extra grazing details for the men. Now his precautions would pay off. He had plenty of horses in the fort to mount a rescue party and recover the stolen herd.

"Thirty volunteers!" he shouted as he hurried down the ladder. "Mount up!"

Ross drew a saddle cinch tight and stepped up on a stirrup to find Gene Dillon mounted beside him. He glanced about and found the yellow-haired

Lloyd. He spotted another of Sergeant Parkhill's squad, then another, then Parkhill himself, the big man leading two horses. One was a lean sorrel. The other was Ol' Chug.

Captain Jones jumped from the fourth rung and took the reins of the big gray as Sergeant Parkhill handed them to him. "Form a skirmish line on the south perimeter and prepare to charge!" he shouted, vaulting into the saddle. "Lieutenant Deihl, you have command of the fort in my absence. Defend it!" He spurred Chug and led the men southward.

Ross wanted to warn the captain about the big gray mare, but the rumble of hooves rose like an explosion around him. He could only rein his mount into the current of horseflesh and head for the battle. Then Julia's shrill voice knifed through the noise and he found her running toward him, his gun belt in her hand, and realized he would have charged the enemy unarmed if not for her.

He held his horse back and veered toward her at the rear of the rescue party, catching the leather as she lobbed it to him. He put his head and one arm through the belt and kicked his pony's ribs to catch up.

Clearing the barracks, he found an uneven skirmish line forming, but before Ross could fall in behind Chug, Captain Jones had given the order to charge and the rescue party was galloping south for the three surrounded soldiers.

Wind filled his shirt, cooling the sweat he had been working up all day. He fixed his hat more firmly on his head and gave his pony rein, preparing to catch Ol' Chug when she bolted.

The Indians fired a few long-range shots at the rescue party, then withdrew up the creek with their stolen horses. Fifty of them stopped on a slanting ridge that angled toward the creek, and watched to see what the bluecoats had in mind.

As the rescue party arrived, two of the three herdsmen stood to greet it. Through the dust, Ross saw the third sitting on the ground, grasping an arrow shaft in his thigh. Captain Jones tightened his reins as he approached the three herdsmen, and started to say something, but Parkhill moved in behind Chug, drew his revolver, and fired a shot toward the distant raiders.

Chug leaped as if slapped on the rump with a razor strop, and a dozen other revolvers opened up. Captain Jones pulled leather, but the big gray took the bit between her teeth and gained momentum, running toward the Indians on the slanting ridge.

Soldiers milled in the confusion, the men from Parkhill's squad staying back, the other volunteers halfheartedly following Captain Jones. Only Ross rode with a purpose. He dodged the faltering mounts ahead of him and took second position in the charge.

"Turn her, Captain!" he shouted, but he was too far back yet. He saw the Indians regrouping on the ridge, their battle feathers whipping in the breeze. He figured he had about a minute to catch Chug before she carried Captain Jones within reach of the raiders.

He looked over his shoulder, saw the other troopers falling back, reluctant to charge fifty braves on high ground. Finding the flap of his holster, he opened it, drawing the big Remington, gripping it surely. He would come alongside and shoot Chug if he had to. The air-chilled sweat around his torso braced him, shivered him with confidence.

"Turn her, Captain!" he shouted again, and this time he knew Jones heard him, for the commander held one rein wide and pulled with everything he had, bowing the gray's strong neck to the right.

Ross began to make up ground, but a flutter on the horizon caught his eye, and he saw fifty braves streaking down the slanted ridge like cloud shadows, each anxious to count the first coup on the two foolish soldiers who had charged too near. Jones saw, too, and pulled so hard on the right rein that he almost fell out of the saddle.

Ross closed in on Chug in seconds. "Let her go, Captain! Jump on with me!"

Jasper Jones hit the ground, rolled, found his footing, raised his arm. He had ordered the men to practice this drill—the mounted trooper picking up the man on foot. He had made a contest of it and felt it pay off now as he landed solidly behind Private Caldwell with war cries stabbing his ears. This soldier was strong, sure of himself. God bless Georgia, he thought. But he wasn't safe yet. The Indians would descend on them like diving hawks. They had to reach the rest of the rescue party.

Looking over the private's shoulder, he saw the nearest soldiers following the appropriate procedure, every fourth man holding the horses while the others formed a firing line. The carbines hurled the first volley at the Indians, and Jones looked back to see a horse drop from under a warrior.

The rest of the raiders, however, remained eager for battle. They chanced a few long shots, having ridden within reach of the two bluecoats. Jones saw an arrow go by, hit the ground in front of him, then pass under him.

The second volley came from the soldiers on foot, half of them reloading as the others stepped up and took aim. The warriors heard the bullets whistle. They scattered, spreading the carbine fire, turning back to the slanted ridge.

"Well done, men!" Jones said as Ross reined in behind the riflemen. "Get down, Private, and let me have your mount."

Ross slid from the sorrel as Sergeant Parkhill and the rest of the rescue party rode up from the rear.

"Sergeant Parkhill!" Jones shouted. "Form a detail of the men from your squad and get that wounded man to the surgeon."

"Yes, sir!" Parkhill growled.

"The rest of you men will come with me to recover the herd. Private Caldwell, tell Sergeant Webber to mount his squad and follow my trail."

"Yes, sir," Ross said as the captain led the party away, leaving him with Parkhill, Gene Dillon, yellow-haired Lloyd, and several other Southerners from his squad—all of them glaring down at him from their horses.

"Caldwell, are you sweet on that captain?"

Parkhill said. "His ass was good as scalped till you rode him down."

Ross shrugged. "I know what it feels like to ride that cold-jawed runaway."

"We could have gotten shed of the son of a bitch," Parkhill replied.

Ross snickered as if the idea were ridiculous. "What's the use? They'd just send some West Pointer to take his place. I'd rather keep Jones."

Parkhill spewed a brown stream of spit onto his mount's rump, then turned back to Ross. "We could all be in the Montana gold fields by the time the next Yankee gets here," he said.

The smile slid from Ross's face. "I haven't heard any talk of such."

"That's because you keep yourself to your wife too much," Gene Dillon said, smiling. "Get out of the house now and then of an evenin', and you'd learn somethin'."

Ross nodded, playing the spy all the way now. "I'll do that. About damn time you boys let me know what was goin' on."

Parkhill turned toward the wounded soldier, lying a hundred yards away among the dead horses, and Ross followed on foot, his legs feeling weak under him. This spy business was more frightening than battle. It was impulse, quick and resistless, that caused him to run stupidly into cornfields after wounded comrades, or rescue his captain from a Cheyenne charge. But this was a calculated march into a hostile stronghold.

And now Ross knew. He wasn't a hero. He was a damned fool.

* * *

Late that night, Captain Jones returned to Camp Marshall, having recaptured only twenty-seven of the more than one hundred horses stolen by the Cheyenne. When he got to his quarters, he found a freshly laundered uniform folded on his dining room table, and in its left breast pocket, a note from his company spy.

EIGHT

"Damn it!" Captain Jones shouted, wadding the piece of paper and throwing it across the room.

The telegraph clerk flinched. "You want me to reply?"

"Yes, tell Colonel Kulp he can . . ." Jones fumed, searching for words.

Lieutenant Deihl bounded into the captain's office, eyes wide with curiosity.

"Tell Colonel Kulp he can rely on me to follow his orders," Jones said, composing himself.

"What's happened?" the lieutenant asked as the telegraph operator left the office.

"I've been ordered to take half my command north to the Crazy Woman River and rendezvous with Colonel Kulp in two weeks."

"For what purpose?"

"Campaigning, of course."

Deihl clapped his hands, rubbed them together. "It's about damn time!"

"Like hell it is! We can't keep the telegraph line open with half our force off hunting Indians. Our scouts don't know a damned thing about the Crazy Woman country. And on top of that, I've got a mutiny to put down."

"What mutiny?"

"You'll know about it soon enough. Why does the army always choose the worst possible timing?"

"You could allow me to make the rendezvous with Colonel Kulp while you continue to command the post," Deihl offered.

"You know I can't do that. The orders are for me. You'll have to take over things here."

Deihl's mouth opened in astonishment. "You can't leave me here. I'm second-in-command!"

"Exactly why I must leave you here, Lieutenant, and you will have your hands full! Now, call a general assembly and let me address the men. And arm a police detail from Sergeant Webber's squad. Six men, and make them ready to fight!"

When Camp Marshall had drawn itself into a formation, Captain Jones ordered his police detail to present arms. "Sergeant Parkhill!" he shouted. "Front and center!"

The burly sergeant obeyed, marching forward from the ranks.

"Sergeant, you are under arrest for attempting to incite the men to mutiny. You will reside in the stockade until such time as you will stand court-martial. Detail, take custody of the prisoner."

Parkhill's face became an instant contortion as

he lunged for the captain's throat with both hands, knocking the commander onto his back. The police detail grabbed the big arms, but Parkhill kicked two of the soldiers off their feet and continued to strangle Jones until a rifle butt clubbed him on the back of the head.

The captain coughed as Lieutenant Deihl helped him to his feet. He rubbed his throat and sopped the tears from his eyes with his sleeve. He tried to speak, but only croaked, then coughed again. Finally catching his breath, the commander stepped up on the board porch of his quarters to watch with satisfaction as the detail dragged Sergeant Parkhill in through the door of the tiny stockade.

"Corporal Dillon, you are now in charge of your squad," the captain ordered hoarsely. "Prepare your men immediately for an extended campaign. Rations for thirty days. Be ready to march at fourteen hundred hours. Lieutenant Deihl, wire Horseshoe Station and Deer Creek. Have each send a squad to rendezvous with me at Bridger's Ferry. Lieutenant Redding will accompany me from there. Dismissed!"

Ross heard the men grumble around him, felt somebody bump him. He turned to see Lloyd glaring at him through pale blue eyes.

"What?" Ross said.

"Nothin'," the high voice said, Lloyd sneering as he turned away.

Ross walked toward his quarters and found Julia waiting there, the door latch in her hand. She let him in, closed the door, bolted it.

"Do they suspect you?" she asked.

"I don't know. I think maybe Lloyd does, but he never liked me, anyway."

She put her arms around his waist. "They won't do anything out there without Parkhill. The captain was wise to order them on the campaign."

"Yeah," Ross said, his hand finding the back of her neck under her hair. "I wonder if he'll want me to testify against Parkhill."

"It doesn't matter. We'll get through it one way or the other." She pulled his shirttail out of his trousers and put her hands on his back. They were cool and soft, having just come out of the washtub. "You've got this campaign to worry about first. What have you heard?"

"No more than you just did. Rations for thirty days. I'll be gone awhile this time."

"Yes, but when you come back it will be almost time to muster out. Then we can go anywhere. Back to Athens if you want to. Or Denver. Even California. We'll be free then."

It was the first time she had talked of what would happen after the army, and he was glad to find her agreeable to staying in the West. When he thought of them growing old, he saw plains and mountains around them. When he thought of his children playing, he saw them riding like Dakota whirlwinds.

"We can start our family," he said, and he kissed her, his dry lips pushing hard on hers.

"We have three hours before you have to go," she said, her hands reaching under his shirt. "Let me have one. The army can have the other two."

Nine

It had been eleven days, and still he could not clear his mind of their parting. She had run at him across the parade ground of Camp Marshall, grasping his knee as he rode away. He had reached down to touch her face and felt her tears run across his fingers. It was in his heart, before his eyes, around his empty stomach.

He was lonely in the wildest country he had ever known. They were camped at the confluence of the Crazy Woman and its south fork, waiting for Colonel Kulp. Since leaving Fort Marshall, they had seen no Indians and little game. About half the salt pork had gone bad for some reason—not cured properly, Ross suspected. Bugs had gotten into the hardtack. At least they had plenty of fresh water from the river. It flowed eastward, out of the Bighorn Mountains, which loomed seductively in the west.

There were grassy hills all around, some rolling, some rather pointed. The summer had given the plains more rainfall here than at Camp Marshall, and the ground undulated with waves of greenery. You could watch that grass ripple for hours, almost hypnotizing yourself, Ross had learned. There wasn't much to do here besides watch the grass and wait.

He sat on his blanket, spread evenly across the ground, a rock on each corner. The pieces of his Remington revolver lay in front of him on the blanket. Meticulously, he cleaned them of dirt, grain by grain. He had to make each task last. Idleness only made him pine for Julia.

The sun burned through the scant shade of the small cottonwood at his back, and what little breeze there was blew hot. The gurgle of the Crazy Woman—a mere brook by Georgia standards—was a mockery. Even the water ran warm today.

He sensed a group of soldiers approaching, but was too intent on his weapon to look up, until a spray of sand rained on his blanket, peppering his gunmetal with grit.

"Oh, damn, how clumsy can I git?" Lloyd said, his ugly mouth set in a grin.

It had been like this every day since Parkhill's arrest, and Ross had taken enough. It swept him up—an impulse of the sort that seemed to dog him when he was away from Julia—and he sprang from the blanket to stagger Lloyd with a shove. Before the yellow-haired private could strike back, Gene Dillon had stepped between them.

"What the hell's wrong with you two? The captain'll put a lash to your back for fightin'."

"I just want to stick a knife in that damn Yankee-lover, that's all," Lloyd said.

"I've told you he couldn't have had nothin' to do with it," Gene said.

"With what?" Ross asked.

"You know what you done." Lloyd sneered.

Gene held Lloyd back with one arm. "He thinks you got Parkhill arrested."

Ross scoffed. "How could I have had a damn thing to do with that?"

"You told the captain about Park's plan."

"I never even speak to the captain."

Lloyd sniffed, and looked Ross over from boots to hat. "Your wife does, and she's a damn Yankee-lover, too. She sure likes that captain. You ought to see her with him when you're out on detail, Caldwell. I'm surprised she's got any left for you."

"Shut your filthy mouth." Ross lunged, swinging a fist, but the blow missed as Gene Dillon caught him around the waist and slung him aside.

"Don't do it, Ross." He stood between the two soldiers. "Damn, Lloyd, are you hell-bent on trouble? Let's git." He turned the yellow-haired Southerner away from Ross and pushed him along the riverbank. "I'm not gonna break you two up again, Lloyd. Next time, you'll get whatever's comin'."

"Next time I'll kill the son of a bitch. I swear to God I'll kill him."

* * *

Jasper Jones was sitting in his tent, smelling the moldy canvas, drumming his fingers on a yellowed map. He hated being here. Hated it so much he wanted to rant and pull hair. This campaign was lunacy to the last detail. Colonel Kulp had actually ordered him to bring two howitzers along. Imagine, fighting the world's finest light cavalry with artillery in a roadless country. It would be like fighting off bumblebees with bricks.

Where is Colonel Kulp, anyway? Lost, probably. Does he know we will soon be starving here? Does he care that my men are restless? Does he realize half my force consists of former Rebels who would just as soon desert as stay another day in this wasteland?

Twilight was coming on, and the heat was lifting. He was wondering if Indians would attack at night. He thought they preferred daylight combat, but he wasn't sure. He would have to call for the civilian scout and inquire. But he hated talking to that damned smart-mouthed scout. Full of himself and his frontier savvy, which didn't impress Captain Jones as being extensive.

If I were an Indian, I would attack now. This force is weak, low on morale, short on rations. The attack is coming. I know it is coming. I must prepare my men. I must . . .

A knock on his tent pole brought him back to the moment. He rose and slung the tent flap aside to find Corporal Dillon. "What are you doing here? Did I send for you?"

"No, sir, but . . ."

"But what, soldier? What do you think you're doing?"

Dillon glanced nervously over his shoulder, hoping no one would see him. "Can I come in, sir?"

"In my tent?"

"Yes, sir. I've got my reasons. Somethin' you ought to know."

Irritated, Jones stepped back so the corporal could come in. "Very well. What is it? It had better be important."

Dillon stood uncomfortably in the tent, his service cap in his hand. "Can I speak my mind, sir?"

"Yes, get it over with."

"Do you know a Private Caldwell, sir? The one married to the laundry gal?"

"Of course I know him. He saved my life. What of him?"

Dillon lowered his voice. "I heard some of the Southern boys talkin', sir. They say they're gonna kill him. They think he's been spyin' on 'em for you. They're gonna kill him and desert."

A pang of remorse struck Jones in the heart. He had brought this on Caldwell. But he showed the corporal no emotion. "Some of the Southern boys? Which ones?"

"It was dark and I couldn't see their faces, sir. I just heard 'em. I don't know none of them Southern boys, anyway. I'm from Indiana."

Jones sneered. "Corporal, you are from Montgomery County, Alabama, as sure as I'm born and bred Boston. Now, which ones said they'd kill Caldwell?"

"As God watches over me, Captain, I swear I don't know."

"Then your intelligence is worthless to me." He glared, and Dillon looked at his feet. "You're sure it's not just talk?"

"It's more than talk, sir. They're gonna do it tonight when Caldwell's on picket duty. They planned it down to particulars."

Jones sat down. He wanted to snap something, tear something to pieces. He might have, if he had had two arms. He rested his head in his palm and thought for a few seconds. "Find Caldwell," he said, getting up. "Tell him to come to my tent at nightfall. Don't let anybody see you talking to him, and don't let anybody see you leave here." He stepped outside for a look across the camp. "Come on, the way is clear. Don't fail me, Corporal."

Ross knocked on the pole and made his salute ready. "Private Caldwell reporting as ordered, sir."

The captain grabbed him by the sleeve and pulled him into the tent. "Forget the damned protocol, Caldwell, just sit down."

Ross took a seat on a three-legged stool.

"Now, listen carefully. You're in danger, Caldwell, and seeing as how I got you into it, I intend to get you out. Some of these Knights of the Golden Circle have figured out that you informed on Sergeant Parkhill and they mean to kill you for it."

Ross nodded. "I know, sir." It was a relief to know the captain actually gave a damn. "But what can I do about it?"

"You're going to desert."

"Sir?"

"You heard me. Saddle a good horse and ride like hell."

"But, sir. What about my wife? What about . . . ? I don't want to be a deserter."

"Look here, Private, I'm ordering you to desert. It won't be a real desertion. I won't report it. Your name won't go down in infamy or anything. Hell, you're due to muster out in a few months, anyway. You've done your service."

"But what about Julia?"

"You'll ride up the Crazy Woman to the Bighorn Mountains. Cross them and you'll strike the Bridger Trail. Follow it to Virginia City and wait there. Get a job at a gold mine or something. When I get back to Camp Marshall, I'll tell your wife where to find you and send her with the first wagon train headed that way."

A hundred thoughts stirred in Ross, but he had known calamity for so long that nothing showed on his face. "When do I go?"

"Immediately. The damned Knights of the Golden Circle have ordered your murder tonight. Take your service revolver and some rations. And keep your eyes peeled for Indians. Colonel Kulp has probably stirred them up like a nest of hornets by now." Jones stood and offered Ross his hand. "Good luck, Mr. Caldwell."

Ross shook the captain's hand. "Just make sure Julia knows," he said, risking a flagrant insubordination. "Sir," he added.

When the private left, Captain Jones sat down at his writing table and lingered over his diary. Something should be set down in writing, he thought. Some record should exist. Finally, he dipped his pen into the inkwell and wrote:

Pvt. Caldwell left at dusk, assigned to special duty for duration of his enlistment.

TEN

———◆———

TWO DAYS HAD passed since Private Caldwell left,
and Jasper Jones had all but forgotten him. He
had other worries. Still no sign of Colonel Kulp.
No game to kill. Food running low. Morale sink-
ing.

This place had not been wisely chosen as a rendezvous point. It was difficult to defend with such
a small force as Captain Jones had at his dis-
posal. Too much low ground. Too many hills for
the Indians to reconnoiter among. This was the
enemy's native soil. He would know it like Jones
knew the streets and alleys of Boston.

Yesterday he had drilled the men, and he felt
good about that. The camp had regained some
semblance of discipline. The pickets looked alert
this morning through his field glasses. Today he

would put them to work digging rifle pits. Maybe he would send scouts out to look for Colonel Kulp.

One thing about these plains—dawn here made a man feel small. Never had Captain Jones imagined such an expanse of quietude. His clamorous urban culture had ill prepared him for this.

He swept the glasses across the hills once more, balancing them on the fingertips of his one hand. He sighed and let them dangle from the strap around his neck. Nothing out there. These false instincts could be damned. Nerves. Cowardice— that was what it was. Nothing more. No formidable force could possibly sneak near enough to completely surprise him, Indian or not.

He rose, dusted the dirt from the seat of his pants. He was about to turn back toward his tent for breakfast when he saw three pickets running toward camp from the east. He knew instantly in his heart that something horrible would follow those terrified soldiers over the near hill, but on its surface he could merely note what an oddly stirring sight it was to see those men sprinting through the grass.

When it came over the hill, he simply stared for the first second, for it enthralled more than it quailed him. Then the terror struck deep and he ran for his tent. He saw the three pickets overwhelmed by a solid line of mounted warriors, a quarter of a mile long. The hill had become a huge canvas for painted faces and horses; fringed shirts and leggings; eagle feathers that groped skyward like fingers.

The yelping voices made him cringe as the Rebel yells had at Kennesaw Mountain, and he felt the old minnie ball shatter his missing left arm again. He suffered the shameful stab of failure and remembered his guns lying on his cot. The first rifle shot came from his camp of surprised men, too late to give adequate warning.

Plunging into his tent, he found his revolver and cartridge belt. An arrow popped twice through the canvas as he charged back outside and added his gunfire to the meager resistance his men had raised. The first wave of warriors swarmed past him now, circling the camp. He saw their faces alive with glory and anger. They were men his own age and younger, but infinitely wiser than he about warfare on these plains.

His soldiers were stampeding toward him in a chaotic retreat. "The wagons!" he shouted, trying to turn them. "Hold the wagons!" As fast as he could shout at them, their bodies sprouted feathered shafts, but a few lucky survivors read his strategy, turned on the attackers, and began blasting painted riders from horses.

The counterattack grew around Captain Jones—a core of resistance in the massacre—and it moved with strange ease toward the wagons.

"Turn 'em over!" Jones shouted. He felt an unseen projectile pierce the right side of his body below the rib cage. Whether it had come from front or back, he could not say, but it hurt like hell.

A wagon box landed beside him and he fell against it between a sergeant and a private. He held his revolver between his knees and reloaded it as the screams and shouts engulfed him. Looking up, he saw Lieutenant Redding leading a small clot of men across the Crazy Woman to the artillery.

"No! Not the damned cannon! Lieutenant!" But

his shouts were lost and he watched the Indians cut the artillerymen down one by one as they tried to turn a howitzer on its carriage. His trembling fingers were trying to slip a primer cap over the last nipple of his revolver when an arrow pinned the stump of his left arm to the wagon box. He grunted, felt the nausea grip his empty stomach.

The sergeant beside him broke the arrow in the middle and yanked the captain's stump off the shaft. Jones looked up as a bullet blew away a chunk of the sergeant's head. The Indians had surrounded the wagon box, rendering it virtually useless as cover. They had captured army weapons. Bullets splintered the wagon bed by the second.

Jones cocked his pistol, found a brave aiming his way, fired, cocked the weapon again, looked for his next target. He mourned a great political career that would never come. He thought of his mother in her kitchen in Boston. The pistol bucked in his grip again as he remembered an old friend, a place he wanted to go, a woman he should have married. Something like a horse kicking him took his breath away, and a thousand notions crossed his mind in an instant.

The battle blurred as he fired again, and he thought of times he had known, aromas he would miss. He relived his old thrills, sorrows, and terrors, tasted flavors bitter and sweet. And for a fleet splinter of a moment, Captain Jasper Jones wondered who would tell Julia Caldwell that her husband awaited her in Virginia City. But gradually, like sunlight flooding the new day, it ceased to matter.

ELEVEN

—————•—————

THE MONOTONY OF the work and the sounds of rushing water had all but drawn him into a trance. Machinelike, he dumped his shovelload of gravel into the sluice box and stepped back into the shallow prospect hole. He slid the shovel along bedrock and scooped up another load of gold-dusted gravel, lifting it without thought or feeling.

Then it happened again. The wave of dread consumed him, sucking him back through the weeks and the miles. Had he forgotten something? What was he doing here? Where was Julia?

Alder Gulch writhed with human enterprise around him. He doubted it had ever been much of a place to look at, but now it rivaled a battlefield in its devastation. Every available stick of wood had long since been hacked and burned. Every stretch of ground along the creek had been staked, claimed, and burrowed into. The once crystalline rivulet of water in the bed of the gulch ran thick and brown with silt.

He beat the wave of dread down to a shudder in his heart and fixed his grip around the shovel handle once more. He had done everything he could do. It was all beyond his control. He would just have to wait for Captain Jones to get back to Camp Marshall. Then wait longer as Julia made her way here. Then they would make yet another start.

One realization had sprung from all the thought he had given his predicament. He was here without Julia because of Sergeant Parkhill and the Knights of the Golden Circle. How stupid he had been to fear them and their visionary scheme. How cowardly he had been for not exposing them like a man, instead of as a sneaking spy. He swore he would never again turn a blind eye to any secret society trying to undermine the law of the land. A man had to learn his lessons, and this one had come hard. His sentence for complicity and complacency was hard labor without Julia.

As he stepped out of the prospect hole and poured his load of gravel into the sluice box, he heard the jingle of trace chains up the gulch, and the crunch of metal wagon tires on the rocks. He glanced, spotted the Summit Shortline coming up from Virginia City, dropped his shovel, and ran to the rutted road. He fell in beside the stagecoach and trotted along beside. "Any women today?" he asked the driver, a familiar face behind a cascade of mustache hairs.

"Two," the driver said. "One just a whore, but

the other one might be your'n. Good-lookin' dark-haired gal."

"Get her name?"

"Nope."

"Where'd she go?"

"Didn't ask." He let the coils play out of his whip and split air over the team as the coach lurched forward.

Ross went back to his prospect hole to find his boss standing there—an old man, veteran of many rushes.

"She here?" the old miner asked.

"Maybe," Ross said. "A woman got out in town."

The old man scooped up some gravel to wash in his prospecting pan. He climbed out of the hole to the sluice box. "Well," he said, filling his pan with water, "it bein' Saturday evenin', you might as well go on down to town."

Ross smiled. "It's a little early to quit."

The old man pulled a small pouch from his pocket. "I'll dock you a little pay, then." He loosened the drawstrings and took a pinch of gold dust from the pouch, flicking it into the air.

Ross caught his week's pay in the pouch as the old man tossed it. "Thanks," he said, turning down the gulch. "See you Monday."

The old-timer stared into his pan of swirling gravel. "I don't look that far ahead."

He hiked past sluices, trenches, rockers, and odd piles of gravel as the music of steel against stone rang from every bend of Alder Gulch. He came to the reservoir above Virginia City and paused briefly in the shade of a lone tree to wipe the sweat from his brow with his bandanna. The clamor of the boomtown reached him here: the hammerblows of workmen punctuating the music from the hurdy-gurdy dance houses.

High rolls of green grass and sagebrush climbed all around the city. Beyond them, the high and distant timber of the Tobacco Root Mountains rose like a crown. An odd setting for a town of ten thousand, but the town showed no inclination toward going away.

Striding down on Main Street, he turned right onto Wallace and went straight to the overland stagecoach office. He asked where the woman had gone who had gotten off the coach earlier.

"You don't mean the whore, do you?" the ticket teller said.

"The lady."

"I believe she went to the newspaper."

"You believe?"

"She came in and asked me where she could find it. I guess she might have gone to get a room first."

Ross continued down Wallace Street, trotting in the dirt to avoid pedestrians on the boardwalks, looking for the offices of the Virginia City *Post*. It was just like Julia to take care of business first. She would ask the editors about her husband, and if they didn't know, she would get them to help with an article or an ad or something. Wouldn't she be surprised when he walked in!

He saw the sign hanging over the doorway and barged in, pausing to catch his breath. Three men were gathered around a dark-haired woman, chatting with excitement.

"What are we going to cut?" a young reporter said.

"My column," a big man in suspenders replied.

"You sure? What's it about?"

"Same old thing: shut down the hurdy-gurdies; clean out the brothels. Wasted ink. Give me an uppercase *C*. Mary, are you sure it was an entire column?"

"It says a detachment here," the woman replied. "About forty-five men."

Ross took his hat off, curled the brim in his hand. "Excuse me. I'm looking for someone."

The three men turned to stare at him, one stepping aside to reveal the woman's face. It wasn't Julia, of course. Ross already knew from her voice. But he had so convinced himself Julia would be here that seeing this lady didn't make any difference.

"Who?" the reporter said.

"My wife."

"You've come to the wrong place," the big editor said. "This is a newspaper. Now, we're busy getting an issue out, if you don't mind."

"A lady came here from the Wells Fargo office," Ross continued. "I think it was my wife."

"And I think I told you you're mistaken," the editor replied, never looking up from his printing plate. "This young lady is my cousin. She's just arrived from the East, and she's brought important news. Now, get out and leave us be."

"Oh, Ed!" the woman scolded. "Can't you see he's asking for help?" She approached Ross, holding a folded newspaper page in her hand. "I rode in on the stagecoach, sir, and there was just one other woman on it with me. I'm sure she was no one's wife."

"Oh," Ross replied, the wave of dread trying to gush up from his chest again. "Sorry, but they said she was a pretty dark-haired lady, and I . . . I see now they meant you."

The woman smiled sympathetically. "I'm sure your wife will be along in time. How long have you been waiting?"

Ross shrugged. "Only a couple of weeks."

The editor turned from his printing plate. "What kind of Indians were they, Mary? Did it say what tribe?"

She glanced at the newspaper in her hand. "Cheyenne, they think. Possibly with some Sioux warriors." She put her hand on Ross's elbow. "Give her more time. It's a long trip here from anywhere."

"Yes," Ross said. "You're right."

"What was that captain's name?" the editor said, situating a lead block in his plate.

Mary handed the newspaper to a reporter. "It's right here," she said. "See for yourself." She turned back to Ross. "Tell me your wife's name. I'll watch for her arrival and contact you when she gets here."

"Captain Jasper Jones," the reporter said.

"Jasper Jones!" the editor bellowed. "No wonder he got massacred—greenhorn name like that!"

The newsmen burst into laughter, but Ross merely stood with his mouth open.

"Your wife's name," Mary said, ignoring the outburst, "what is it?"

Ross stormed across the room and snatched the newspaper from the young reporter's hand.

"Hey, what's the idea?" the reporter said, but Ross swatted him aside.

As he read, the wave burst from his heart. Colonel Kulp had attacked a village of Indians and driven them west—directly into the camp of Captain Jasper Jones and a detachment of K Company, 11th Ohio Cavalry. Every last man in the column had been killed, stripped, mutilated.

This was the dread that had lived in his heart for weeks, and now it overwhelmed him as he came to understand it. Julia wasn't coming at all. He had no idea where she might be, and no way of communicating with her.

"I'll take that, if you don't mind," the editor said, yanking the newspaper from Ross's hand. "What's wrong with you, mister? Have you lost your mind? What did you say your name was?"

"Never mind," Ross answered. "It doesn't matter now." He felt his pocket for the pouch of gold dust and turned for the door.

TWELVE

JULIA WAITED IN the parlor, sitting primly on a sofa, her back straight, feet together on the floor, hands clasped in her lap. The house included some of the finest appointments she had seen anywhere in the West, but it was obvious that Colonel Kulp didn't know what to do with them. There was no flow in this room. No theme, no pattern. Just furniture bunched together. Oh, well, the man was a soldier, not an interior decorator.

How much longer would he keep her waiting? Was he really that busy or just hoping she would go away? She would not go away, of course. She had questions to ask. The official report had failed to satisfy her.

She had refused to cry the day Lieutenant Deihl came to her room at Camp Marshall and told her the news. Ross could not have been killed. She would have had a dream or something, felt his soul's embrace. It was true that something had overwhelmed her the day Ross left, but that was just sorrow in seeing him ride away again. She didn't care if there was a massacre. They had not proven to her that Ross was dead.

"Mrs. Caldwell," a bespectacled corporal said, "the colonel will see you now."

Julia smiled and rose, her heart beating crazily, as if she would enter the office and find Ross there. She found, instead, a fat, aging, oily-haired man in crisp uniform.

"How do you do, Mrs. Caldwell?" he said, coming around his desk to meet her. He was a big man and he looked down on her with a smile and sad eyes, his head cocked to one side. "I wish we could have met under happier circumstances."

Julia took his hand. She hadn't expected him to behave like an undertaker, and she didn't like it. Why did everybody act this way? She was here for answers, not sympathy.

The colonel gestured toward a chair as he lumbered back to his seat behind the desk. "If it is any consolation at all, I can assure you that the savages who murdered your husband will be punished most severely." He put a pair of grimy lenses on his face and shuffled a few papers. "I've arranged for you to collect your late husband's pay." He pushed a voucher across the desk, followed by a small brown envelope. "And the men took a collection for the widows' fund. It's not much, but it will help you get back East."

"I'm not going back East," Julia said. "And I don't want any part of any widows' fund." She shoved the envelope back at the officer. "I want to know what makes you so sure my husband was killed."

Kulp's mouth gaped for a moment, then he took in a long, rattling breath. He removed his glasses. He had encountered this kind of widow before. The angry kind. What did she expect? Her husband had joined the army. "The entire detachment was wiped out. Your husband's name was on the roster."

"Show me his personal effects."

"Ma'am?"

"I want his wedding ring, his watch, his revolver. Where is his uniform?"

"I don't mean to upset you, Mrs. Caldwell, but you must understand that the Indians leave nothing behind. They take all weapons. They cut off fingers to get rings. They strip their victims of everything."

The colonel's tone was making her mad. "Do you know what my husband looks like?"

"I cannot know every soldier in my command."

"Then no one recognized him on the battlefield?"

"Even if I had remembered his face, Mrs. Caldwell . . ." He looked down at his paperwork.

"What?"

"The Indians scalped them. They cut out tongues, slashed faces, mutilated arms and legs. Opened . . . opened the body cavities and took the organs out. It was plain that Captain Jones offered some resistance, but he was hopelessly outnumbered. It was a total defeat, Mrs. Caldwell. No one could have survived. Every last officer and man was killed, I assure you."

"How many?"

"The entire detachment."

Julia clenched her fists and glared across the desk. "How many dead bodies did you find on the battleground?"

The colonel scowled for a moment, then yanked at a desk drawer. He removed a file, opened it, put on his glasses. Licking his fingers, he thumbed through leaves of hand script, finally pausing to peruse one. "Forty-two by one account. Forty-four by another."

Julia gasped. "You didn't count them yourself?"

"I did not."

"Which count is accurate? Forty-two or forty-four? Or shall we average them and call it forty-three?"

The colonel's jowls trembled. "You weren't there. Men wept as they buried the dead. The stench was horrible. You have no idea what a battlefield looks like, Mrs. Caldwell. You wouldn't have had the stomach to count, either."

"I once worked as a nurse on a battlefield, Colonel, and I placed exactly fifteen legs and twenty-two arms in a pile outside the hospital tent. I would have counted."

The colonel's eyes twitched with surprise. "You would have wasted your time. It's quite possible that wolves dragged some of the corpses away. The Indians themselves might have taken live prisoners to torture. An exact count would have meant nothing."

Julia scoffed. "It means a great deal to me. How many men were assigned to Captain Jones's detachment? Do you have an exact count on that?"

Kulp's face reddened as he leafed through his file again. "Two officers and forty-four men."

"That makes forty-six total. If an *average* of forty-three were killed in the massacre, wouldn't that leave three unaccounted for? Hasn't that occurred to you? Three soldiers could be in the hands of the Indians as we sit here!"

"They are all dead, Mrs. Caldwell."

"Let me see the reports," she demanded, holding her hand across the desk.

"I don't have the authority to allow that."

"Damn your authority!" She sprang from her chair and lunged for the files.

"Corporal!" Kulp shouted, retreating with his documents.

Julia heard the door open behind her and knew the corporal was there. "May I ask one more question?" she said.

"There are some questions I cannot answer."

"Did you know Captain Jones would be bivouacked on the Crazy Woman?"

"Captain Jones followed his orders."

"Then why in the name of God did you drive hundreds of enemy warriors directly into his camp?"

"Corporal, see Mrs. Caldwell out."

"You should be court-martialed," Julia said, her voice scathing.

"You are impertinent, Mrs. Caldwell."

"*You* are incompetent!" She felt the corporal's hand on her arm, wrenched herself free of his grasp. She snatched the pay voucher from the colonel's desk, leaving the envelope from the widows' fund.

When she had collected Ross's pay, she left the fort and went to the stage stop to wait for the next

coach west. She sat on a bench in front of the
whitewashed board building, her bags at her feet.
The day was pleasant and the sunshine felt good
on her legs. A cool snap had blown down from the
north. The long summer was over. She put her
hands on her stomach and fought back the urge to
cry.

If he had died like that, she would have felt
something. She refused to mourn him until she
knew for certain. She had followed him before and
found him. She could do it again.

It was different this time, of course. Finding
him would be fraught with difficulties. This time
she had lost him beyond the frontier. This time she
was pregnant. She was going to have Ross's baby.
He could not have died out there on the Crazy
Woman.

THIRTEEN

Ross WORE A beard ten months old the day he
rode back into Virginia City. The horse he straddled was not much to look at, hell to ride, but
bent on getting there. Ross called him Ol' Whitey.
He was the color of milk spilled on the barn
floor.

Against his saddle bounced his sack of posses-
sions, around his hips a gun belt, in his boot a bag
of Colorado gold dust. As he approached town, he
realized that Virginia City was where he had last
put a razor to his face. Even if anyone here remembered him, they wouldn't recognize him. The
beard had covered his jaw. The soldier's haircut
had come bristling out under his dusty hat. Tons
of ore had left scars and calluses on his face and
hands.

Julia, if he found her here, would not know him. But he had learned to moderate his hopes of finding her. He would never stop looking, of course, but a disappointment in every town had tempered his expectations.

He heard Virginia City coming two miles down the mountain: brass horns, gunshots. It was July 4, a rare miner's holiday. For Ross it was a day to change strategies. No more drifting from town to town, searching, writing letters, sending wires. He was going to stay put for a while. Maybe he and Julia had missed each other coming and going. Maybe she would find out somehow that Captain Jones had sent him to Virginia City and would turn up here if he gave her time.

As he reached the edge of town, he slowed his horse to a walk and began habitually shooting glances at the faces of women. Most of them on this side of town were harlots, and they returned his looks with calculated glances of their own. But Ross hadn't touched a woman since he reached down to brush the tears from Julia's face at Camp Marshall.

He rode past two blocks of hurdy-gurdies, an occasional dollar-a-dance girl attracting his attention. He had to wonder if time had exaggerated Julia's beauty in his memory, for none of these women even remotely compared.

When he turned the corner onto Wallace Street, the full force of the celebration hit him, and even his tired horse perked up. A boxing ring had been erected in front of the Virginia City *Post*, and two men were sparring in it, bare-chested and bare-fisted. As he rode closer, he recognized the larger man as the editor of the *Post*.

He rode up behind a band uniform at ringside and stopped. The man in the uniform had a trumpet slung over his shoulder on a string and held a mug of beer in one hand. "What's this all about, partner?" he asked.

The man looked up, misty-eyed, and saw Ross for fellow pick and shovel man. "You just ride in?"

Ross nodded.

"Welcome to Sin City, friend."

Ross reached down for a handshake.

The trumpet player gestured toward the ring with his mug. "The big fellow puts out the newspaper. Name's Ed Johnson. The little dried-up fellow's Bob Hodges. Runs the Break o' Day Saloon." He pointed down the street.

"I take it the editor's against wet goods." Ross seemed to remember a puritanical streak in some editorials he had read here ten months and more ago.

The crowd roared as the pugilists came together, the editor snapping the saloon man's head back, and the saloon man burying a fist in the editor's flab.

"Against it wholesale, but particular at the Break o' Day. He wrote in the paper that Bob's been waterin' down drinks and short-weightin' his scales."

Ross leaned across his saddle horn. "Looks like that riled ol' Bob."

"No, Bob let that much go. Laughed about it, in fact, and said you could pan that editor out clear down to bedrock and not raise a color. Now, when

Johnson got a earful of that, he dared Bob to fight him boxin' rules come the Fourth, and there they stand."

The saloon owner whipped a sudden uppercut into Johnson's chin and the big man hung on the ropes for a second, then hit the rough-sawn floor. Someone at ringside struck a brass bell with a mallet and Bob went to his corner for a shot of whiskey while a reporter for the *Post* poured a bucket of water on Johnson.

"How many rounds is that?" Ross asked.

"Eight or ten," the musician said. "They're just gettin' started good."

"Who'd you put your money on?"

The happy miner raised his mug. "My heart's with Bob, but my dust is on the big fellow."

Ross grinned and reined his mount around the spectators as he saw the editor getting up. He didn't wish any loss of dust on the trumpet player, but he was hoping the newspaperman would take a good whipping today. He remembered the editor's ill temper ten months back, the day he went looking for Julia.

He had left Virginia City that day, the very hour he heard about the massacre on the Crazy Woman. The stage took him south to Fort Bridger, the nearest telegraph station by his reckoning. He sent a wire for a Mrs. Caldwell at Camp Marshall, receiving an almost immediate reply. Mrs. Caldwell had gone away.

He didn't go to Camp Marshall. They would recognize him there, wonder why he hadn't been massacred, suspect him of desertion. In fact, he became so worried about getting arrested for desertion that he invented an alias: R.W. Colby. It matched the initials carved into his pistol grip. He himself didn't know what the *R.W.* in his alias might stand for, but it didn't matter. It wasn't considered polite out here to ask.

He let his beard grow out as a disguise as he headed for Denver. He and Julia had talked about going there, but he found no trace of her. When he ran out of gold dust, he went to work in the Gregory Gulch diggings, replenished his funds, drifted farther south.

He wasted part of the fall on a virgin farm near Pueblo, helping get the harvest in, then drove a bull train to Julesburg. From there he sent a wire to the folks back in Athens, thinking Julia may have gone home.

"Ross!" the reply read. "Army claims you were killed! No word from Julia. What goes on?"

His only answer was to say that he would find her. Somehow he didn't feel the need to explain it all to his folks, or Julia's. They had never lived out here. They wouldn't understand the difficulties.

He returned to Denver through a blizzard. He found the name of a Mrs. Caldwell in a hotel register there, but it wasn't written in Julia's hand. It didn't make sense. He was the one who was supposed to be lost, but it was Julia who had vanished without a trace.

Winter in Boulder was miserable. He got out as soon as the weather broke and started heading for Montana again.

When he reached Fort Laramie, he worked up the nerve to enter the post and ask Colonel

Kulp's clerk if anyone had heard from Julia Cald-well.

"Who are you?" the corporal said.

"Name's R.W. Colby. I'm a friend of her folks back in Georgia. They haven't heard from her in a long time and asked me to look around for her."

The corporal nodded. "She was here last September to collect her husband's pay. He was killed with Captain Jones on the Crazy Woman."

Ross merely nodded. "Where did she go?"

The corporal shrugged.

It was the first lead he had turned up, and it had grown cold as an ice-clogged river over the winter. There was nothing to do but go back to Virginia City and hope.

The brass bell rang as he dismounted in front of the Break o' Day Saloon, and the boxers began stalking each other again. He had a notion to go in for a drink, but knew he should case the town for Julia first, so he walked to the first hotel down the street and began his search.

"Can I see the register? I'm lookin' for some-body."

The hotelier turned the book around so Ross could read it.

He ran his finger down the list of current guests and curled his mouth in a practiced frown. "I'll be in town a while. If I don't find who I'm lookin' for at some other hotel, do you mind if I come back and look through the back pages of your register?"

The hotelier shrugged. "All right with me."

By the time Ross had inquired at every hotel and boardinghouse in town, Ed Johnson's left eye

was swollen shut, and Bob Hodges had a stream
of blood running from his nose.

"How many rounds?" Ross asked, stepping up
beside the trumpet player at ringside.

"Must be twenty-five or thirty. I think Bob
would whip him in another couple of rounds if
he'd lay off the panther sweat."

Ross chuckled as he watched the fighting saloon
man throw back a shot of liquor. "Well, he's got to
prove his point his own way."

He walked back to the Break o' Day Saloon,
pushed his way inside, and stood at the bar until
the bartender found time to glance at him.

"What's the whiskey like?"

"Got three kegs of valley tan fresh from Salt
Lake."

"I'll have a taste of that and a cigar," Ross said,
reaching into his boot for his pouch of dust. He
traded the pouch for his drink and a long cigar,
watched the bartender sprinkle dust until the
scales leveled out at two bits' worth.

"Torch?" the bartender said, handing Ross a box
of matches with the return of his gold pouch.

Ross nodded and lit his smoke. He had taken to
smoking an occasional cigar in Boulder after hearing a drunken mule skinner recite a line of barroom verse:

> When weary I are,
> I smokes my cigar:
> And when the smoke rises
> Up into my eyeses,
> I thinks of my true love,
> And, oh, how I sighses.

He had laughed when he heard it. Then, having a few drinks under his belt, he had almost cried. Now the smoke was in his eyes again, the sigh on his lips. He was weary indeed, and thinking of Julia. The valley tan had a scalding edge to it, and he heard the brass bell ring outside.

Fourteen

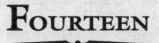

HE CLENCHED THE stub of his cigar in his teeth as he stepped outside to see how the fighters fared. The clean mountain air carried smoke into his lungs, and his head droned with a whiskey hum. The pugilists had to have gone fifty rounds by now. Each staggered, leaning on the other. Johnson was hurt, his face swollen and bloody. Hodges was merely drunk and a little tired.

A volley of gunshots drew Ross's attention up the street, beyond the fighting ring. He saw a freight wagon coming, bristling with gun barrels. A dozen voices sang, hollered oaths. As the wagon rumbled nearer, he sensed the fight spectators dispersing. A pistol round shattered a second-floor window and Ross recognized the familiar drawl of Dixie in the rough voices.

His instinct, though whiskey-clouded, told him

this was a good time to take his horse to a livery.
But he looked a little closer at the wagon and saw
a familiar figure holding the reins. He didn't have
to wonder. Men like Parkhill didn't come in pairs.
He was wearing an old Confederate cavalry cap.
His shoulders sprawled against his shotgun riders, and he sat spraddle-legged on a whiskey keg,
driving his team of four wantonly into the throng
at ringside.

"Hey!" he yelled, drawing rein and nudging one
of his men. "Don't I see that Yankee editor?"

A lean, squint-eyed rake steadied himself on
Parkhill's shoulder from behind. "What's left of
him."

"What was that he said about me in his paper?"

"Said the way you treat them poor Chinee bastards, you might as well have resurrected the
slave trade of the wretched Old South in the
Rockies."

"Now, Wink, are you sure he said 'wretched Old
South'?"

Wink whipped a newspaper from behind his
back and pointed out the line for Parkhill as the
men in the wagon began an ominous moaning.

"I believe that calls for an ass-whippin'," Parkhill said, jumping down from the wagon. Wink
tripped out behind him, catching a boot heel on a
sideboard and landing on his shoulder. Several
other men jumped from the wagon, picked Wink
up, and followed Parkhill to the boxing ring.

As Parkhill started to climb through the ropes,
someone grabbed him by the arm.

"Wait a minute, Parkhill," the trumpet player
said. "This here's a prizefight. We've got side bets.
You can't git in there."

Parkhill shook the man off, but the feisty miner only grabbed him again. Two of Parkhill's men pulled the musician back by the trumpet looped around his shoulder while a third clubbed him over the head with the barrel of a Navy Colt.

Ross sank his teeth into his cigar and stepped off the boardwalk as Parkhill climbed into the ring.

"I'll finish him off for you, Bob," he said, pushing the saloon man aside.

Johnson was scarcely coherent, smearing blood around his eyes with the backs of his fist, searching for his opponent. Parkhill pushed up his right sleeve as the editor staggered. He wound his arm a few times as if cranking a mill. Then he slammed a fist into Johnson's nose and watched the editor stumble back into the ropes and bounce on the floor.

Ross pushed his way among the laughing Parkhill men, picked up the trumpet player, and helped him to the boardwalk, where he could sit down. When he turned back to the ring, he saw Parkhill stomping the unconscious editor in the ribs, forcing him under the ropes and out of the ring. The saloon owner was standing in the far corner, looking suddenly sober.

Parkhill grabbed the prize purse full of gold dust as he stepped between the ropes. "Drinks for Dixie at the Break o' Day!" he shouted, waving the pouch, and his men stormed the saloon.

"You all right?" Ross asked.

"Yeah," the musician said, rubbing the back of his head, checking his fingers for blood.

"What's the deal with that big Reb?"

The musician blew some dust from his trumpet

valves. "Name's Parkhill. He owns the hydraulic works up the gulch. Only hires Chinese, except for his overseers, and they're all Sesech. He also freights some. Owns another claim up at Last Chance Gulch and runs a weekly stagecoach up there. Says the road's his and he'll whip anybody who won't pay his toll."

"Looks like he means it."

"One fellow thought he didn't," Fritz said. "Pennsylvania boy tried runnin' freight to Last Chance and wouldn't pay the toll on Parkhill's road. They found that boy dead. Had three numbers painted on his freight outfit."

"Numbers?"

"Three, seven, seventy-seven."

"What's that mean?"

"Vigilante code they used to use in California. Nobody knows what it means for sure, but a grave is about three foot wide, seven foot long, and seventy-seven inches deep, ain't it?"

Ross threw the stub of his cigar down in the street and watched the reporter for the *Post* trying to revive Johnson. "So Parkhill's a vigilante?"

"Make up your own mind about that," the trumpet player said. "Once was the time we had to have vigilantes around here for the likes of road agents, but now what we need is law for the likes of the vigilantes. I believe in checks and balances, and the damned vigilantes have gone too far."

Ross looked toward the Break o' Day and saw a steady stream of men coming out. "What's your name, friend?"

"Fritz."

"Pleasure to meet you. I'm R.W. Colby. You bet-

ter have somebody look at that head. Clean it out
or you'll get the lockjaw."

"I know a gal across town that'll look at it,"
Fritz said, getting up. "But if she cleans anything
out, she'll start with my pockets." He slapped
Ross on the back and headed up the street.

The laughter of the Parkhill men rang from the
saloon, and Ross felt a strange urge to join them.
He had cursed Sergeant Parkhill and the Knights
of the Golden Circle a thousand times over the
past months. If not for them, he would never have
lost Julia. Of course, he might have been massacred on the Crazy Woman instead, but Parkhill
deserved no credit for that chance stroke of luck.

Right now Ross had just enough whiskey in his
stomach and felt just enough frustration in his soul
to desire some retribution. It was like that day in
the cornfield. Like riding after Chug with Captain
Jones on her back. It was as good as done, fool-
hardy or not.

"Hey!" Parkhill shouted as Ross entered the saloon. "Let's drink to the Sons of Liberty!"

Their voices rallied, then died for a second as
the liquor poured down their throats.

"To the Knights of the Golden Circle!" Wink
said, lifting his drink again. He threw the last of
it past his teeth as his squint searched the room.
"Hey, Bob," he said to the saloon owner. "Come on
and have a drink with us."

Hodges was looking in the mirror of his backbar, cleaning blood from his swollen face with a
wet cloth. He merely glanced at Wink's reflection.

Parkhill's lieutenant strutted to the bar. "I said
drink to Dixie, Bob."

"I'm all drinked out," Bob answered.

"You're still standin'. Ain't you from Dixieland?"

"Maryland."

"Hell, that's Dixie! Drink up, Bob, I'm buyin'!"

Bob turned around to look at the drunken mine foreman. "I didn't fight for the Confederacy. I ain't no rich plantation owner."

Wink turned his head and sneered. "You didn't turn Yankee, did you?"

"No. Came out here to stay neutral. Couldn't fight against my home state." He filled Wink's glass, hoping he would take it and go away.

"Neutral, hell," Wink said. "You're a Southerner, boy. Let me hear you whistle 'Dixie.'"

"My lip's busted."

"Hum it."

Bob glanced at Parkhill, as if for help, only to find the big man grinning. "I can't carry a tune in sack, Wink. Leave me alone."

Wink shoved the drink back at Bob. "Then drink to Dixie, damn it."

"No."

Wink's bloodshot eyes widened and glared. He pulled a small revolver from his belt, cocked it, and pointed it at the saloon owner. "Drink!"

"Go to hell," Bob said.

The revolver erupted, knocking Bob against the backbar. He sank to the floor, holding his left side.

"Goddamn, Wink," Parkhill said, coming to look over the bar, his boots thundering across the floor in the midst of the sudden silence. "You better run for a doctor. Then just keep runnin'. Hide out till things settle down."

Ross let out the breath he had been holding since the gun fired. He saw Wink put the revolver in his pants and stroke his stubbled face nervously.

"I said git," Parkhill ordered, leaning over the bar. "He ain't dyin'. Don't worry about it. Just git."

Wink staggered toward the door, staring blankly at the light of day through the open doors.

Before Ross could contemplate, he felt his Remington in his right palm. He reached under Wink's left arm as the foreman passed him, grabbed the little revolver from the top of Wink's pants, and put its muzzle under Wink's chin. His Remington rose smoothly and covered the rest of the saloon as he pulled the foreman in front of him as a shield.

Every eye in the smoky room turned to stare. Then Bob Hodges rose from behind the bar, holding his rib cage.

"Put your hands behind you," Ross said to Wink. He paused to swallow, to breathe, to think. "Now stick them through your belt. That's right, now clasp them together. You try to get those hands loose, and I'll put a bullet right through your head."

"Who the hell are you?" Parkhill demanded. "Turn that man loose before you get hurt."

Ross covered the big man with his revolver, looking right over the sights, amazed to find them so steady. "Send an unarmed man for the doctor."

"If you don't stop givin' orders, you're gonna need the goddamn doctor."

Ross watched his pistol sights float to the high ridge of Parkhill's cavalry cap. Send a shot over his head, he thought. Let him know you mean business. He squeezed his trigger, felt the satisfying recoil, saw Parkhill standing wide-eyed and hatless. Damn, Ross thought, didn't mean to get that close!

"Frank," said Parkhill. "Take your guns off and fetch a doc."

Bob Hodges climbed onto the bar and lay down as if waiting to be examined.

With a jab of the pistol barrel under Wink's chin, Ross pulled him backward toward the door. "We're goin' to the jailhouse," he said.

"All right," Wink answered. "Careful with that piece, it's got a hair trigger."

They backed out of the bar and into the street, Ross's boots scuffing against Wink's. He kept his Remington trained on the door of the Break o' Day and saw Parkhill appear there, his hand on the revolver at his gun belt.

As he stumbled over ruts, Ross watched the Parkhill men follow at a distance. He risked only glances in the direction of the jailhouse, trusting Wink to lead the way. He knew he was there when he saw the wall at his shoulder. The jailhouse had been built of sawmill lumber laid flat, each layer overlapping at the corners. The walls stood eight inches thick, solid wood, bulletproof.

The stale smell of dust greeted him when he entered with his prisoner. He slid his Remington into its holster as he closed the door behind him and bolted it. He shoved Wink toward a cell, grabbing a key on an iron ring from the sheriff's desk. Before he pushed the foreman in, he took the time to frisk him, finding a knife in a boot scabbard. The iron door made a solid sound when it slammed, and the key slipped into the hole as if it knew the way. He tested the door: locked tight.

Ross put Wink's revolver on the sheriff's desk

and sat down. Whirlwinds of dust swirled in the sunlight beaming through the tiny window. He glanced at the gun rack: empty. He raked a finger across the desk, leaving a trail. He felt something unusual on his right palm and found his initials raised in reverse from the flesh.

Boots scuffled outside. Parkhill's fist pounded on the door and a shadow filled the window.

"How long's Sheriff Jackson been gone?" Ross asked.

"Jackson?" Wink said from the cell. "He's been dead two months."

Ross shot a glance into the cell. "What happened to him?"

"Somebody killed him on the road to Last Chance Gulch."

The fist pounded on the door again, harder this time.

"Who's the law around here now?" Ross asked.

Wink stared at him through the iron grating. "You mean, it ain't you?"

Parkhill's voice bellowed from outside: "Open up, lawman, and let's talk this over!"

FIFTEEN

THE WHISKEY HUM had left his head, and a dull ache had taken its place. Ross was sitting in a lawman's chair, trying to figure out what to do next. His only consolation was the fact that Parkhill had finally quit pounding on the door and gone away.

He stared at the dust suspended in the sunlight until he heard another pair of boots on the boardwalk.

"Open up!" a slurred voice said.

"Who is it?"

"The Virginia City *Post*."

Ross lifted the bolt and cracked the door to find the swollen face of Ed Johnson. The editor held a pencil and a pad of paper in his hands.

"What do you want?" Ross asked.

"I want to know what happened."

Seeing as how he needed information worse than Johnson right now, he figured he might as well let the editor in. "This man shot the owner of the Break o' Day Saloon," he said, opening the door, "so I put him in jail. How's the wounded man?"

"Unconscious right now, but the doc stopped the bleeding and says he'll pull through all right."

"It was an accident," Wink said from his cell. "My gun went off."

"It'll do that when you pull the trigger," Ross replied.

"What's your name?" the editor asked.

"R.W. Colby," Ross replied.

"You the deputy marshal we've been waiting on?"

"No."

"What kind of lawman are you?"

"I'm not a lawman at all. At the moment."

Johnson cocked his head back to see through his left eye—the one that wasn't quite swollen shut. "But you've heard we've got no law here."

"I heard your sheriff got killed a couple of months back."

"So that's what you're after," Johnson mumbled. "You sure know how to start a campaign, but there's no need for one. Nobody will run against you. Nobody wants the job."

"What job?"

"Sheriff."

"I'm not so sure I want it." Ross rubbed his temples as the whiskey throb grew.

"It's a good job for a lawman. You get a cabin on the edge of town, good pay, and support from the county and the city."

"I'll think about it."

"If you want the job, I can print ballots tonight,

announce a special election in tomorrow's issue, and have you in office in a couple of days."

"What am I supposed to do until then?"

"Guard your prisoner, I guess. I imagine the mayor will be by directly to appoint you town marshal until we can arrange the county election. That will give you jurisdiction in Virginia City for the time being. Where did you say you were from?"

"I've been on the drift."

Johnson shrugged. "Doesn't matter. Talk's all over town already. You sure know how to make an entrance."

"It just happened, that's all."

"What's the charge against Wink?"

Ross kept a straight face while his mind scrambled for some kind of legalism. "Attempted murder."

"I've got to get this story on the press," Johnson said, looking up at Ross as his hand continued to scribble notes. "I'll come back for a more detailed profile on you tomorrow. Anything I can do for you till then?"

Ross rubbed his stomach. "See that my horse gets to a livery, if you would. Bring me my bedroll and something to eat."

"You bet," Johnson said through his swollen lips, and he took his leave.

"I wasn't tryin' to shoot him, Colby," Wink said. "Honest."

"I wasn't tryin' to arrest anybody today, Wink. But these things happen."

Ross heard a fist beating on the jailhouse door and woke up staring at the bottom of the sheriff's desk. It would have been almost impossible to get a bullet under the desk from the little window, so he had slept there for the night. It seemed a little ridiculous now, and he decided he had been overly cautious.

"Who is it?" he said.

"Fritz."

Ross opened the door to find the trumpet-playing miner holding a tray of steaming food and drink.

"Thought you and Wink might want a little breakfast."

"Obliged," Ross said, inhaling the fragrances of coffee and biscuits. When he allowed Wink a share of the food, he noticed the prisoner's right eye twitching uncontrollably. "Got somethin' in your eye?"

"Nervous twitch. Runs in my family."

"I didn't see any twitchin' yesterday."

"I was drunk yesterday. It quits when I'm drunk."

"It don't quit," Fritz said. "It goes to your trigger finger."

Ross chuckled. He took his share of the breakfast and ate at the desk.

"You had me fooled yesterday," Fritz said. "I thought for all the world you were a prospector."

"What about you?" Ross said. "Not workin' your claim today?"

"Sold it."

"Worked out?"

"No, there's plenty of color left in it."

"Then why'd you sell?"

"I was thinkin' of runnin' for sheriff till you showed up. I'd settle for deputy."

Ross slurped coffee and wiped his mouth with a napkin. "What's your last name, Fritz?"

"Green."

"Where you from?"

"New York City. I was a police officer there for a year."

All night Ross had been feeling like a prisoner of his own impulses, locked up in a musty jailhouse on account of a hasty decision. He had slept cowering under the desk, for heaven's sake, afraid to step outside even to relieve himself.

But this Fritz Green—this new friend of his—had brought the light of dawn back into his thinking. This was no way to live. He got up, flung the door aside, and stood in the open portal. Nobody shot him dead, so he turned back to Fritz.

"Deputy Green, guard the prisoner. I have business to attend to."

Sixteen

With a hard snap, Hector Beauchamp tested the horsehair rope he had just twisted. It was sound, as usual, from end to end—a stout measure of bristling line long enough for making a bosal or a set of reins. He was in no hurry to make anything of it right now, though. He had to kill his time wisely. Maybe he would take a nap first.

"When we were stealin' ideas from the Mexicans," he said aloud to himself, "who was the dumb-ass who left out the siesta?" He stretched the rope again. "We got horsehair ropes, but we forgot the siesta. And tortillas. Why the hell didn't we get tortillas?"

He coiled the rope and looked southward down the street. "Beats the hell out of me," he said, answering himself. Denver was hot today; most folks staying in the shade. Only a few people moving around out of necessity. There went Tim Elliot in his lumber wagon, dragging a cloud of dust down the dirt street.

"I'd hate that. Every day, drive the damn wagon up the street, down the street." He looked north. "Load it, unload it." He waved at a friend turning into a log-walled saloon with a canvas roof. "Son of a bitch," he said. "Probably just sobered up."

Things were mighty dull today, but Heck wasn't complaining. He considered his job the best a lawman could have. A lot of benefits came with being a sheriff in a wide-open town like Denver. People tended to take care of you when they needed you as bad as Denver needed Heck Beauchamp.

He had two good permanent deputies and half a dozen reservists he could call on anytime trouble arose. He also carried a deputy U.S. Marshal badge, which gave him jurisdiction outside of his county. This allowed him to hire out as a detective to anyone who could afford his fee when he occasionally got bored with town life. Yes, this would be quite a setup if outlaws would quit shooting at him, and drunks would quit vomiting in his jail.

A woman came around a corner two blocks away. Carrying something. A baby? "Who the hell is that?" He watched her walk a block, her auburn hair bouncing on her shoulders. "She don't waste no time, do she? Got a stride, by golly."

When she angled across the street for his office, Heck Beauchamp rose from his chair, tucked his shirt in, stomped his pant legs down inside his boots, repositioned his hat, and twisted the handlebars of his mustache.

He could see her face now, and she was pretty.

Her look of determination concerned him a little. Whose baby was that? She wasn't a sporting girl, was she? Didn't look like one, now, but he had seen some of them clean up almost proper. But, no, he would have remembered her, even painted up in some dim social parlor. He breathed a sigh of relief.

"Afternoon, ma'am," he said.

She walked up the steps, uncovering the baby's face under the shade of the gallery roof. "Are you Sheriff Beauchamp?"

He brushed his finger across her baby's cheek and made dovelike noises. "Hector Beauchamp, ma'am. My friends call me Heck."

"I'm Mrs. Rossiter Caldwell. I need help finding my husband. I was told to come to you."

Heck tickled the baby under the earlobe. "I'm not generally in the business of trackin' down runaway husbands, Mrs. Caldwell."

"He didn't run away. He's lost. The army says he's dead."

Heck pulled the horsehair rope across his palm. "And you don't believe the army?"

"They have shown me no proof."

He stood back to admire the mother and child. "How old is she? It is a she, ain't it?"

"Yes. Her name's Fay. She's two months old."

He made baby noises at the infant again, then turned adult to address the mother. "How long has Mr. Rossiter Caldwell been lost?"

"He doesn't know he's a father."

Heck put his hand on his chin and pretended to contemplate. He was not at all in the business of tracking down husbands, whether they were lost or dead or whatever. But he had gone a long time without having a conversation with a woman like Mrs. Rossiter Caldwell. "Come in and let's talk about it," he said. "Maybe I can help."

Heck came to one conclusion rather easily as Mrs. Caldwell told her story. The poor woman's husband was dead and she just didn't want to admit it. She wanted her baby to have a father. The whole thing was a little sad, but it had the ring of opportunity. Hector Beauchamp was thirty-one years old, and at the present time enjoyed no prospects for lifelong female companionship.

"You have to know how to put a ring in the army's nose," he said, twirling one end of the horsehair rope. "Shouldn't take much sniffin' around to find out what they know. It usually ain't much. If the army doesn't know anything, the Indians will."

"What Indians?" Julia said.

"The ones that massacred that column on the Crazy Woman."

"But you can't just go out there and talk to them."

"Why not? I get on famous with Indians. I know the hand signs."

"But they're hostile."

"Oh, they tend to get a little bloodthirsty when the army rouses 'em from their pallets with a bugle charge and tramples their papooses into the ground. But they'll calm down after they take a few scalps to even the score. I hear they've been quiet this summer on the reservation."

Julia stared at his face, glanced at the twirling rope end. "The same Indians who massacred Captain Jones's column are now on a reservation?"

Heck nodded. "Eatin' government rations. That's Indian policy, ma'am. Don't make much sense, do it?"

Julia pursed her lips and looked down at the baby in her arms. "We should discuss your fee," she said. "I might be a while in raising it."

Heck slapped his hands against his knees. "Mrs. Caldwell, you happen to be in luck. I have to go up through Fort Laramie and the Sioux country on another investigation. Seein' as how your case won't require much pokin' around, I'll just take it on as a favor to you and little Fay. Why, come to think of it, I wouldn't take a fee from such a good-lookin' pair if you were rich as you are pretty."

"I can raise the money in time," Julia said. "I don't expect any favors."

"We've already settled that. Now, where are you stayin'?"

"Mrs. Masterson has been kind enough to give me the use of a room until she gets a paying boarder. I've been helping her with the cooking and cleaning."

Heck shook his head. "I'm glad you came to me, Mrs. Caldwell, because one of my deputies, Elliot McDaniels, is married and lives in a house with an extra room."

"Oh, no, I couldn't," Julia said.

"They're expectin' a baby of their own in a couple of months and Elliot was telling me just the other day how he wished he had a woman around who could help his wife with her chores, and I said, 'Elliot, why don't you help her yourself?' And you know what he said? He said, 'Heck, you won't find no biscuit dough on my pistol grip.' But that's just the way Elliot is." He got up and urged Julia toward the door.

"This really isn't necessary," she said. "I didn't come here to beg charity."

"You'll be doin' 'em a favor. I'll borrow a buggy and we'll drive up there together. You'll like Elliot's wife. She's a Southern gal, too."

Julia felt the baby squirm in her arms. Well, if they were nice people, and if she could stay for a while, what was the harm? She had to have a place to live until she found Ross.

"At least meet 'em, for heaven's sake," Heck said.

She sighed. "Oh, all right. I suppose it wouldn't hurt to meet them."

SEVENTEEN

YOU SEE HIM?" Ross shouted over the roar of the spray.

"He ain't here," Fritz answered. "I don't see him nowhere."

A rainbow hung over the Parkhill Hydraulic Works—the only pretty thing about the place. Ross had seen streams and gullies pretty well carved up by placer miners, but this hydraulicking ate at the world like a locust. There had been a hillside here last year, he recalled. A gentle slope covered with high grass and studded with young pines. Now there was a ragged bluff seventy feet high and a gaping void where tons of gravel had lain for eons.

Three men were operating artillerylike nozzles, spraying jets of water onto the exposed hillside.

The lawmen had hoped Wink might be among them, but he was nowhere to be seen.

"Where are all the Chinamen, Fritz?"

"They work the sluices below and the reservoirs above."

"The hard work," Ross suggested.

"Yeah, and dangerous. Four of 'em's been killed."

Ross watched the jets undercut the raw bluff. "Avalanche?"

"Two were killed in an avalanche. One drowned when he was sucked into a pipe. The fourth was cut damn near half in two by that hydraulic spray."

Ross shot a glare at Fritz. "How the hell could that happen?"

"Talk was that Parkhill executed him with that nozzle for tryin' to lead a wage strike. I saw the body. It was a damn hell of a sight."

Ross's lip curled and he spotted Parkhill riding toward him across a ridge. "Here comes the big bastard now." As he watched, the mine owner twisted quickly in the saddle, spitting on his horse's rump. It drove Ross's thoughts back twelve months and more, and he suddenly felt himself riding Chug in Parkhill's repair detachment. He had to grin, feeling the advantage he had. Parkhill still hadn't recognized him, though he could tell the big man had been trying to place him.

"What brings you out here, Sheriff?" Parkhill asked, drawing rein in front of the mounted lawmen.

"Checkin' on Wink. Makin' sure he hasn't jumped bail." Ross caught himself putting gravel in his voice, subconsciously disguising it.

"Hell, if he jumped bail, I'd be after him before you. I was the one put the money up. Besides that, I can't do without him. He's my chief engineer. Wink's the one brought the pipes and nozzles and all the Chinamen from California."

"So where the hell is he?" Fritz said.

"He's got a work gang on a new flume around the bend. Come see for yourself if you want."

Ross nodded at his deputy and they nudged their horses up the gulch.

"Sheriff," Parkhill said as they rode, "I keep gettin' the feelin' I know you from somewhere. Have we met before?"

"I'm a stranger out here."

"Where do you come from?"

"Nowhere."

They rode in silence for a minute.

"Some operation you've got here," Ross said. "Where'd you get the capital for it?"

Parkhill turned to spit. "Where do you think? It's root, hog, or die out here, Colby. I staked a claim in Last Chance Gulch that paid six dollars to the pan, and diggin's was shallow. Then I made some improvements on the road between here and Last Chance, so the legislature awarded me a franchise for the toll road."

"What kind of improvements did you make?"

"Cut down trees, dug up rocks, blasted. I even put in some corduroy road where it washes out regular."

"Fritz tells me this road of yours is plagued by outlaws."

"Nothin' you can do about that," Parkhill said. "Them road agents are gonna steal from you out here. Course, they don't bother me, because I take precautions. I send a shotgun rider with every stage and freight outfit I put on the road. Out here you take care of those things yourself, Colby. No offense, but lawmen ain't much use in this country, except maybe for collectin' fines from whorehouses."

Ross smirked. "When did you start this hydrau-lickin'?"

"Just this spring. When Wink showed up with all the trappin's, I bought him out and hired him as engineer. He's a good man."

"His gun goes off easy," Fritz said.

"Nobody can help accidents," Parkhill replied. "Part of life."

As they rounded the bend, Ross spotted the work gang wielding picks, carving a notch in a hillside for a flume. The Chinamen wore their distinctive hats and ragged work clothes. A couple of them went barefoot. Wink was looking down on them from his horse, his leg hitched lazily over the saddle horn.

Ross reined in his mount. "What do you pay those poor devils?"

"They get a fair wage. They don't complain."

"Wouldn't be healthy for 'em if they did," Fritz added.

"Shit, if it wasn't for my payroll, they'd starve. Every damn one of 'em's just glad to have a job."

"I've seen enough," Ross said. "Let's go."

"Don't you want to say howdy to Wink?" Parkhill asked.

"Yes," Ross replied. "In court."

The lawmen spurred their horses to a trot and put the bend between themselves and Parkhill.

"Fritz, I want to have a look at those China-men's living quarters."

"All right, but I hope your horse is gentle."

"Why?"

"Because, if he ain't, the rats and mice are lia-ble to spook him clean to Idaho."

Ross sat staring, his eyes squinted, nostrils pinched. Even from the edge of the shantytown he could see rodents crawling among the hovels in broad daylight.

"The hell of it is that they're spreadin' up into Virginia City," Fritz said. "We'll be overrun by the damn things by the time summer's over."

"Aren't there any cats in town?"

"There's three toms that I know of, and Lester Shinn has one old she-cat over at his livery barn."

"Why don't they breed a litter?"

"They tried," Fritz explained. "That ol' she-cat whipped every one of them toms. Mort Frawley trapped a bobcat and tried to breed that to her, but she whipped him, too. Course he was missin' one foot where the trap got him."

They rode in among the first of the shacks and Ross shook his head. The Chinamen had used old boards, logs, brush, pieces of wagon sheets. They had tried to establish winding streets, but rains had turned them into gullies on the hillside. A child sat in one of them, playing with rocks. The mother worked nearby, scrubbing clothes in tubs made of whiskey barrels sawed in half.

A sudden pang knifed at his heart as he remem-bered Julia laboring over the laundry barrels at Camp Marshall, and he knew he had to do something. "How come they don't fix these places up a little?" he asked.

"Parkhill works the men long hours at the hydraulic works. They don't have no time for fixin' up their houses. Even if they had the time, they don't have the money to buy lumber. They gotta pay their rent first."

"Rent?" Ross scanned the hovels again. "Parkhill?"

"Takes it out of their wages before they ever see it. Nobody wants 'em here, anyway, R.W. They work too damn cheap. Any more of 'em, and they'd put all the American miners out of a job. But, damn, nobody ought to have to live like this."

Ross reined his horse back toward town. "I've seen enough. Let's go."

They were three blocks from the jail when Ed Johnson burst out of the barbershop with the towel still around his face. "Sheriff! You better get down to the Break o' Day!"

"What for?" Ross said.

"Bob Hodges is leaving town!"

Ross and his deputy loped to the saloon, only to find it deserted. Across the open door, just under the etched-glass window, they found three numbers scrawled in red paint:

3-7-77

"Bob!" Ross shouted, entering the barroom. He found Hodges coming down the stairs from his room above the saloon, carrying a bag stuffed to bulging. "Where do you think you're going?"

"Salt Lake City."

"The grand jury expects you to testify next week."

"No, it don't. I dropped the charges against Wink. Decided it was just an accident."

"What the hell did you do that for?"

"You seen the numbers!" Hodges shouted, jutting a finger toward the front door. "I'm a dead man if I stay in this town."

Ross's eyes followed the saloon owner behind the bar. "I'll put you under guard at the jail where nobody can get you," he offered.

"So you can be a dead man, too? Forget it, Sheriff. We're whipped. It was an accident."

"But what about your saloon?" Fritz asked.

Hodges was lining the bar with pouches of gold dust, tying them together. "I sold it."

"Let me guess," Fritz said. "Parkhill."

Hodges nodded.

"How much did he give you for the place?"

"None of your damn business." The saloon man stuffed the gold dust in his traveling bag and turned toward the door.

"Think about what you're doin'!" Ross pleaded.

Hodges stopped on the threshold and slung his bag on his back. "The only thing I have to think about is catchin' that stage to Salt Lake. You don't know these vigilantes, Colby. If you're smart, you'll let the matter rest and go back to collectin' fines from whorehouses and hurdy-gurdies." He glanced at the numbers painted on the door of his former saloon. "Virginia City ain't ready for no law yet."

Hodges left, his heavy boots clogging against the boardwalk.

"Well," Fritz said, slapping his hat against the bar. "We might as well have us a drink on Parkhill." He reached for a whiskey jug.

Ross felt the anger boil up in him until he could no longer hold it back. He lashed out, kicking a table, flipping it onto its side.

"Hey," Fritz said, "take it easy, R.W."

But Ross didn't hear; didn't even feel the deputy's presence anymore. Parkhill's secret societies and contempt for everything just had taken him again from a blind side and swept him up in a whirlwind of anger. Was Parkhill following him in life, or what? Maybe that was it. Maybe God was throwing obstacles in his way to test him. Do something about Parkhill, and you can have Julia back.

"R.W. R.W.!"

Ross blinked and found Lester Shinn standing next to Fritz. "Huh?" he said. "What is it, Lester?" He hadn't even seen the livery man enter.

Lester fumbled with the hat in his hands and looked at the floor. "Well, you know this mornin', when I loaned you that bay mare, so your old white horse could rest?"

"Yeah." He was hardly listening to Lester. Something else was trying to speak to him.

"Well, I didn't tell you at the time, because I thought maybe he'd get over it."

"Over what?" How do you hurt a man like Parkhill? he was thinking.

Lester glanced sheepishly at Fritz. "Well, I must have left his stall unlatched last night, and Ol' Whitey got into a pile of green alfalfa hay I had stacked in the barn. Colicked hisself. I didn't want to tell you this mornin', so I loaned you the bay. Thought maybe I could walk it out of Whitey, but he sat down and wouldn't get back up."

"What are you sayin', Lester?" Ross asked.

Lester forced himself to look the sheriff in the eye. "He's deader than hell, Sheriff. I'm sorry. I'll give you any mount in my stable in trade."

Ross sighed and looked at his bearded, weathered face in the mirror behind the bar. "Ol' Whitey's dead, huh?" He could feel himself on the verge of a wild idea. "Guess I better drag him out of town and burn him."

"I'll take care of it," Lester said. "It was my fault."

Ross put his hand on Lester's shoulder. "He was my horse, Lester. You understand. I'd better do it myself."

EIGHTEEN

$\blacktriangleright$━━━━$\bullet$━━━━$\blacktriangleleft$

Ross PULLED HIS pocket watch out to check the time. Four-thirty in the afternoon, and still no sign of the Parkhill stagecoach. It should have passed here by this time. This waiting was torture.

A woodpecker drummed suddenly against a hollow tree behind him, making him flinch. He liked this high country: the cool pine-scented air, the long views. These Tobacco Root ranges along Parkhill's toll road to Last Chance reminded him of the Bighorn Mountains Jasper Jones had ordered him to cross. Hard to enjoy them today, though. Other things on his mind.

He wasn't sure he was going to go through with it now. He could always go back to town and let the Parkhill men drive by unmolested as if he had never come up with the idea in the first place.

The white horsehair beard he wore was starting to make him sweat and itch, but he didn't dare scratch at it for fear he would pull it out of place and show his real whiskers. The disguise was the most important part of the scheme. If it failed, he was ruined.

Maybe the gold shipment from Parkhill's diggings at Last Chance Gulch wasn't coming today, after all. That would be both a relief and a disappointment. Maybe he hadn't thought about this thing long enough. It might be well to go home and sleep on it a few more nights.

He sighed and tucked his watch back into his pocket. It's just as well, he thought. You never could have gone through with it, anyway. You're good on a whim, boy, but premeditation never was your strong point.

Just as he was getting up to leave, he heard the crack of a whip and the crunch of wagon wheels on rocks below. His heart jumped like a startled animal trying to burst from his chest. Looking down the grade, he saw the coach coming up the road, a passenger's elbow jutting from one of the windows.

The vehicle slowed as it mounted the steep grade. The driver cracked his whip over the six mules, turned to his partner to continue some story he was in the middle of. The shotgun rider bounced on the seat, listening, grinning, his weapon across his lap.

Let them go by, Ross thought. You can't do this. It was a ridiculous idea in the first place.

But when the stage neared the top of the grade, he felt his body surge ahead through the trees. He put the stoop in his shoulders, the gravel in his throat, and—in a moment of invention—a limp in one leg. He stepped into the road just as the lead mule prepared to drop down the next slope, and the big animal balked when it saw him there. The coach stopped, rolled back a foot as the mules tossed their heads.

"Git your lazy asses up!" the driver roared, drawing his whip back. Then he saw the old man in the road pointing the double barrel at him, and the strength left his arm. The burly old highwayman's tattered hat covered the top of his face, and the long white beard hid the front of his dirty vest.

"Set the brake!" Ross ordered, scarcely recognizing his own voice. "Don't lift that scattergun, boy!" He saw a head jut momentarily from a window.

The shotgun rider put his hands in the air, leaving his weapon on his lap.

"What do you want, old man?" the driver said. "Git the hell out of the road!"

"Shut your mouth, you scrawny little pup. You boys work for Parkhill?"

"Yeah."

"Good. Throw down the strongbox."

The stagecoach men looked at each other.

"Now!"

The driver glanced down the twin barrels of the old bandit's shotgun, then reached for the box behind him. He had to put one knee on the seat to heft it. He slid it over the edge of the coach roof and let it drop to the ground.

"Now, git!" Ross ordered. "Anybody looks back'll see buckshot comin'."

The whip cracked and the coach dropped quickly down the grade, leaving Ross alone with the silence of the high country, and the strongbox, a small wooden trunk braced with iron straps. He felt suddenly sick, but stuck to his plan, dragging the box into the trees. He put a steel bar in the padlock and twisted, popping the latch off the box. He threw back the lid and found rows of white sacks. Lifting one, he knew it contained gold dust.

Dizzily, Ross began stuffing the bags of dust into his saddlebags, but there was too much to carry. He couldn't seem to catch his breath. He left half the gold in the broken box and ran back to the road.

Looking to make sure no one was coming, he crossed to the other side and ducked into the timber. He ran a hundred yards with his shotgun in one hand and the saddlebag slung over his shoulder until he reached the buckskin horse Lester Shinn had traded him for Ol' Whitey. He flung the heavy bags on behind the cantle and tied them down. He stripped his costume off, revealing his own clothes underneath. He dropped the fake beard, the garments, and the sawed-off shotgun onto the waiting blanket and made a bedroll of them.

After securing his things, he mounted and took a high trail across the mountainside. The way he had it figured, the coach was just now arriving at the dead tree he had pulled across the road. The coachmen would have to unhitch a mule to clear it out of the way. He could push his horse hard and arrive at his cabin fifteen minutes before the coach got to town.

"God, you've done it now," he said to himself as he whipped his horse with the ends of his reins.

But he felt a grin crawling under his whiskers as he imagined the look on Parkhill's face.

He stopped to look across the gulch before he approached his cabin. It was almost dark now, and his place stood at the far corner of town, so he would probably not be seen. Even if someone heard him riding, they would think nothing of it. Darkness tended to bring a lot of activity to Virginia City.

He trotted his tired horse across the gulch and up to his shed. The bay horse he had borrowed from Lester this morning waited inside. He stripped his saddle from the buckskin, then hustled to his house carrying his saddlebags and bedroll, leading the fresh bay. He tied the bay to his rickety picket fence and hurried into the cabin.

Locking the door behind him, he pushed a heavy table aside and pulled up a floorboard he had loosened. He dropped the bedroll and the stolen gold into the hole and covered it again, positioning a table leg over the loose plank.

Walk, he told himself. Act natural. He stepped casually outside, trying to whistle through his dry lips. He led the borrowed bay horse down Cover Street, tipping his hat to the occasional greeting along the way.

"Lester," he called, sticking his head into the barn. "I brought your horse back."

"Howdy, Sheriff," Lester said, coming out of the feed room. "You do any good prospectin'?"

Ross smirked. "I found a little color."

"Where'bouts?"

"I ain't tellin' you, Lester. You'll stake it before I can pan it out."

"You didn't go far, judgin' by this horse."

"Oh, it's handy," Ross said.

"How's that lame hoof on that buckskin?"

"It wasn't as bad as I thought. He'll be all right in a day or two." He listened for the whip of the Parkhill stage driver. "Anything happen while I was gone?"

"Couple of fights is all. Fritz broke 'em up. Nobody hurt bad."

The sheriff nodded approvingly. "Well, thanks for the loan of the horse, Lester."

"Anytime."

He went to the jail to find Fritz turning the key in the front door.

"Evenin', R.W. Didn't expect to see you till tomorrow."

"I had forgotten how dull prospectin' could get. Any trouble while I was gone?"

"Not a lick. I was just fixin' to make a round and go home."

"I'll walk with you."

They strolled down the street, checking locked doors, eyeballing thirsty miners on their way to favorite saloons. As they passed in front of the bakery, the Parkhill stagecoach suddenly thundered around the curve onto Wallace Street, Parkhill himself holding the reins.

"Colby!" Parkhill bellowed, stopping the team. "Saddle up! My stage got robbed!"

Ross looked at his deputy, then back at Parkhill. "Robbed? Where?"

Shaken passengers began pouring out of the coach.

"Comin' up Bear Pass," the driver said. "An old

man held us up and got the strongbox full of dust."

Ross crossed his arms over his chest and cocked his head. "I thought you took precautions against road agents, Parkhill. Why didn't you take care of it yourself?"

"Because I wasn't there!" Parkhill roared. "These chickenshits just picked me up at my wagon yard on the way into town!" He elbowed the two stage men flanking him. "Now, you saddle up and go out there and catch the bastard! What kind of a lawman are you?"

Ross pulled a cigar out of his pocket and rolled it between his fingers. "Didn't you tell me just a few days ago that lawmen weren't much use in this country? Except for collectin' whorehouse fines?" He bit the end from the smoke, spit it toward Parkhill.

"I've *found* a use for you!" Parkhill shouted. "Go out there and find that road agent!"

Ross took a match from his pocket, struck it on the brick wall of the bakery, touched its flame to the end of his cigar. "Bear Pass, huh? That's across the county line, ain't it, Fritz? That's out of our jurisdiction."

"Since when do we have a county line?" Parkhill snapped.

Ross laughed smoke into the breeze. "Settle down, Parkhill. I'm just needlin' you a little for gettin' yourself robbed. I'll go have a look in the mornin'."

"You'll go right now!"

"What good would it do? Maybe spook that bandit into the high country is all. I'll have a look in the morning when I can see something, but I doubt it'll do any good. Like you told me the other day, Parkhill, outlaws are gonna steal from you out here. That's just all there is to it."

Parkhill spit a stream of tobacco juice in front of his shotgun rider. "You're worthless, Colby. How the hell did you ever get elected sheriff?"

Ross shrugged, fighting to keep the laughter down inside him. This was better than he had ever imagined. "I guess I was just in the right place at the right time. Sort of like that fellow who robbed your stage."

Parkhill hissed and shook his reins, driving the coach down the street.

"Damn," Ross said, turning to Fritz. "You'd have thought I robbed the damned stage myself."

NINETEEN

Y̶OU KNOW HE'S dead," Heck said to himself as he trotted his horse past the rows of troop tents outside of Fort Laramie. "Would you let a wife like that run loose if you wasn't dead?" He bounced along in silence until he was almost to the sutler's store. "If he ain't dead, he's about the sorriest outfit I ever heard tell of."

"Hold it, mister," a soldier on sentry duty ordered. "What do you want?"

"Government business. I'm Deputy U.S. Marshal Hector Beauchamp here to see Colonel Kulp." He peeled back his vest to reveal his badge.

"Come with me," the soldier ordered.

Heck followed the private around the sutler's store and along the borders of the parade ground. They stopped in front of "Old Bedlam," the building that housed the bachelor officers and served as post headquarters. The private ordered him to wait outside as he stepped into the commander's office. He got down and gave his mount some breathing room in the cinch. He tipped his hat back, enjoying the breeze that cooled the sweat on his forehead.

Three lieutenants rode up to Old Bedlam and jumped down from their mounts, leaving their horses at the rail. After they went inside, Heck walked to the horse nearest to him, patting it on the rump to let it know he was there. He grasped the top of the horse's tail with both hands and, in one smooth stroke, ran a tight grip all the way down the tail, harvesting a single horsehair. He went to the second mount and got another hair. As he was pulling his hands down the third horse's tail, the sentry came out of the headquarters building.

"What the hell are you doin'?" the private said.

Heck wrapped the tail hairs around his fingers, making a small coil. "Buildin' a horsehair bridle for a lady friend of mine." He tucked the coil into his vest pocket. "You ain't gonna tell the President I took these, are you?"

The private smirked. "The colonel's clerk wants to see you."

Heck walked in, holding his hat. "Howdy," he said.

The clerk glanced up and down at him. "Howdy yourself. What's this official business you have with the colonel?"

Heck pulled up a chair and fanned himself with his hat. "Well, to tell you the truth, it ain't all that official or anything. You can probably take care of it yourself without even botherin' the old man."

"That's usually the way. Now, what brings you here?"

"I was first cousins with Captain Jasper Jones, the fellow who got hisself scalped last summer."

"I know who he was."

"Figured you did. Well, his mother—my aunt—wired me from Boston and said she never did get Jasper's personal things from the army. Asked me if I'd find 'em and send 'em to her."

"That's all?"

Heck shrugged. "That's about it."

The clerk leaned his chair back on its hind legs. "Captain Jones's things were held here until after the investigation. I think they're still in the warehouse."

"Can I look?"

"No, but I can."

"Can I go with you?"

He rocked forward in his chair as he got up. "I guess so. Let's see if the stuff is still there."

They left Old Bedlam, walked across the parade grounds, passed the infantry barracks, and proceeded to the warehouse. After inquiring with a few soldiers, the clerk located Captain Jones's personal effects stacked in a dusty corner.

"I'll see that it gets sent out today," the clerk promised. "My apologies to the family for the delay. You know the army."

Heck's eye caught a splinter jutting from a small portable writing desk. "This looks like a bullet hole," he said.

"That was found in Captain Jones's tent on the battleground."

Heck sighed and shook his head. "Poor old Jasper. Do you mind?" he asked, removing a stack of folded uniforms from the desk so he could open its top. He scanned a few leaves of paper in the desk, then his hand touched a leather-bound book with a buckle on it. "What's this?" He opened it and found a dated notation on the first page. "Why, it's Jasper's diary."

"Is it?" the clerk said.

"Corporal, do you mind if I express this one item to Boston and let Jasper's mother know the rest of his things will be comin' soon?"

"I guess that would be all right."

He clasped the corporal's shoulder in his hand. "The family'll be grateful to you, Corporal."

Heck sat down in the shade of the sutler's store and began with the last entry in the diary, something about drilling the men today and feeling good about the restored discipline. After turning just two pages back, the name of a Private Caldwell leaped up at him from the diary.

He read aloud to himself: "Private Caldwell left at dusk, assigned to special duty for duration of his enlistment." He looked up at his horse. "What the hell kind of order is that?" He looked down at the diary, then back up at his horse. "Damn, that sorry outfit didn't git massacred, after all. He might still be alive somewhere."

He tore the page from the diary and stuffed it into his pocket. "If he's alive, he ain't worth spit," he said as he got up. "If she was my wife, I'd find my way back to her, by God."

TWENTY

THE BAND WAS playing a waltz when Ross entered. He stood for a moment to let his eyes adjust from the glare of the afternoon to the dim smokiness of the hurdy-gurdy house. The dance floor came into focus first: only three couples waltzing, but it was early.

He focused on the orchestra next: five men sitting in a corner, each with an instrument or two and a glass of something within reach. A rail separated the band from the dance floor, and it led Ross's eyes all the way around the room. Near the bar he saw two miners standing inside the rail, ogling something against the wall. He sauntered that way and finally made out a row of women sitting against the wall on a bench. They paid little attention to the two miners judging them from across the rail.

"You. Hey, you, darlin'!" one of the miners said. "You and your friend care to dance?"

Two girls got up to speak to the men. They wore fine gowns from back East and really looked quite proper in the gloomy light. After a moment of conversation, they directed the miners to the scales where the bartender measured out a dollar per man in dust, then they stood waiting for the next song to begin.

"How about you, Sheriff?" a giggling voice said.

Ross found a young blonde emerging from the dark. "Pardon?" he said.

"I'll dance with you. Dances are on the house for you."

She wasn't more than seventeen, he thought. "No, thank you, miss. I'm here to see the proprietress."

"Oh," the girl said, her enthusiasm wilting. "I'll tell her."

The waltz ended and one of the hurdies had to fight off her dance partner, who insisted on kissing her.

"Let her alone," Ross warned, his voice rasping across the dance floor. "Kissin' ain't part of the deal."

The miner left grousing, and the band struck up another number.

"She'll see you now," the young blonde said, appearing at Ross's shoulder. "This way."

He followed her to a dark corner, the wooden floor creaking under his feet. She opened a door, blinding Ross with daylight that streamed in through lace curtains, falling like spray on the form of a woman sitting at a small desk. She seemed to glow, as if the light were hers and not the sun's. He squinted, shaded his eyes, glanced through another door to see a canopy bed draped with lace, silk ropes, and tassels. The blonde girl closed the door behind him, shutting the music out.

"Sheriff Colby," the woman said, getting up from her desk to approach him. "I finally meet you."

For a moment he thought she was smiling, but it was just that the corners of her mouth turned upward in a misleading way, like dangerous barbs to her full painted lips. Her eyes sparkled through fronds of darkened lashes. Curls of reddish-black hair strayed onto her round cheeks, her shoulders, her bare throat. The eyes were . . . What color *were* they?

"Can I get you something to drink?" she asked, placing her right hand in his.

"No, thanks."

She gestured toward a chair and Ross nodded. He sat down, put his leather case on his lap, and removed a ledger book. "I don't believe I know your name," he said. Looking up, he noticed a small safe on the floor beside her writing desk.

She turned to a small mirrored bar and watched him in the glass as she pulled the top on a decanter of amber drink. "Sage."

Ross smirked. "Sage what?" He was expecting something like "Lovejoy" or "Darling." Already today he had collected fines from hurdies and sporting women with names such as Ranche Belle, Scarlet Valentine, Goldie Rush.

"Just Sage," she said, filling a second glass with liquor. She turned back to Ross, offering the drink to him.

"This is a business call," he insisted.

"A short whiskey's good for business." She swirled the drink seductively in front of his eyes.

Ross looked past the liquor to find her looming over him, standing uncomfortably close. She was smaller than average, but her presence overwhelmed him. The enticing curve and swirl of the whiskey in the glass seemed to flow from her, through her fingertips.

He took the drink, his eyes following the contours of her dress to her lips. Was she smiling, or was that just the way her mouth turned? Her face seemed to say that she just really did not give a damn about anything.

"Thanks," he said, and she turned away, giving him room to breathe. "Now, what's the name of your establishment?"

"It doesn't have one." She sat upright at her desk chair, crossed her legs, and clasped both hands over a knee.

"All I have here is a description of your place," he said. "I have to put in a name for the business."

"Then make one up."

He sipped the whiskey. It was good smooth stock: not some cheap valley tan or flash of lightning. He put it on a glass-topped lamp table at his elbow and opened his ledger book. "I'll just call it Sage's Place."

She locked her elbows and inhaled a sigh that pushed swells of white flesh up from her neckline. "That's really not very imaginative. Why not call it the Golden Sage?"

She turned her head to look across the room at nothing and he noticed a small black beauty mark under the curve of her jaw. "All right," he said. "The Golden Sage." He wrote it down, then paused for another sip of whiskey. "Now, Miss Sage, I suppose you've heard that the city has an ordinance against dance-for-pay places, or hurdy-gurdies, or whatever you want to call 'em."

"Are you going to shut me down?"

"No, but the town is charging you the annual four-hundred-dollar fine for operating."

"That's ridiculous. If you're not going to shut me down, then it's not a fine. It's a license to operate."

He looked for indignation in her eyes, but found only that hollow indifference. When he concentrated on the corners of her mouth, he could almost convince himself that she was enjoying his company. "Call it what you like, but if you don't pay it, I *will* shut you down. That's the way the ordinance works."

"It's ridiculous, and you know it. I can see it in your face. You detest it, don't you? It's not as if I were operating a brothel or something."

"Are you going to pay it or not?"

She rose and smoothed the fabric hugging her waist. "Of course I'm going to pay it."

He picked up the whiskey and watched her kneel in front of the little iron safe. As he watched her work the combination, he inhaled the aroma of whiskey and enjoyed a sip. He put the glass on the table again and looked up to find Sage standing there—just standing—as if waiting for him to watch her. She approached and handed him a pouch of gold dust.

"I already weighed it," she said. "I've been expecting you."

Ross put the dust in his leather bag and made the entry in his ledger book.

"I'll have a receipt," she said, taking her seat at the desk. "And since I'm purchasing this license to operate, I feel entitled to say that a portion of that revenue should be used for relief instead of all of it going into the pockets of the town bureaucrats."

"Relief?" Ross said.

"Men sleeping on saloon floors because they have no homes, mothers and children begging for food, and those Chinese people living in those shacks outside of town. It's all a disgrace. The city should establish a relief fund."

Ross closed his book, tucked it slowly into his leather bag. He could feel his eyebrows hunching up on his forehead. She was right. He had thought of it often. There was enough gold dust blowing down these streets to feed every empty stomach in town. He had enough under the floorboards of his cabin to put roofs over every miserable soul. The question, up to this moment, had been how to distribute it.

"What?" she said, reading the look on his face.

He took up the whiskey glass. "I have a better idea. Establish your own relief fund. If the city did it, the bureaucrats would just bleed it to death, anyway. A private charity would be much more effective."

Her eyes angled away. "Where would I get the money?"

"I'll collect it. You distribute it."

Until now, she had prophesied his every move and word. He was just a man, after all. A lawman at that—one of the easiest breeds for a woman in her profession to predict. But this suggestion was extraordinary, and she caught herself feeling suddenly unaware of what message her features were sending back to him.

"How about it?" he said. "Do you want to help those unfortunate wretches out there or not?"

"You can use my safe." She turned in her chair and kicked the door of the iron box shut. "I'll contribute the first hundred dollars myself." She shrugged. "Maybe the publicity will be good for business."

He poured the last swallow of whiskey down his throat, buckled his leather bag, and got up. The thought of Parkhill's money buying food and shelter for his Chinese laborers tickled him so much that a grin formed on his face. He took a step toward Sage and held his open hand out to her. "Congratulations, partner. You and I just became philanthropists."

She looked at his palm for a second, then put her left hand against it and used it to steady herself as she rose.

Strange handshake, Ross thought. Why does she stand so close? How old is she? Twenty-five? Thirty-five? She seems childlike and innocent in a way. Is that smile genuine? He caught himself staring at her lips, felt Julia over his shoulder.

The band stopped playing and a girl screamed outside. Ross yanked his hand from Sage's and rushed to the dance floor to find a group of miners laughing, one of them holding a girl on his back.

"Here, now, put her down!" he ordered.

"Hell, Sheriff, I would if I could shake her off. She jumped on me."

"What for?"

"A big ol' rat ran across the dance floor!"

Sage came to Ross's side. "The vermin situation in this town is deplorable. The City Council should do something."

TWENTY-ONE

SAGE JUGGLED THE figures a dozen ways, and still came up short. That orphan Turner boy had to be sent back to Iowa before winter came on. Men were still sleeping on the bare floor in the relief barracks. The hospital needed a new shipment of medicine and supplies. And those Chinese families in Parkhill's tenement town still didn't have enough food to go around.

Sheriff Colby had raised more than she expected, but it was already gone. Now she would have to test his commitment. She wasn't at all certain she had him figured out yet.

Deputy Green had delivered all the contributions. Sage hadn't seen the sheriff since the day he sold her the license to operate her place. She had expected to work directly with him in this relief fund, but he was obviously avoiding her. She knew she had gotten to him that afternoon in her office, so why hadn't he come back around? Shy? She didn't think so. Probably had something to do with another woman. Women were always ruining men before she could get her hands on them.

She smiled and stuck her pen in the stand. She should meet with the sheriff personally on this budgetary matter, she thought, and there was no better time than now. Evening was coming on and he would soon be stopping at his favorite saloon for a whiskey on his way home. Maybe he would like to sample some more of the Golden Sage's reserve stock.

She got a shawl from her bedroom, paused to apply a drop of perfume to her throat, and set out for Wallace Street. As she passed the *Post*, she heard a knuckle wrapping on the inside of the glass. Glancing, she saw Johnson trying to wave her into the office. She ignored him, and kept walking, but heard him storm through the door behind her.

"Miss Sage, I need some clarification," the editor said. "Is that Turner boy going to make it back to Iowa or not?"

"He will be among his relatives before the first snow."

"Do you have enough in the relief fund for the Turner boy *and* the cots in the relief barracks? The public has a right to know where their contributions are going."

"We'll manage to meet all the needs of this community somehow, and the public can come look at the books if they wish."

"Just wondering," Johnson said, pacing with

her down the boardwalk. "What kind of salary do you take for managing the funds?"

"The kind that brings business into my dance hall."

"So you admit that your philanthropy is motivated by personal gain."

Sage stopped and turned on the editor. "How much have you contributed to our fund?" she asked.

He straightened and tugged his vest down over his stomach. "What I contribute is more valuable than gold dust."

"And what might that be?"

"Publicity. To your cause I contribute my lexicon."

She smirked. "Not everyone in town has learned to eat words as well as you." She turned her back on him, stepping down to the street.

She crossed to the other side so she wouldn't have to walk in front of Parkhill's Break o' Day Saloon. But even across the street, one of the drunks spotted her through the open door.

"Miss Sage!"

She didn't have to look to know it was the voice of Parkhill himself.

"I've got some boys in here need some charity."

She set her jaw to the burst of laughter and continued to the jailhouse.

"Evenin', Miss Sage," Fritz said, springing from his chair. "What brings you here? Trouble at your place?"

"No," she said, not bothering to look at him. "Where is Sheriff Colby?"

Fritz was trying to shape his hair to its best advantage. "He went fishin' this mornin'."

"When will he be back?"

"Well," Fritz said, coming around the desk to approach her, "if he catches a mess of trout, he might come on back tonight. Otherwise, he'll probably stay out another day. Can I help you with anything?"

"No. I need to meet with him regarding the relief fund."

"Well, I've been helping him with the collections," Fritz said. "If it's anything I can help you with . . ."

Sage was already halfway through the door. "No, thank you." She shut Fritz inside and stood for a moment. She could go back to the Golden Sage and try again tomorrow. Or she could check the sheriff's cabin on the edge of town. Maybe he was back from fishing. Maybe he would feel more comfortable on his own ground.

She turned for the cabin, snugging the shawl around her neck against the evening chill. The light faded as she made her way through town, ignoring the dozens of miners who tipped their tattered hats on their way to the saloons. It was almost dark when she saw the cabin. The tiny window revealed no light from inside. Still, she had come this far. Why not wait a few minutes?

As she walked through the fading dusk toward the cabin, she heard hooves clacking against rocks in the gulch. She stopped and listened. A rider was approaching the cabin; she heard the squeak of saddle leather. She stepped behind the woodpile to watch. In the low light she could just barely make out the form of the rider entering the shed.

She smiled and loosened the shawl to reveal her throat. Sheriff Colby was in for a surprise.

Tiptoeing, she made her way to the cabin porch. She sat on the steps and waited. Within a minute she heard the sheriff's boots scuffing the ground as he approached. She sat perfectly still as he came quickly around the corner, carrying a bedroll under one arm, his saddlebags slung over his shoulder.

Ross's foot was almost on the step before he noticed her. He jumped back and reached for his Remington, but recognized her shape, even in the twilight, and took his hand from the pistol butt.

"I didn't mean to startle you," she said.

"Miss Sage." He panted, his heart pounding against his ribs. "What are you doin' here?"

She stood, making his path up the steps a narrow one. "I came to discuss the relief fund."

He adjusted the saddlebags on his shoulder, forced the rising wave of panic back down his throat. "I was thinking about that when I was out fishin' today," he said. "I'm gonna start a new campaign for contributions. Can you come to my office tomorrow and talk about it?"

"That will be difficult," she said. "I'm busy tomorrow. Why not right now?"

He shuffled for a second or two. "Let me put my things away and we'll walk to my office."

"No need to go all the way down there. We can talk here."

He stood in silence. "Wait here, if you don't mind." He brushed past her and disappeared in the darkness of the cabin.

Sage waited, listening. She heard the heavy saddlebag hit the floor, recognized the rattle of the coal-oil lantern. The light wavered through the window and the sheriff opened the door.

"It's a nice evening," he said, closing the door behind him. "Let's talk out here." He hung the lantern on a stob and gestured to the bench against the log wall. "Now, what did you have in mind for the fund?"

She fought off a shiver as she sat down, but she wouldn't think of covering her bare skin with the shawl now that the light was on her. "The problem is the irregularity of the contributions. I realize that you and your deputy have just so much time to collect for charity."

"We'll redouble our efforts," Ross said, glancing toward town as he sat a safe distance from her on the bench.

"I believe I've thought of an alternative. A system to keep the contributions coming in regularly."

Ross looked at her face for the first time, the lantern light sparkling in her eyes and glowing along the curve of her fair cheek. "What do you mean?" He saw that hint of a smile still lingering at the corner of her mouth.

"We've had a problem with certain businesses in this town short-weighting their customers," she explained. "They use loaded counterweights on their scales and overcharge for every purchase. The amount is usually so small that no one notices, but it adds up."

"I'm familiar with the trick," Ross said. "What does it have to do with our relief fund?"

"What if we *encouraged* businesses to short-weight their scales—openly and deliberately? But instead of pouring the extra gold into their pockets, they would contribute it to our fund. We could get the newspaper to list the participating businesses, so it would be free advertising for them."

The idea made him smile, in spite of the whirlwind of nerves spinning in his stomach. He leaned toward her, resting his elbows on his knees. "Short-weighting for charity."

"In my business, for example, every time a gentleman purchased a dance with one of my girls, he would contribute a few pennies to help his fellows, and he would scarcely notice the loss."

"I like it," Ross said. "Are you willing to give it a trial run at the Golden Sage?" He saw her eyes narrow at something on his shoulder.

"Yes," she said. "I think it will be good for business." She scooted toward him on the bench and reached for his lapel.

Ross straightened, craned his neck nervously as her fingers closed on nothing and withdrew. Then he saw it: a long hair shining yellow in the lantern light, blowing on the chilly breeze.

"What's this?" she said, a tease in her voice.

"Must be a horsehair," he said, brushing his shoulders for anything else she might find. A knot tightened in his stomach.

"Your horse is a buckskin." Her smile became genuine now, a taunting flare of red lips. "This looks rather blond."

"Yes, but . . ." He looked toward town. "My horse was lame a while back and I borrowed a paint from Lester. I must have been wearing this coat."

She let the hair slip from her fingers and blow away on the breeze. "You should be careful of what you pick up while you're out . . . fishing. I don't suppose you caught anything. I would hope not, anyway."

Ross squinted and scooted an inch away from her. "I'm not sure what you're . . ."

A rumble of hooves interrupted him, erupting like an avalanche as the riders rounded the corner of a warehouse down the street. Four men galloped to the cabin, drawing rein in the light of the lantern hung on the porch.

"Colby!" Parkhill shouted. "The damn stage got robbed again!"

"What!" Ross said. "Where? Same place?"

"No," the stage driver said. "It was at the top of the corduroy road this side of Rebel Creek. The same old bastard with the long white beard!"

Sage looked away from the men and found the pale hair snagged on a log end at the corner of the cabin, waving lazily on the breeze. She saw through the yellow coal-oil light now and found the whiteness in the sheen. It streamed like a banner in the sunlight for a sharp eye.

"I want something done this time, Colby," Parkhill was saying.

When she looked back, Sage caught Parkhill following her eyes into the night, trying to find what she had been looking at beyond the end of the porch. She drew his attention with a subtle flourish of her skirt, and stepped to the edge of the porch to sit on the rail, moving between the lantern and the corner of the cabin, casting her shadow on the long white hair.

TWENTY-TWO

J̲UST LIKE LAST̲ time," Ross said, staring down at the open strongbox. "Looks like he left more than he took."

"He got thousands," Parkhill growled. "Anyway, I don't care if he just took a handful, it's stealin'."

"Wonder who he is," the sheriff muttered. "If he was a pro, he'd take it all. The old codger must have it in for you, Parkhill. You must have jumped his claim or somethin', and now he's gettin' even."

"Wonder why he pulls that tree onto the road?" Wink said.

"Probably wants to slow the coach down," Ross said, "make sure it's dark before the law gets the word. He's picked the dark of the moon for both robberies. Doesn't want a posse chasin' him in the night. I wouldn't send any more gold shipments on the dark of the moon if I was you, Parkhill."

Parkhill spit over his shoulder, splattering a brown stream against his horse's rump. "It ain't your job to tell me how to run my business, Colby. Just find the old fart."

"It's not gonna be easy," Ross said. "If it's like last time, he'll pick a hard mountain trail and lose us in the rocks. He knows these mountains."

"He's gonna make a mistake sooner or later," Parkhill said. "And when he does, I don't care how old he is, I'm gonna stretch his goddamn old neck."

"You do, and I'll have you in jail on murder charges," Ross snapped. "Everybody gets a fair trial in this county."

Parkhill glared at the sheriff until he heard hoofbeats coming.

"We found where he mounted!" Fritz hollered. "This way, R.W."

Ross spurred his horse in front of Parkhill's and followed Fritz back across the corduroy road and into a ravine where several Parkhill men were waiting. The deputy jumped down to point at the sign on the ground.

"Here's a boot heel in the dirt," Fritz said. "Looks like he rolled his blankets into a bedroll over there where the grass is pressed down. The horse tracks lead down the coulee."

Ross squinted at the sign on the ground as if he intended to follow it. Fritz made a pretty good tracker for a former city cop, he was thinking. "Comb every inch of this area for evidence." He frowned and shook his head. "Parkhill, I wish you'd keep your men out of the way when I'm conducting an investigation. They've trampled more sign than they'll ever find." He nudged his horse along the trail, leaning to his off side as if he had to read sign to know where he had ridden the day before.

As the sheriff followed the trail down the ravine, Wink leaned toward his boss and spoke low. "I'll say one thing for that Colby. He sure reads sign good. Follows a trail faster'n anybody I ever seen."

Ross didn't have to look when he rode past the *Post*. He knew Johnson would be watching for him. He heard the door fly open and ignored the editor's call except to point toward the jailhouse. Johnson was there before Ross could shut the door behind him.

"Any clues?" the editor asked.

"If I had any, I wouldn't tell you. You'd print 'em and scare the old man off."

"You have a suspect?"

"Not exactly."

"Now, Sheriff, I don't want to have to make my speech again."

"What speech?" Ross said, putting a Henry repeater on the rack.

"The one about you being a servant of the public, and the public having a right to know what you are doing about lawlessness in this region, and . . ."

"Oh, that speech," Ross said, tipping his hat back to rub his forehead. "All right, Johnson, sit down. Give me a second to collect my thoughts, and I'll give you something you can print." He skidded his chair back and plopped down behind his desk as the editor clutched his pencil in anticipation.

"We've got two robberies," Ross said, heaving with indignation. "We don't have a suspect yet, but we're startin' to get an idea of who the bandit is. He's an old man, of course. Probably a prospector, judging from his description. Both times he's struck just before nightfall, on the dark of the moon. He picks a spot where the stage has to move slow and robs it on foot with a scattergun."

Johnson scribbled furiously on his notepad.

"Both times he's left more gold than he's taken. Leads me to believe he's not in it for the gold. I think he's got a grudge against Parkhill. He's crafty and careful. Plans everything to the last step. Both times his trail has led to a dead end. He knows all the creek beds and rocky places where his tracks won't show. I'm guessin' he's a loner or a hermit. Lives up in the high country."

Johnson's pencil scratched along the bottom of the page. He tapped a period and flung a fresh sheet into play. "That's it?" he asked, looking up at the lawman.

Ross shrugged. "Except to say that I've advised Parkhill to send a double guard with his gold shipments and be wary of places where the coach has to slow down. And of course, I've told him not to ship any gold on the dark of the moon."

"But what about the manhunt? How close are you to the bandit?"

Ross smiled knowingly. "Closer than you might think, Johnson."

"What does that mean? Do you know his whereabouts?"

"Maybe."

Johnson sighed and rolled his eyes. "Is there *anything* else?"

"Yes, as a matter of fact." Ross leaned his chair back and propped his feet on his desk. "There is one other thing I want to talk to you about. We need some publicity."

"For what?"

"Miss Sage has come up with a new moneymaking idea for the relief fund. She calls it short-weighting for charity . . ."

TWENTY-THREE

MOST OF 'EM'S drifted into the Black Hills for the winter," the translator said. "But ol' Bad Wound was too weak to go, so he come here."

Hector Beauchamp had his horsehair reins in his hands, leading his mount away from Fort Reno, walking toward the lone tepee on the plains. "Was he there?"

The translator nodded his greasy head in a succession of jerks. "Oh, yeah. He knows the massacre good. Been paintin' pictures about it since the day."

Heck flipped the collar of his wool coat up around his ears to turn the sharp north wind funneling along the eastern slopes of the Bighorns. A gray blanket of clouds hung overhead, but he could sense no rain. "Will he talk about it?"

"If he's of a mind to. Don't let him gall you. He's not liable to like you."

When they reached the tepee, Heck dropped his reins and let his pony stand. The translator rapped his rifle barrel on the lodgepole, then flung the skin aside and stepped in, muttering something in the Cheyenne tongue. "Come on in, Heck," he said, his head emerging from the oval.

Heck ducked into the hide lodge, his nostrils instantly flaring at the familiar scent of the nomadic people. Some called it a stench. Heck knew better. It was not exactly his favorite aroma, but he had been raised with houses and towns. Even a dog had sense enough to know that every tribe of people God had ever put on this earth reeked of its own culture. Heck knew he smelled like a horse most of the time himself.

He found the eyes of an aged warrior looking up at him, set deep among sagging pockets of flesh. A single eagle feather stood above his head, its dark tip almost invisible against the shadowy interior of the lodge. White hair hung across a blackened buckskin shirt, parting to reveal a necklace of bear claws and elk teeth.

Heck nodded and smiled, but Bad Wound just looked back at the hide spread across his lap. The gnarled fingers gripped a feather he was using as a paintbrush. As Heck watched, the old artist moistened the tip of the feather in a tin of water, then dipped it into a small buckskin bag filled with red powder.

As the translator spoke to Bad Wound, Heck squatted and took his hat off, noticing piles of soft hides around him, different sizes, all painted. The horses caught his eye first. Dark horses, pale horses, paints, and Appaloosas. They had thick bodies and stiff legs. Each carried a rider.

He dragged a small hide from a pile and studied it closer. In the scene, the rider of a spotted horse wore long braids, carried a bow in one hand, and had a fringed quiver on his back. In front of the Indian pony, a soldier lay flat, an arrow standing on its point on the bluecoat, blood streaming across the ground.

The old Cheyenne spoke softly as he lay his feather aside. He moistened a finger on his tongue and stuck it into a buckskin bag of blue powder.

"Says they're all dead and that's all there is to tell," the translator reported.

Heck grunted. "I wouldn't answer you no questions, either, if you just busted into my place and started wantin' to know things." He held the hide painting up to catch a beam of light coming down from the smoke hole. "Warm up to him. Ask him what he makes this paint out of."

The translator asked, and as Bad Wound replied, he thrust the blue finger toward Heck before applying it to his painting.

"Says the colors all come from different things. The red's made out of clay and roots. The green's made out of plants and dirt. That blue he's got on his finger is made out of mud, boiled rotten wood, and duck shit."

"Ask him who this is," Heck said. Then, catching the old man's eye, he signed the question himself, pointing at the figure in the painting, waving his right palm, flicking his index finger forward in front of his mouth.

Bad Wound muttered something as he touched

his blue finger to a soldier's uniform on the large hide spread across his lap.

"Says that's Crazy Thunder killin' a bluecoat that tried to get away."

Bad Wound pulled the folds out of the robe he was painting, spread it out, and pointed to a pair of figures along one edge. It was Crazy Thunder again, riding the same horse, wearing the same identifying design on his leggings, looking down on the same dead soldier.

Heck pulled another small painting from a pile: a mounted warrior teetering in his saddle, blood gushing from his chest. "And this feller?"

Bad Wound shifted the hide on his lap, pointed to the same figure near the middle of the scene, and spoke in a wheezing voice.

"Says it's Circlin' Dog where the White Captain shot him."

"Looks like he listened to all the stories of the battle," Heck said, "and painted each warrior's part on a little piece of hide. Now he's puttin' it all together in one big scene."

"I don't believe I'd stick my finger in duck shit," the translator said.

Heck rocked forward onto his knees and pulled the last folds out of the big hide the old man was painting. The simple figures of Indians, soldiers, and horses took breath and he sensed the wind streaming through braids and war bonnets as the braves attacked. He heard war whoops, rifle shots; smelled powder; and actually felt the rumble of the ground under the hooves. Blood streaked the Crazy Woman.

"He ain't much of a artist, is he?" the translator said, rasping a laugh.

The battle shrank back into the hide, but its echoes circled Heck in the lodge as he glanced his disapproval at the white man. He turned to the old warrior and signed a question: where is Bad Wound?

A gnarled finger straightened slowly and pointed. In the vortex of the carnage, Heck made out a rider holding a rifle. A line led from the barrel to a blue-coated figure pressed against a box with spoked wheels. The old veteran muttered as his steady finger hovered over the painting.

"Says he killed the captain hisself. First time he'd ever shot a gun. Says he shouted Good Medicine out of that gun barrel and chanted it home, whatever the hell that means."

Heck only nodded, absorbed as he was with the battle scene. Then Julia entered his mind. "Ask him if anybody left the soldiers' camp a day or two before the battle."

The translator spoke haltingly and the chief dipped his feather in the tin of water and swirled it. Placing the feather across the top of the tin, he signed with both hands:

Tracks. West. One rider. Two sleeps. Catch the Eagle follows. Soldier ride much in river. Bighorn Mountains. Big wind. Dirt hide tracks.

Heck stared into the steady old eyes for a moment, almost able to see Ross Caldwell riding for his life up the Crazy Woman. He usually saw Ross as sort of a dried-up, rat-faced character, although he doubted Julia would fall for that sort. No, he was probably a silver-tongued rake blessed with a bit of good looks.

Either way, he was a sorry excuse for a husband, if he wasn't dead. Any man who wouldn't fight off a whole tribe of Indians to get back to a wife like Julia didn't deserve her, anyway. He may have gotten away from Bad Wound's Cheyenne, but there were other bands out there, other tribes. Not to mention outlaws and grizzlies.

"What's that?" the translator said. "You're mumblin' to yourself."

"Huh?" Heck focused on the squinted face of the translator. "Tell him I want to buy one of these pictures from him." He shuffled through the hides until he found one representing four warriors surrounding a dead soldier, the bluecoat stuck with half a dozen arrows. "This one here."

"He wants to know what you're gonna pay him with."

Heck stepped out of the tepee, returning with a coiled length of horsehair rope. He let it play out in front of Bad Wound's eyes so the old man could inspect his workmanship. Bad Wound took it in his hand, pulled on it, looked up at the white man, and nodded.

Heck put his hat on, rolled the painting and tucked it inside his vest. He didn't know a farewell sign—didn't think there was one—so he touched his hat brim before he stepped out of the lodge.

"He took to you," the translator said outside. "Never seen him talk sign to a white man before."

Heck gripped the horn and rose on the stirrup.

"What are you gonna do with that picture you swapped him out of?"

"Keep it," he said, patting the roll flat against his chest. "That's history, sure as our books."

"Shit. Damn stick figures. You'd have got more use out of the rope."

"When he dies, you ought to see that those pictures get in a museum somewhere. That big one's as good as a photograph of the Crazy Woman massacre."

"I'll see what I can git for 'em."

Heck frowned, suddenly feeling as lonely as old Bad Wound. He pulled his coat collar tight around his neck and spurred his horse south for Denver.

TWENTY-FOUR

FRITZ DREW A breath to steady his nerves and let it out as a cloud of vapor. Frost had come to the high country. Some of the seasonal miners had already gone south. The owners of the best claims would stay until ice choked their sluices, but they would be drifting soon, too. Fritz knew that if he was going to impress Miss Sage, he would have to do it before winter froze the flow of revenue.

He stepped into the Break o' Day and felt the silence spread from his feet to the far walls. He walked briskly to the end of the saloon, turned his back to the corner, and hefted the wooden box to the surface of the bar.

"Get out from behind there," he said to the bartender.

"What the hell do you think you're doin'?" the Southern voice drawled.

"Investigating a fraud. Move."

"Like hell I will."

Fritz put his hand on his revolver. "I'll give you one more chance to get out of my way, then I'll arrest you for interfering with an investigation."

The bartender snarled and threw a rag down on the bar. "All right, have it your way, Deputy. You want me to move, I'll move right upstairs and get Park out of his office."

"I'd appreciate that." Fritz let the bartender squeeze by and watched him stomp up the first few steps of the staircase. He slid the dovetailed box to the Break o' Day's scales, opened the brass-hinged lid, and removed a set of measured weights, checking the bar patrons occasionally for signs of trouble.

"What are you lookin' for, Deputy?" somebody asked.

"Got a tip about some short-weighting going on here." He opened the saloon's box of weights, put twenty ounces in one pan and twenty ounces of his own in the other. He waited for the needle on the scale to settle, then shook his head in disapproval. Some of the drinkers began to grumble as Fritz added smaller weights, one by one, until he made the scales balance. "How 'bout that," he said. "Twenty Parkhill ounces is equal to twenty-one of the genuine article."

Two pairs of boots stomped down the stairs.

"Get the hell away from my scales!" Parkhill roared.

Fritz quickly looked the saloon man over for weapons as he descended into view. "Do your customers know they're paying a nickel on the dollar more than you advertise?"

The murmur of voices grew.

"Those are the same scales Bob Hodges left when he sold me the saloon. If they're short-weighted, it's his fault."

"You're responsible for checkin' 'em," Fritz said.

Parkhill sauntered toward the scales. "Who made you inspector? Where's Sheriff Colby?"

"He went deer huntin' today."

Parkhill sneered. "He oughta be huntin' that old bandit. You both oughta be huntin' my stolen gold instead of comin' in here to take more."

"Don't change the subject, Parkhill."

"You oughta be out there guardin' my stage-coach. I can't afford to pay all them extra guards. They cost me more than the damned old bandit did."

"I wouldn't worry about it today," Fritz said. "The new moon's a week off yet. I'd worry about these scales if I was you."

"You sure that lead is weighed right?" Parkhill stepped up to the scale and squinted at the weights.

"To the grain."

"Well, I'll be damned. You're right, Deputy Green. Ol' Bob Hodges short-weighted these scales. I thank you for pointin' it out to me. Jim, give the deputy a drink on the house."

"You can't buy me off with a drink," Fritz said. "You're going to have to make restitution one way or the other."

"What do you mean? You're not gonna try to charge me with anything illegal, are you?" Parkhill swaggered back a step or two from the bar and stood defiantly.

Fritz put his weights back in the wooden box. "I

could, according to city ordinances. Then, again, I might assume you've been short-weighting for charity, like every other business in town. If that's the case, I'll just take your contribution and go."

Parkhill smiled and turned to his customers. "Now, that's reasonable, ain't it, boys? What'll I give? Fifty? Sixty?"

"Seventy-five!" somebody said.

"That's mighty low," Fritz said. "I figure you take in a couple of hundred a night average. At a nickel on the dollar, that would come out to ten dollars a night, and short-weighting for charity's been runnin' a month now. Let's call it three hundred and be done with it."

Parkhill couldn't hold the smile up any longer. "Three hundred! How the hell can a man make a livin', givin' that much to bums and drunks?"

Fritz shrugged. "The fine's five hundred, if you'd rather pay that."

"Shit!" Parkhill blurted. "Jim, give him three hundred."

The bartender reached under the counter and produced three sacks of dust. Fritz lined them on his box of weights and headed for the end of the bar. "Miss Sage will be grateful to you, Parkhill."

"Don't come back for any more. I'm gettin' those scales fixed. And don't give any of my gold to those Chinamen. You've spoilt 'em bad enough as it is!"

Fritz sidled out of the saloon, his right hand hovering over his revolver. He was anxious to put his weights back in the jailhouse so he could deliver the gold to Miss Sage. This was bound to impress her. Not even Sheriff Colby had brought in three hundred in one lump. And from Parkhill, at that!

He flung the door of the jailhouse open to find Ross putting his Henry repeater in the rack.

Ross jerked the rifle nervously from the rack before he recognized his deputy. "Damn, Fritz. You're liable to get shot bustin' in here like that."

"I thought you went huntin'."

"Nothin' was movin'," Ross said. "I didn't even get a shot at anything." He noticed the bags of dust and the box of calibrated weights. "Whose scales you been checkin'?"

Fritz grinned. "The Break o' Day's. And look what I collected for the relief fund." He dropped the three pouches of dust on the desk.

"Son of a gun, Fritz. It's a wonder you didn't collect a bunch of knots all over your head at the same time. Why didn't you wait for me?"

The deputy tugged at his gun belt and puffed his chest out. "Parkhill didn't even put up a fight. I'm gonna take this over to the Golden Sage right now."

"I'll do it," Ross said. "I need to discuss some charity business with Sage, anyway. Looks like we might get through the winter all right with what we've got, thanks to Parkhill's contribution."

"You sure you don't want me to go?" Fritz said, each word taking a little wind out of his chest. "I don't mind."

Ross chuckled. "I don't guess you would, the way those hurdies fall all over you in there. Walk over with me, if you want to."

Fritz stared longingly at the three bags of gold

for a moment. "Well, if you're goin', there's no need for me to go. I'll lock up and make the rounds before I walk home."

"Good man." Ross slapped Fritz on the back, put the three bags of dust in his coat pockets, and struck out for the Golden Sage.

TWENTY-FIVE

THE SMELL OF burned wood and hot stovepipes drifted in and out of the streets and alleys as he kept an ear tuned for the Parkhill stage. He nodded to the passersby who greeted him, reasoned that the coachmen must have run into trouble moving the dead pine he had pushed down on the road. He heard the Golden Sage orchestra playing a quadrille and paused at the door to light a cigar.

It seemed the publicity generated by her charity work had done wonders for Sage's business. Even with Virginia City's population falling off as fast as the temperatures, the Golden Sage continued to attract crowds. Ross stepped inside, stayed to the outside of the rail to avoid the dancers. He tipped his hat to the ladies as he made his way to the corner. He knocked on Sage's door, took the cigar from his mouth, and blew smoke rings at the wall lamp.

Sage opened the door, and he saw her lips tell him to come in, though the band drowned out her voice. She shut the noise behind them and slid her hand across his lapel, petrifying him.

"May I take your coat?" she said.

"Let me get the gold out of it first."

She hung the coat on a brass hook and poured him a drink as he put the three sacks of dust on her writing desk. She was wearing lavender tonight, and it warmed the glow of her pale skin. He had never seen her wear the same gown twice. She must have a closet stuffed full somewhere. Suddenly he realized he was staring at her through his cigar smoke. He glanced at her face in the mirror, saw her looking back, and knew she knew.

"This is a surprise," she said, handing him the whiskey, taunting him with that perpetual smile. "But I'm glad you stopped by. I went looking for you earlier. Your deputy told me you were out for the day."

"What was on your mind?" He inhaled the aroma and took a sip.

"The relief fund. Revenues are up, but it's going to be a long winter." Her sleepy eyes glanced languidly at the three sacks of dust on her desk. "Those will help."

"Deputy Green just collected that from the Break o' Day." He smiled, imagining the looks that must have crossed Parkhill's face. "Caught Parkhill short-weighting his customers."

"Still," she said, "it's going to be a long winter."

"Don't worry. I've been doin' some fund-raisin' of my own. We'll have enough to get us through."

Sage questioned him with a tilt of her head as she glided to the sofa facing his chair. She sat down, kicked her shoes off, and stretched her legs out on the seat. "You don't mind my getting comfortable, do you?"

Ross glanced at his glass, thought about guzzling it and getting out of there. But the whiskey was too good. "Why should I mind?"

They sat in silence for a moment, Ross looking vacantly at her. He thought about Julia, remembered her wholesome beauty, contrasted it to the soft paleness of this dance hall siren. What would Julia think if she saw him sitting here? Some people in town already had the wrong idea. But Ross trusted himself. He came here for business purposes only, though Sage tempted him in her silent way.

Julia . . . The image of Sage blurred as he thought of her. Where was she now? With whom would she be sitting tonight? If he didn't hear from her soon, he would hear nothing until spring. He had to find her. Without her, life would continue to ricochet like a bullet among the rocks. She was the one constant that could keep things from . . .

"Are you going to tell me about it?" Sage said.

Ross snorted, as if waking suddenly. "About what?"

"Your fund-raising."

He took a sip of the whiskey, tapped the ashes from his cigar. "That's what I came here for." He shifted in his chair. "I've managed to get pledges from a number of businesses to contribute so much a month through the winter. So, I'll be sending small amounts of gold to you at regular intervals until spring."

"Sending?" She toyed with a curl that brushed against her neck. "Why don't you deliver the goods yourself?"

Ross chuckled. "I wouldn't deprive Deputy Green of the pleasure. I think he's got a sweetheart among your girls. Every time he comes back from the Golden Sage, his eyes look like marbles in a moose head."

Sage seemed irritated. "I've seen the same look in your eyes."

Ross felt the smile slip from his face as his grip tightened on the glass of whiskey. He was getting anxious to leave now. Why didn't he just get up and go?

"Deputy Green said you went hunting today. Did you catch anything?"

"Catch?" he said. "You don't catch anything when you go huntin'; you shoot to kill. You're thinkin' of trapping. Trappers catch their game."

"Are you a trapper as well as a hunter?"

Ross looked into his glass and felt her eyes on him. They were whiskey-colored, he realized: intoxicating. "I've done some of both."

Layers of petticoats rustled as she pulled her legs into them. "What kind of animal would you like to catch, Sheriff Colby?"

Ross looked up at her, sifting for suggestion in her voice, trying to think of a reply. He was about to attempt something clever when the door flew open, letting a blast of dance music in.

Ross sprang from his chair, sloshing the good

whiskey as he whirled and reached for his Remington.

Parkhill kicked the door shut behind him as he brought a scattergun out of his coat. "Take your hand off that pistol, Colby. You've got some questions to answer."

"What is this?" Sage said, scrambling off the sofa. Her eyes flashed a frenzy. "Get out of my place!"

"Not until the sheriff tells me where he was this afternoon. And I mean *exactly* where he was."

"It's none of your damn business where I was," Ross said, his thoughts racing, wondering what he had left undone. Nerves wrenched his stomach into a bundle. "Get out before I arrest you for trespassing."

Parkhill latched a hammer back on the double-barrel. "Talk Colby. Your deputy said you were huntin'. I want to know where and you'd better convince me."

"South of town, if it's any concern of yours."

"Where's your game? What'd you kill?"

"I didn't see anything to shoot at. What's this all about?"

"My stage was robbed by the old man again today, and somethin' dawned on me. Where were you the day of the first robbery?"

"Hell, I don't remember."

"Prospectin'. Where were you during the second robbery?"

Ross stiffened as if he were getting mad. "What's your point, Parkhill?"

"You were fishin'. Where were you today? Huntin'. Looks like you're out of town every time the old bandit robs me."

"So what?"

"Who knows when the shipments come? You do. I've been a damn fool enough to tell you myself."

"Half the hard cases that work for you know when you ship gold. Ever think of that? Any one of them could have leaked the information in some saloon."

"Who told me to double my guard on the dark of the moon?" Parkhill's eyes glanced around the room, found the three bags of gold from his saloon.

"What's that got to do with it?"

"It ain't the dark of the moon today. How'd that old road agent know to change his game?"

"If I could read his mind, I'd have caught him by no v."

Parkhill set his jaw, showed his teeth. "I think you know somethin', Colby. I think you know who the bandit is. I think you're in it with him."

"Then you're a bigger fool than I expected."

"Where did you go huntin' today? And I'd better be able to find your tracks there tomorrow."

Ross glanced at the twin muzzles. Now what? Bluff? Yes, bluff, and you'll have the night to think of something. "Well, let's see," he said, stalling. "Hard to say exactly where I was. I was huntin', not blazin' a damn wagon trace." He rubbed his head, tried to get his mind to come up with something.

"You might as well tell him the truth," Sage said. She stepped to his side and stood with him in the path of the buckshot.

"What?" Ross said.

"He's caught you. You might as well tell him where you were."

"What are you talkin' about?" His innards throbbed with terror.

"Sheriff Colby wasn't hunting today." She put her arm around Ross's waist and ran a hand across his chest as if smoothing his shirt. "He was here with me."

Ross held his breath as he let her words sink in. She knew. Sage had known since the night she found the long white hair on his coat. She could have turned him in a month ago, but now she was offering him an alibi.

"With you?" Parkhill said, his eyebrows gathering. "Doin' what?"

"Running his trapline, what do you think? Do I have to spell it out to you?" She looked up at the sheriff. "I know you wanted to wait, darling, but this is as good a time as any to let it out."

Ross put his arm around her shoulder. With her heels off, she was smaller than he had realized.

"What about the first two times?" Parkhill said, his suspicions giving way to intrigue.

"Are you an idiot?" Sage said. "You found us together at his cabin the day he was supposed to be fishing. It doesn't take a detective to figure it out."

Parkhill lowered his shotgun and grinned. "Huntin' today huh? Huntin' the wildcat!" His laughter erupted like gunfire. "The newspaper's gonna have a fit with this one." His grin turned quickly to a scowl and he put his hand on the doorknob. "It don't change the fact that my stage was robbed again, Colby. You'd better get on the trail of that old outlaw pretty damn quick or you'll be huntin' a trail out of Montana."

The band music burst in on them, and then Parkhill was gone.

Ross tried to step away from her, but she held on.

She turned to face him, looked up at him with flashing eyes. "I don't like lying for a man," she said, "but I'll make an exception in your case."

He felt her hands interlock at the small of his back. "What do you want from me?" he asked.

She faked a look of astonishment. "Nothing. That is, nothing any other woman wouldn't want. Just a little gratitude and devotion."

He shook his head. "There are things you don't know about me."

"I know you've got some woman on your mind. I can make you forget her."

"It's not that simple." He tried to pull her arms away, but she locked her hands together tighter. He felt like a weakling.

"Now, listen," she said, a vicious new note in her voice, "I just told a lie for you. I think you owe me something."

He had thought about what it would be like with Sage in that adjoining room. "Owe you something? Like what?"

Her painted lips lifted in a true smile—not the false look of indifferent bliss she usually wore, but a visage of wicked amusement. "Let's start with tonight."

His voice came wheezing up his throat. "And what if I told you I already had plans for tonight."

She released him and went to her safe to open it, looking back at Ross as she picked up the bags of gold dust and threw them into the iron box. "That would be risky. I might have to tell Parkhill the truth. Otherwise, what would be in it for me?" She kicked the safe shut, walked to the doorway leading to her bedroom, and waited for him to decide which way he would turn.

Ross faltered for a moment, trapped in her snare. He felt smothered with foolishness, consumed by guilt for the base desires he held for her. Finally he approached her, stood over her whiskey eyes.

She grabbed a handful of his shirt and pulled him in. "It's going to be a long winter," she said.

TWENTY-SIX

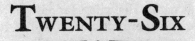

JULIA WINCED AT the board creaking under her foot. She looked over her shoulder to make sure she hadn't wakened Fay, or Hanna McDaniels—who was sick in bed with some mysterious ailment that to Julia looked suspiciously like laziness—or Hanna's baby, Elliot, Jr. To her relief, they all continued to sleep.

She took her shawl from a peg and turned the brass knob quietly, opening the door by degrees until it was wide enough for her to get outside. She felt her fatigue as she tiptoed to the porch step, pulling the shawl tighter around her shoulders.

The mixture of cool air and warm afternoon sun felt good where she sat. She looked down on the crooked little city of Denver as she relished the first break from labor she had had all day. What a strange, barren spot to locate a home, she thought. The winter wind would surely freeze them all through the cracks in the thin board walls of the McDaniels house. She hated staying here.

Deputy Elliot McDaniels grumbled from the moment he woke up in the morning until he went to sleep at night. His wife, Hanna, was worse, because she was there all day. "If you're gonna stay with us, you'll be expected to pull your weight," she had told Julia the day they met. Since then, Hanna had apparently decided that Julia was to pull most of her weight, too. She took sick on a regular basis and thought nothing of ordering Julia around like a house servant.

This was a miserable existence. Hector Beauchamp had been gone for weeks and she was beginning to think he would never come back. A thousand calamities could have befallen him between here and the Sioux country. Would she ever find out what had happened to Ross?

She thought often now, in her moments of rationality, that Ross must be dead. The chances of his escaping the massacre seemed slimmer every day. And yet she still experienced a moment now and then that made her look over her shoulder to see if he was standing there. A mind could play tricks on a tortured soul.

She glanced back toward the smoke trails of Denver and saw a rider trotting up the hill toward the McDaniels homestead. Hector Beauchamp had been gone so long she thought she had forgotten what he looked like, but she recognized him instantly. The hope and dread clashed in her stomach again as she rose unconsciously and started to walk toward him.

They met on the treeless hillside, a few dried tufts of grass whistling, bending in the wind. Heck got down from his saddle and let his horsehair reins dangle. He smiled, but he did not look happy.

"Hello, Julia."

"Sheriff Beauchamp. What did you find?"

Heck sighed, reached into his pocket, and pulled out a folded scrap of paper. "I tore this out of Captain Jones's diary. He wrote it two days before the massacre."

Julia had only seen the captain's handwriting a couple of times, but she recognized the heavy pen strokes. She read the words, gathered their meaning. "He wasn't there," she said. "Ross wasn't at the Crazy Woman." Her eyes grew wide with hope, but she saw something in Heck's face that kept her joy from leaping.

"No," Heck said. "If he had been, there would probably be no way to ever prove how he died. But he was on the prairie alone when it happened."

"When what happened?" she said. "What are you talking about?"

"My guess is that Captain Jones sent your husband out to find Colonel Kulp. You know he relied on Ross."

"Yes, but if he wasn't at the Crazy Woman, he wasn't killed in the massacre."

Heck turned to his saddlebag, opened the flap. "No, he wasn't at the Crazy Woman. He was a day's ride east when a Cheyenne scouting party found him." He pulled a rolled piece of tanned hide from his saddlebag.

Julia felt a cold lump in her stomach pressing hard against her heart. "How could you know that?"

"I talked to the leader of that scouting party. An old warrior named Bad Wound. He described Ross perfect. Said Ross gave 'em one hell of a chase before he finally holed up in a buffalo wallow. They charged him several times, but he held 'em off. He ran low on ammunition, Julia. He knew it was over. Bad Wound said it was the bravest thing he ever saw. Ross came out of the buffalo wallow and charged the whole Cheyenne scouting party. They shot him full of arrows, and he died quick."

Julia shook her head, slinging a tear across her cheek. "No. I don't believe it. It could have been any soldier."

Heck bit his lip to steady himself. "Bad Wound showed me his gun, Julia. The old Remington revolver with his initials carved on the grip. It was him."

Her mouth opened, and her eyes darted helplessly.

He hated doing this to her. He had dreaded it for days. But he was sure of himself. There was no doubt that it was the best thing for *him*. And he had also decided it was best for Julia. He unrolled the painting he had bought from Bad Wound and gave it to her.

"When the Cheyenne have a great battle, they paint a picture about it. This is Bad Wound's picture about the death of Ross Caldwell. I've never seen such a thing done for a single white man. I know it doesn't help any now. But in time you'll be grateful you know how it happened."

Julia threw the painted hide back at Heck.

"No!" she shouted, almost doubling over with sobs. "I don't believe it!"

Heck took her by the arm but she shook free. He grabbed her again, and she pummeled him with her fists, but he held on, pulling her closer. He took a pretty good beating from her until she gave up and buried her face in his shoulder.

He held her for a long time as his horse wandered a short way off to graze on a tall clump of grass. He had to squint hard to keep tears from coming out of his own eyes, and he felt a nagging guilt for the lies he had told her. But he knew he would get over it in time. And he knew Julia would get over Ross. It wouldn't take her long. They had already been separated for over a year.

Right now this felt like the worst thing he had ever done. But he knew in the long run it would be the best thing that had ever happened to him. And he would prove to Julia that it was the best thing for her and little Fay, too. He was holding her now in her moment of greatest sorrow. He would hold her someday in rapture.

Heck heard the front door of the McDaniels house slam and looked up to see Hanna standing there shielding her eyes against the afternoon glare. He heard the raspy voice rattle down the hill:

"Julia! Where the devil did you go? The baby's cryin'!"

TWENTY-SEVEN

❖

SENSATIONAL CRIME!

PARKHILL STAGE
ROBBED AT GUNPOINT!

HERMIT HIGHWAYMAN COMMITS
FOURTH DARING HOLDUP!

Ed Johnson trembled with excitement as he positioned exclamation points. It had been a long, dull winter, but now news was busting out everywhere. He had been putting together a good issue even before the robbery. Now he was looking at the biggest edition ever.

His ink-stained fingers groped for capitals in the tray as he composed the headline for his second front-page story:

TELEGRAPH SERVICE REACHES
VIRGINIA CITY

He had waited two years to print this story. To editor Johnson it meant access to national news almost as it occurred. The *Post* would flourish. He might even go daily.

In fact, the telegraph had been his lead story until yesterday, when he heard Parkhill roaring in the street about the robbery. He had sprinted with Parkhill and Deputy Green to the sheriff's cabin. They had knocked furiously on the door until it opened to reveal the infamous Miss Sage standing there in her dressing gown—one thin layer of silk between her curvaceous skin and editor Johnson's bulging eyes.

He shook his head and put his mind back on business. He might have printed something about catching Sheriff Colby in a tryst with the most notorious woman of soiled virtue in town, but that was hardly news. It had been going on all winter.

The important news about the sheriff concerned the shoot-out at the Golden Sage three nights ago, told here at the bottom of page one:

SHERIFF WOUNDED IN GUNFIGHT
WITH DRUNKEN BANDIT

Something like this happened about this time every year. Some miscreant would get cabin fever just before the ice began to thaw, get drunk, and commit some absurd crime.

This particular culprit was a mule packer from Idaho who had decided to rob the relief fund in Sage's office. She had caught him trying to throw her safe through the window, and he had forced her to open it at gunpoint. When he reached in for the gold, she slammed the door on his hand and he had shot at her as she ran from the office.

Sheriff Colby, who happened to be in the Golden Sage, charged the office and exchanged gunfire with the bandit, disabling him with a bullet that hit him in the face, shattering his jaw. A piece of flying glass from a shattered lantern globe had cut Colby on the cheek. It wasn't much of a wound, but it made for a compelling headline.

And there was still more sensational news to print, spilling right on over to page two:

PARKHILL LINE LOSES MONOPOLY ON LAST CHANCE ROAD

Oh, this was a fine piece of reporting! Rumors of corruption in the territorial legislature had led to an investigation of so-called road franchises granted to certain freight line operators who just happened to hail from Dixie, as did most of the legislators.

The executive branch, made solely of Union men, had now declared the roads public property, but Parkhill—and this was deliciously inflammatory—had vowed to continue operating the Last Chance Road as a tollway in clear defiance of the territorial government.

And there was still more!

RODENT POPULATION EXPLODES! CHINESE INFANT BITTEN BY RABID RAT!

Well, nobody was sure it was rabid, but Johnson was relatively certain it was a rat, although it could have been a big brother who slept with the infant. The point was that Virginia City had a serious vermin problem, and nowhere was it worse than in Parkhill's Chinatown.

Oh, mercy! What a week for news!

The brass bell on the door clattered and Johnson looked up to see Mary.

"Hurry, cousin," she said, "the ceremony's about to start!"

Johnson glanced at the clock. "Where has the morning gone?" He grabbed his overcoat and hat and escorted Mary toward the new Western Union office on Main Street.

The Virginia City Marching Band was there, Fritz blaring on his trumpet. To one side of the band, the townspeople stood dressed in fluff and finery. To the other side, the telegraph line construction crew waited in dirty work clothes and bearded faces. Among them, a few miners and prospectors stood to witness the ceremony.

Under the canvas awning of the telegraph office, Sheriff Colby stood with the mayor and a Western Union representative. Behind the telegraph key a boy of about nineteen years sat wearing full telegrapher's uniform—eye visor, white shirt, black sleeve garters, bow tie.

Johnson pushed his way through the crowd with Mary and whipped out a notepad and pencil. His searching eyes caught sight of the notorious Miss Sage standing near the band, her white skin like porcelain in the light of day. She stared longingly at the sheriff, seemingly aware of little else. Scandalous, he thought.

As the band finished honking its march, the crowd applauded and the mayor stepped to the edge of the boardwalk.

"That's enough speeches and fanfare, ladies and gentlemen. Now the moment we have all been waiting for. Time for Virginia City to join the age of modern communications. I have been asked to choose someone to send the first telegram to the Western Union offices in St. Louis. For this honor, I have chosen someone with an appreciation for the language, a person who is well known and highly regarded in our community. Reporter for the Virginia City *Post* and president of the Virginia City Literary Society, Miss Mary Johnson!"

The editor smirked as his young cousin gasped beside him. The mayor, that lecherous old bachelor, had been after Mary for months. She took the mayor's hand and sprang up to the boardwalk, so excited that she could scarcely speak.

"This is such a surprise," she finally said. "I have no idea what to say."

Ross took the cigar from his mouth, put his hand around Mary's arm, and whispered something in her ear.

She giggled. "How shall I compose it?" She pondered a moment, then began writing on a sheet of paper at the telegrapher's elbow. She shook her head, scratched something out, scrawled another line.

The crowd raised a common grumble, and Ross looked on as Mary scribbled. When she was done, she showed the message to the sheriff, and he nodded in approval. She handed the note to the young telegrapher. The boy shrugged, and began tapping the key.

"Well, what the devil does it say?" a miner yelled.

The telegrapher paused, looked at the mayor. The mayor gestured approval. Haltingly the key operator read the message aloud as he sent it east, his voice breaking as he began:

"Greetings ... St. Louis ... from Virginia City ... Montana Territory ... Gem of the Northern Rockies ..." The boy paused as the crowd applauded. "Help! Our city ... has been ... invaded by ... tribes of natives ... Save us ... Send cats."

Laughter sprang from the crowd, the bandleader brought the musicians to attention, and a brassy waltz began to plod from the bandstand. Johnson looked up from his notepad to see his cousin offering her hand to the sheriff. The sheriff gallantly threw his cigar aside. The editor felt himself flush with embarrassment as Mary began to dance with the famous philanderer of the Golden Sage.

The girl was so ridiculously naive, he thought. Really, she didn't have the sense of a goose. The crowd, however, was loving it—raising quite a round of applause. All except for Miss Sage. Her hands were clenched in little fists. Her lips seemed to smile, but her eyes glared.

When the waltz ended, the crowd began to break up, most of the celebrants drifting off to various saloons. Johnson saw Sheriff Colby pull the young telegrapher aside for some sort of serious conversation. The editor put his notepad in his pocket and grumbled to himself. Nothing of interest to add to the telegraph story. Except maybe the message Mary had composed. That was rather ingenious, even if Colby had helped her think of it.

He looked for his cousin, anxious to escort her back to the office and get back to work on the paper. He spotted her stepping down from the board- walk, but as she reached the bottom step she stopped. Sage was standing in her path. Mary smiled. Sage drew an arm back and hit Mary across the cheek with a roundhouse blow that knocked her flat on her back on the boardwalk.

As Mary tried to get to her feet, Sage sprang on her, smiling wickedly as she pummeled the presi- dent of the literary society with her fists. Mary shrieked, kicked Sage away, and sprang to her feet.

The crowd surged. Ross tried to push his way through spectators. Fritz jumped over the band- stand rail with his trumpet. Johnson rushed for- ward to protect his cousin, but Sage had grabbed her by the ankle and pulled her off her feet. The smiling wench was on Mary again, pulling her hair viciously. Wild-eyed, Mary threw an elbow in Sage's stomach and leaped free.

Sage lunged again, but Sheriff Colby caught her around the waist and lifted her from the board- walk. Fritz leaped in between the two women, protecting Mary. Johnson tried to catch his cousin as she stumbled backward, but she fell on the cracker barrel at the general store, scattering a nest of mice living within it.

"My God!" Johnson shouted.

The miners and construction crewmen laughed, the townspeople gasped, and Ross struggled to control Sage. She continued to scratch and kick in Mary's direction, her face contorted with insensible anger—except for the smiling corners of her paradoxical mouth.

"Arrest that woman!" Johnson shouted. "She should be thrown in jail!"

The sheriff appeared mortified with it all, unable to respond.

Fritz helped Mary to her feet among the cracker crumbs and rodent droppings.

"No," Mary said, composing herself, smoothing her dress, and raking her hair back from her face. "She didn't hurt me."

"But she attacked you!" Johnson roared. "Something has to be done!"

"I said no!" Mary snapped. "It's not worth the trouble. I'm going home." She nodded at Fritz. "Thank you, Deputy Green," she said, and walked away with all the dignity she could muster as some of the miners, for some reason, awarded her a round of applause.

Johnson glared back at Sage. She was hanging from the sheriff's arms like a rag doll now, and she still had that idiotic smile on her face.

"This does not bode well for you, Miss Sage," the editor declared, drawing himself to his full height. "Nor for you, Sheriff Colby." He straightened his top hat and turned for his office, relishing the befuddled look on Colby's face. He could already feel the lexicon boiling inside him, aching to burst out and splatter all over the editorial page.

The telegraph key began to tap wildly and the young operator reached for his pencil. Fritz lost his view of Mary as she entered her boarding-house down the street, so he sauntered toward the telegraph operator and looked over his shoulder.

"Well, what does it say?" the mayor asked.

"They misunderstood," Fritz said. "They think we're really under attack. Says, 'Clarify. Message reads *cats*. Do you mean caps? Firing caps?'"

Sage suddenly wrenched away from Ross, smiled defiantly up at him, and strode away toward the Golden Sage.

Ross sighed. "Better clear it up or we'll have the damned army marching up here. Tell 'em *felines* this time."

TWENTY-EIGHT

Ross SPREAD THE *Post* to its full width in front of his face and stared dumbfounded at the editorial page. Johnson had vented a journalistic thunderclap over yesterday's brawl between "Sheriff Colby's depraved concubine" and "Virginia City's quintessence of female purity."

He read one passage aloud: ". . . but behind the facade of their vaunted relief fund lurks a union so perverse and scandalous that it would shock even the vilest class of humanity, nay, even the rats that propagate under our houses . . ."

And this Ross could not deny. He had once been a devoted husband. Now he robbed stagecoaches and consorted with lewd women. This was life after Julia.

But he was trapped. Sage held a noose around his neck that she threatened to tighten every time he tried to distance himself from her. If he had known how possessive she would become, he would never have used her alibi. He would have taken his chances with Parkhill. But now he had lost all control.

It had started enjoyable enough—except for the guilt, and even that could be explained to almost nothing. He was being blackmailed, after all. Sage had shown him pleasures he had never conceived. But when the veneer of her charms began to fall off, Ross saw their true nature. She used her sensuality as leverage to lodge him where she wanted him; as reward for behavior she expected. She trained him like a dog, taking no pleasure from him in return, feeling nothing for him but a desire to control.

He had only heard about the first attack. Sage had fired one of her girls, run her off to another hurdy-gurdy. Ross had heard she roughed the little thing up pretty bad, but figured the hurdies must have exaggerated the beating. Now, after seeing Sage tear into Mary Johnson, he realized how bad it must have been.

All winter he had kept his sanity by consoling himself with the same rationale. This had started as a way to punish Parkhill, and Parkhill deserved it. If Ross hadn't robbed the stagecoaches and spread the gold around, people would have starved and frozen to death this winter— particularly the Chinese. Parkhill had been so preoccupied with the Hermit Bandit that vigilante activity had practically ceased around Virginia City.

He couldn't have foreseen Sage finding out,

Sage blackmailing him, Sage going berserk with jealousy.

The jailhouse door opened and Ross let the newspaper collapse in front of him. He saw Johnny Tibbits, the young telegraph operator, stepping in.

"That editor let you have it pretty good," the boy said.

Ross forced one side of his mouth into a smile. "Nobody takes Johnson too seriously."

Johnny glanced at the jail cells. "Is that the robber you shot in the Golden Sage?" he asked, seeing the man with the bandaged face sleeping on a cot.

"That's him. The doc says he's gonna pull through to stand trial."

The young man sat down in front of Ross's desk. "Is it true what the paper says? Is that lady, Sage, your . . . concubine?"

Ross folded the paper with a flourish. "Don't believe everything you read in the newspaper. And don't ask so many damned questions. What have you got for me?"

Johnny drew a Western Union envelope from his pocket. "A telegram came in your code name. A reply to the one I sent to Georgia for you yesterday."

Ross straightened suddenly and glanced at the prisoner in the cell. He put his finger over his lips to caution the boy. He took the envelope handed to him and opened it hastily.

Ross! Heard from Julia recently. Wrote from Denver to say you were killed on Crazy Woman. What has happened? Reply!

"You all right, Sheriff Colby?" the boy said. The sheriff had stared at the telegram long enough to read it three times. Then he had looked blankly at the wall. Then he had read the telegram again.

"Huh?" Ross said, springing to his feet. He paced to the gun rack, put his hand on his Henry rifle, walked to the jail cell, looked at the wounded prisoner.

"What's it mean?" Johnny asked.

Ross felt Julia's warmth in the telegram pressed against his palm. The boy's words got to him as he moved aimlessly to the window to look toward Denver. "It's all in code," he said. "It has to do with some outlaws I've been after a long time. You don't tell anybody about this, you understand?"

"Yes, sir," Johnny replied. "You want to make a reply?"

"Does Denver have telegraph service yet?"

"No, sir."

"No reply, then." He could scarcely think for the wild fluttering in his stomach.

"Anything else?"

"No, that's all." He heard the boy get up and open the door. "Wait, Johnny. Has the Wells Fargo stage left yet?"

"No, sir."

"Tell the driver to wait for me. Tell him I'll be there in ten minutes."

"Yes, sir."

"And, Johnny. After I leave, deliver a couple of messages for me. Deputy Green's out on the road to Last Chance today, scouting for sign of the Hermit Bandit. When he comes in, tell him I had to go to Denver on urgent business. Tell him somebody's tryin' to jump my mining claims up Gregory Gulch. And give the same message to Miss Sage. Tell her she'll have to start the spring charity drive without me."

"Yes, sir," Johnny said.

Ross grabbed his gun belt and slung it around his hips. "Hurry! Hold that stage for me!"

Johnny tried to bound through the doorway, but ran into the barrel chest of Parkhill and bounced back into the jailhouse.

"Sorry, sir. Excuse me."

"Watch where you're goin', boy," Parkhill said as Johnny skulked past him and ran out of the jailhouse. Wink came in behind him, his eye twitching like a bug in an ant bed.

"What do you want, Parkhill?"

"I want to know what in the hell you're doin' about that damned old bandit."

"Got Fritz out lookin' for sign right now."

Wink laughed and went to the jail cell to look at the wounded prisoner.

"Hell, Fritz couldn't track a stuck pig to the butcher. You're the one reads sign so damn good. You ought to be out there yourself."

Ross slapped his hat on. "There's more than one kind of sign to read." He forced his arm through a sleeve of his coat.

"What the hell is that supposed to mean?" Wink said.

Ross grabbed the door handle.

"Where are you goin'?" Parkhill said. "I ain't done talkin' to you."

The sheriff looked back and forth at the two men. "All right, I guess I'd better tell you what's goin' on, just in case I don't make it back alive."

He glanced at the man in the cell and motioned for Parkhill and Wink to step outside.

The sheriff looked up and down the street before he started talking. "There's been a stage robbery in Colorado that sounds like the work of our old hermit."

"How the hell would you know what's goin' on in Colorado?"

"The wire, Parkhill. Don't you know anything about telegraphs?"

"I used to ride guard on the telegraph. Hell, I used to fix the damn thing."

"I'm sure you did," Ross said sarcastically. "The point is, I just got a telegram from a Colorado lawman about this stage robbery and he thinks he has a lead on the bandit. I'm goin' down there to help catch the old codger."

"Colorado?" Parkhill said.

"Makes sense. Our road agent probably went to spend your gold down there and couldn't resist doin' a little business while he was at it. Now, if you'll excuse me, I have to grab a few things and catch the stage."

He could barely keep from grinning as he turned his back on Parkhill and headed for his cabin. The long winter was over and he was heading south into spring and summer. Julia was waiting for him down there. Poor thing. She had been grieving for him almost two years now. Oh, to see the look on her face when he found her. He could almost feel her now. They would start over again. Head for California. And he would never see Parkhill, Sage, or Virginia City again as long as he lived.

TWENTY-NINE

WHEN ROSS ARRIVED at Denver, he felt every mile he had traveled in the small of his back. For day after solid day he had ridden the rollicking stagecoach, stopping only to eat and change teams. He had slept with his feet on someone's shoulder, someone else's head on his knee, one arm dangling out of the window.

But Julia was near. He knew it. There was no time to rest now. He had to find her.

"Hey, partner," he said to the man unhitching the mule team. "Who's the law here?"

"That'd be Sheriff Hector Beauchamp. Everybody calls him Heck."

"Where can I find him?"

The harness man pointed. "His office is on Broadway."

There had been more than enough time to think

on the trip south, and Ross had decided to go to the local law first. He knew virtually every permanent resident in Virginia City, so he figured the lawman here would know his town equally well. If this Heck Beauchamp could tell him where to find Julia, it would save him a lot of snooping around in hotels and boardinghouses.

He felt dizzy walking down Broadway, passing the slower pedestrians, listening to the rattle of buckboards and buggies. He wondered if it was the long trip or the prospect of finally finding his wife that made him so light-headed. Passing a dry-goods store, he glanced at his reflection in a large plate-glass window. God, what a sight. Would Julia recognize him? Maybe he should clean up before he actually approached her. Get a bath and put on a clean suit of clothes.

He saw the sign over the sheriff's office and broke into a trot. He angled across the street, dodging traffic. He stomped up the steps and reached for the knob before he saw the scrap of paper closed in the crack of the door: "Out to Lunch."

He pulled his watch from his vest pocket. Sheriff Beauchamp employed rather liberal luncheon hours. It was almost two o'clock. His eyes spotted a barbershop across the street. There was an option. Trim the hair and beard, watch for the sheriff's return. Why not? If Beauchamp had not returned by the time he left the barbershop, he would find Julia on his own.

Ross ran in front of a milk wagon and leaped to the barbershop door. "Howdy," he said, looking over the shop as he stepped in. A one-chair outfit. The barber's hand hovered around the head of a dandified customer, scissors snipping like some chirping bird.

"Have a seat," the barber said. "Be with you in a minute."

He took off his coat, sat in a chair that gave him a view of the jailhouse. He picked up a copy of the *Police Gazette*.

"You gonna take a little more off over the ears?" the customer said.

The barber sighed. "I ought to charge you double every time you come in. You take twice as long."

"I look twice as good when I leave," the customer replied.

The scissors snipped, then paused. "You mean half as ugly."

Ross glanced through the window. Busy out there. A man in a big hat approached the sheriff's office, but walked on by. Ross turned the page as if he had read it.

The scissors chirped for a while, then clattered against the counter. The barber picked up his hand mirror to give the customer an all-around view. "How's that?" he asked.

The customer craned his neck, inspecting every angle. "Put some of that oil on," he said. "The smelly stuff."

"Smelly stuff, huh? Where you goin'?" He rubbed a splash of tonic between his soft palms and stroked it onto the customer's hair.

Through the glass, a man stepped into Ross's view and seized his attention as if in a hawk's talon. He knew the look of a lawman. A glimpse told him that was Hector Beauchamp.

With a grin, the customer yanked the apron

from his neck. "Someplace where the service is more cordial than here and you get more for your money."

Like a flash of blinding light, Julia appeared at the lawman's side. Ross froze, the newspaper lurching with every mighty throb of his heart. He wanted to call to her, but his breath was stuck in his chest. For a moment he floated in halcyon bliss. Then an unnamed panic began to grow.

"Not if you complain as much there as you do here." The barber laughed and took the customer's money. "You're next, mister."

Ross stood, but he hadn't heard the barber. Heck Beauchamp had his arm around Julia's waist. Julia was carrying a child. A little squirming toddler. The customer passed in front of him, disrupting his view.

"You're next, mister," the barber repeated.

"Who is that?" Ross asked, pointing.

The barber looked past the painted letters on his window. "That's Sheriff Beauchamp."

"I mean the woman," Ross said.

"His wife," the dandy replied, easing a derby down over his new haircut. "Julia Beauchamp."

The couple stood at the door to the office as Beauchamp put his key in the lock. Julia smiled at something he said, carried the baby inside as he opened the door for her.

"Hey, you're next," the barber said. "You gonna sit down or not?"

Ross grabbed his coat and stepped outside, bumping the smelly dandy out of his way. He stepped into the street, heard someone holler, saw a horse veer from him. He stopped, traffic passing in front of him, behind him. Through the sheriff's

office window, beyond the reflections of false
fronts across the street, he saw Julia move as he
had seen her in a thousand dreams. He walked
blindly into the path of a delivery wagon, hardly
noticing the horse that balked to keep from running into him.

"Watch where you're goin' there!" a voice
shouted.

He stepped onto the boardwalk and peered
breathless through the window. Beauchamp's
back was turned. His arms were around Julia.
She was turning her cheek, pushing against his
chest. Ross felt his hand move to the pistol grip of
his Remington as his anger reached an instant
boil.

Her smile shined through the dusty window-
pane. She moved the baby to her other arm,
slipped a hand behind Beauchamp's neck. She
kissed him.

His grip felt feeble on the revolver. She hadn't
waited. She hadn't searched. She hadn't mourned
or grieved or cried. She had taken up with a lawman. No wonder he had found no trace of a Mrs.
Ross Caldwell. She was Mrs. Hector Beauchamp
now. Judging from the size of that child, she had
been Mrs. Beauchamp for quite some time.

The door opened, and he turned away, standing
at the street as if waiting to cross. He gathered
his shoulders and hunched his back, partly to disguise his build, partly to ease the stranglehold in
his stomach.

"What time is supper?"

"About six o'clock."

Her voice brought a tear to his eye.

"What are we havin'?"

"Oh, hush. We just ate lunch. You just be home on time."

Ross heard her shoes tap down the boardwalk, and they seemed to slow for a stride or two as she passed behind him.

"*Adiós*, honey," Heck said.

THIRTY

HE WOKE NOT knowing where he was. For long minutes he stared at the strange ceiling above him. Oh, yeah, Denver. The dim light of day shone through the window. Had he slept a night, or a night and a day? Was it dawn or dusk?

Rolling out of bed, he sat up for a few minutes, then walked to the window. He saw bright sunlight on the mountains west of town. It was morning. He tasted paste in his mouth, remembered the saloon and the things he had learned about Hector Beauchamp from his drinking companions.

What a nightmare. In his dream he had killed this Beauchamp, the tall sheriff with the handlebar mustache. Shot him in the back. But when the sheriff fell, Julia was standing there with the baby. The bullet had gone through the man, hit the baby, the mother. He had killed them all. What a horrible dream.

But as the dream haze lifted from his thoughts, the reality struck. He remembered the barber and his customer talking. He hadn't heard them at the time, but he recalled every word now. The customer was talking about going to a whorehouse. He wanted scented hair tonic. He and the barber had joked with each other as if there were nothing wrong.

But something had gone terribly wrong. Julia was kissing the sheriff. Heck Beauchamp: man hunter, tracker, detective, county sheriff, deputy U.S. Marshal.

He got dressed, left the hotel. He had no appetite. Maybe because he could smell himself. He hadn't bathed since Montana. He stopped to look at himself in a shop window. The mining camp beard put ten years on him. His clothes held a cloud of trail dust.

He didn't know where he was. The sun was high. He smelled leather, looked at the lettering on the window: "High Plains Saddlery." His eyes focused on something beyond. An angry face looking back at him. He barely heard the voice through the glass:

"Go on, git out of here. Move on, you tramp!"

He must have stood there longer than he thought. He looked for the mountains, got his bearings, wandered back toward the middle of town. He recognized the stagecoach office and remembered that he had left his bag there yesterday. He checked. It was still there.

He should buy a ticket to somewhere, he thought. But where? Virginia City? Why? What did he have there besides a job and a lot of trouble? California? No. Not without Julia. Texas? New Mexico? Georgia? Remember Georgia? Before the war? The honeymoon, the simple plans they had made.

There was a saloon across the street. A whole row of saloons. Maybe a drink or two would help him decide.

From his table at the window, he saw the stage-coaches come and go. Black Hawk, Dodge City, Santa Fe. He had to go somewhere. He couldn't stay in Denver. A hazy thought had dogged him all day. He saw himself shooting Hector Beauchamp dead right in his own office. The foggier this saloon grew, the clearer the image became. If he didn't get out of Denver he would get one of those impulses that always got him into trouble.

He poured another shot into his glass. No one had come near him since he came in. Must be smelling pretty fierce. They probably wouldn't let him on a coach until he cleaned up. A bath and a meal were what he needed. He'd rather sit here and drink. Finish the bottle. Hell, you paid for it.

The muffled rattle of another coach came through the pane, and he glanced to see where it had come from. What the hell?

Cage upon cage rode atop the coach. Poultry cages four tiers high. Ross had seen that kind of shipping crate on trains and farm wagons back East, each one carrying a live turkey or chicken. But wait. Those weren't birds in those cages. Those were . . . Cats!

And there were more cages inside the coach! Cats to the ceiling! Cats in the boot! Through the dust he saw graceful waves of red and yellow lettering on the coach door:

Fort Worth and Jacksboro Shortline

Two cats were squalling. Fort Worth? Wasn't that in Texas? A crowd of boys appeared in the dust of the coach as the team of six came to a stop.

Only now did Ross look at the driver's face. If it wasn't a black man! The driver set the brake and jumped down from the seat, the tails and cape of his long blue coat flying behind him, affording a glimpse of a side arm holstered butt-forward on his left hip. He coiled a rawhide whip as he turned to smile at the boys running up from behind.

Ross left his whiskey on the table and stepped through a crowd of onlookers on the boardwalk.

"Sorry, boys," the black man was saying. "These cats is headin' north. No, I ain't got no dogs!" He laughed. "Don't want none, either." His ambling felt brim shaded a close-cropped beard and two sharp eyes.

"Where did you get all those cats?" Ross asked.

"Caught 'em in Dallas and Fort Worth. Strays. They got more cats than they knows what to do with down there."

"Where are you takin' 'em?"

"Virginia City, Montana Territory. Folks up there got rats like a dog got fleas." He laughed again.

"How did you find out?" Ross said.

"It was in the newspaper. Virginia City got 'em a telegraph while back and the first telegram they sent says 'Send cats!' God have mercy! Must be rats up there like dust on ol' Brownie!" He slapped the rump of his wheelhorse, raising a cloud of alkali.

"Mice, too," Ross said. "You can get fifteen dollars a head for those cats. Maybe more for the toms."

"You been to Virginia City?" the driver asked, taking a more discriminating look at this stranger.

"I'm the law there. Sheriff R.W. Colby."

The driver narrowed one eye, glanced Ross up and down.

Ross brushed his lapel. "I've been on the trail some time after a road agent."

"Cyrus Rose." He jutted a hand toward Ross. "Call me Cy. When you goin' back to Montana?"

"Directly, I guess."

"Be happy to have you ride with me." He swept his arm toward the high seat overlooking the team. "Be obliged, in fact. I don't know the trail."

"Hey, boy."

Ross and Cyrus Rose looked back at the coach to see a burly red-haired man poking a finger into one of the cages. A pearl gun butt gleamed inside his coat.

"Give me this big ol' tom."

Cyrus put his hands on his hips, casually sweeping the blue coat back. "Sorry, mister. Them cats ain't for free. Fifteen dollars a head."

The redhead sneered. "Like hell." He drew back to strike, smashed the poultry crate open with a forearm and fist.

Ross saw Cyrus square himself with the redhead and put a hand on his Colt revolver. As the redhead reached into the cage, the big tomcat hissed, wrapped both forepaws around the hand, and sank its teeth into the thumb.

The Colt sprang from Cyrus Rose's holster as the big redhead hollered and slung the tomcat to the ground. The animal hit on all fours and kicked dirt in its first leap for freedom, but the stage driver's Colt sprayed fire and black smoke, rolling the tomcat in a bloody heap.

"You'll pay me for that cat," Cyrus said, covering the man with his Colt.

The redhead clutched his bitten thumb in his left hand and glared at the muzzle of the pistol.

"What's the trouble here?"

Ross looked through the gun smoke to see Heck Beauchamp trotting toward the coach. He felt his muscles tense, yearned for the grip of his Remington.

"This man just bought hisself a dead cat," Cyrus said.

Heck looked at the redhead. "Buck?"

Buck snorted with hatred, whistling his breath through his nostrils like a maddened bull. "The son of a bitch's got mad cats, Heck. That one bit me."

Heck looked at the dead cat on the ground. "Stranger, you can't expect a man to pay for a cat if you shot it dead. What's a man gonna do with a dead cat?"

Ross found his voice, took a big step forward. "Either he pays for it, or you arrest him for tryin' to steal it." He felt his eyes glaring at the lawman.

"Now, who the hell are you?" Heck said.

"Sheriff R.W. Colby. I'm here to escort these cats to Virginia City, Montana."

Looking over his sights at the redheaded Buck, Cyrus could not keep himself from grinning.

"Escort for a load of goddamn cats?" Buck yelled.

"Well, Buck," Heck said, "Montana tends to breed peculiar folks, but they generally mean what they say. Now, you've got a lawman here who can testify you stole a cat if you won't pay for it. The choice is yours. I'd just as soon you paid for it and get it over with."

Buck heaved a sigh that made his lips flap. "Oh, goddamn it, all right, Heck. Goddamn cat-freightin' black-assed son of a bitch, anyway." He pushed his bleeding hand into his pants pocket and pulled out a handful of coins. Sorting out three five-dollar pieces, he tossed them onto the dirt at Cyrus's feet.

"Pick 'em up!" Ross ordered. "Pick 'em up and hand 'em over proper."

"Now, that's all right, Sheriff," Cyrus said, resting the hammer on his Colt. "I don't mind stoopin' to pick up my pay." He slid his Colt into the holster and bent at the knees to reach for the coins.

As the coach driver's eyes turned to the ground, Ross saw the redhead reach into his coat for the pearl handle. He brushed his own coattail aside and groped for his Remington.

Beauchamp's big fist snapped upward and slammed into Buck's nose, then opened as it swept down and slapped against his pistol grip.

Ross began to pull, but found Beauchamp's muzzle swinging up on him as Buck hit the ground on his back and Cyrus's coach whip played out behind him in his left hand.

"Easy, men," Heck said. He glanced between them.

Trembling, Ross took his hand off his pistol grip and pulled his coat over it. He was stunned by the fast draw, enraged and shamed.

Heck put his gun away. "You two headin' for Montana anytime soon?"

Cyrus began coiling the whip. "I got to dope the axles, trade for a fresh team, and get some meat to feed this livestock, but then we'll be gittin' out of here faster than a rooster with socks on."

Heck looked at the Montana sheriff. If eyes could damn a man to hell, he thought . . . Hello, Satan! That was one lawman who didn't like to have a gun pulled on him. "I'll keep Buck locked up until you're on the trail." He glanced at the cats and shook his head. "Good luck."

Fighting an urge to test the nightmare he had dreamed last night, Ross watched the big sheriff lift the redhead to his feet and lead him away from the coach.

"I'd like to get a bath and a change of clothes before we leave," he said after Heck had gone.

Cy nodded. "Like the preacher told me, 'Cleanliness is next to godliness, because that devil's one dirty son of a bitch!' "

THIRTY-ONE

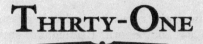

Ross DIDN'T MENTION it for three days on the trail, and Cyrus Rose, not knowing this sheriff well, avoided stirring him up with a lot of talk. Cy had been teaching the lawman to drive the team, and Ross had the reins in his hands when the subject finally came up.

"Whatever possessed you to shoot that cat?" he asked.

Cy laughed loud above the jingling chains and crunching wheels. "That cat was gone, anyway. Figured I might as well make him talk."

"I didn't hear him say anything."

"Ol' redheaded peckerwood Buck sure did. Cat say, 'Look here, Buck! Brother Cy don't go that route. Brother Cy don't give up nothin' that easy!'"

"Brother Cy sure shoots straight."

The coachman laughed as he whistled his whip through the air and cracked it over the team. "See, you heard that dead cat talk!" The stage approached the top of a long grade. "Don't nobody take something I call mine that easy. If it's worth me havin', it's worth me fightin' for it. That's one thing, Sheriff. Brother Cy ain't afraid of no fight."

Ross shook the reins as the divide passed under the wheels. "That Sheriff Beauchamp sure pulled that gun out quick."

Cy whistled, remembering. "Punched the man in the nose and grabbed his gun before the man hit the ground!" He braced his boot heels on the footboard as the coach rocked down a hill. "Now, that's a lawman!" He glanced at Ross, saw the eyes flashing, and decided to speak no more on the subject. Professional jealousy, he assumed. This R.W. Colby didn't like being beat to the draw.

Two days later, they came down from the Medicine Bows and camped on the North Platte. Cy was cleaning cat cages in the river when he looked up the bank and saw Ross standing on top of the coach, waving a handkerchief, looking out over the vast grasslands of North Park.

"Oh, shut your mouth," Cy said to a cat protesting the water running across the bottom of the crate. He looked up again and saw Ross kneeling on top of the coach now, holding his Henry repeater, still waving the handkerchief. Curiosity got to him, so he crept up the bank to see what the white man had in mind.

Between the wheels of his coach, Cy spotted a white patch of fur standing above the grass, and focused his eyes on a pronghorn buck approaching cautiously, still a couple of hundred yards away. The crooks of the black horns stood above a set of bulging eyes that seemed fixed on the waving handkerchief. Cy knelt and watched as the creature came nearer. Then the Henry erupted and the antelope dropped from view.

"There's dinner," Ross said, tossing the repeater down to Cy.

"How'd you know he'd come up?"

Ross stepped from the seat to the rim of the front wheel and sprang to the ground. "I hunted 'em when I was in the army at Fort Laramie. One fellow I knew there used to bring 'em up by standin' on his head and wavin' his feet. They're curious devils."

Cy walked with the white man toward the downed pronghorn, anxious to try a fresh antelope steak. "You was in the Union Army?"

"For a while."

"You sound like you come from down South."

"I do. Georgia. It's a long story."

Cy wanted to hear it, but he had just seen where curiosity had gotten the antelope.

"How 'bout you?" Ross said. "How'd a black man from Texas come by his own stagecoach?"

"Bought it from old Boss Rose. I was born a slave in Louisiana. Boss Rose bought me when I was a boy and told me he'd let me buy myself free for a thousand dollars. He paid me a little on his farm there, where I worked, and I made extra money fixin' harnesses and stuff."

Ross was stretching his neck to see the dead antelope in the grass. "If he wanted you to be free, how come he didn't just let you go?"

"I asked him that one day. He said, 'Cyrus, ain't

nobody gonna give you nothin' in this ol' world, now you might as well learn how to work for it.' I was free five years before the war."

They came to the carcass of the antelope and stood over it for a moment. Ross pulled his knife from his gun belt scabbard.

Cy knelt and grabbed the rough black horn of the buck, the first he had lain his hands on. "Well, it ain't like a deer, and it ain't like a sheep," he said. "It's somethin' like a goat, I guess." He looked over the sleek coat of the animal. "No, it ain't no goat, either. He just is what he is." He helped Ross roll the animal on its back and held two legs up so Ross could make the cut up the belly.

"You didn't say how you came by the coach," Ross said.

"Ol' Boss Rose had him that stagecoach. Had him a store and a freight line and a farm, too, but I wanted to drive that stagecoach. So I asked him, after I bought myself free, if he'd hire me on to drive it. He said I could earn my way up to it if I tried, and he started me driving a freight wagon. Little buckboard. Well, that was all right, but them mules was slow, and I wanted to sit up high and pop that whip at them horses, you see. So I stayed with it, and kept pesterin' ol' Boss Rose, and after three or four years, he let me try it."

"You must have liked it," Ross said.

"Sheriff, I thought I was God's reason for wheels. When I felt them six horses get up, I knew what I wanted. I bought that stagecoach when the war started and moved it west. Made the run from Fort Worth to the Butterfield Line in Jacksboro twice a week. Did all right, too, but I got tired of driving that same ol' road. I hear there're lots of new roads in Montana and lots of miners headin' up 'em, so here I am."

"With a load of cats," Ross said, groping through the viscera of the dead antelope. "You want these innards to feed 'em?"

"Just the choice pieces. I don't want to ride with no gut eaters." He watched as Ross cut the heart out of the antelope. "You don't eat no chitlins, do you, Sheriff?"

Ross looked up at him and chuckled. "I haven't yet," he said. "But you never know what life will serve up for you next, Brother Cy."

The next day they came over a roll in the prairie to find a mounted Ute warrior waiting near the road. As they passed, the warrior paced them, slowly closing. Ross glanced at his rifle once, but kept his hands away from it. The warrior had a bow case and an arrow quiver slung across his shoulder, but the bow wasn't strung and the Indian merely seemed curious about the strange cargo lashed to the top of the coach.

It wasn't until the warrior veered away and disappeared that Ross noticed the look set on Cy's face. "What's wrong, Brother Cy? Haven't you ever seen an Indian before?"

Cy glared. "I can show you places where Comanche arrows hit this coach. Hell, I can show you where one hit me." He handed the reins to Ross and pulled his trouser leg up over his left calf to reveal a jagged scar. "Iron point stuck in the bone. The doctor in Jacksboro had to get the blacksmith to pull it out with a pair of tongs."

"Comanches bad down there?"

"They sure was during the war. The Union

Army pulled out, you see, and the Comanches took back a lot of land they'd been beat out of. Raided Jacksboro so much that half the people left. Didn't hurt my business none, though, because most of the other shortlines out of Fort Worth quit runnin'."

Ross shook the reins and crooked his left wrist to steer the lead horse back into the wallowed-out ruts. "Well, these aren't Comanches up here, they're Northern Utes. As long as we don't go shootin' at 'em, they'll probably let us be."

"I don't want no trouble with 'em," Cy said, sweeping his eyes across the vastness of the park. "Ain't no place to hide out here, and we ain't got that much ammunition."

"We could always stampede the cats over 'em," Ross said. He smiled, then chuckled, the laughter easing for a moment the hollow sickness of Denver in his stomach.

THIRTY-TWO

AN HOUR BEFORE sundown, they saw the Indians coming. The dust trail in the sky clearly showed their path out of the Park Range.

"Looks like a bunch of 'em," Ross said.

"I'd say twenty or twenty-five," Cy replied. "How far is the next stage stop?"

"It's up on the Muddy. Too far to outrun 'em. We'll just have to take our chances."

As the riders closed on the stage road, Ross handed the reins to Cy and picked up his Henry, resting the butt on his thigh so the barrel would stand in the air as a warning. "Is your shotgun loaded?"

"Always."

The Indians cut across the grasslands and waited on the road in front of the coach.

"You're the coachman," Ross said. "What do we do?"

"Stop. If it comes to shootin', we can aim better standin' still. We can't drive through that many Indians, anyway. Too easy for them to take a horse down." As he approached the warriors, he reached under the seat for his scattergun and let the team slow to a trot. "Be friendly, but don't give 'em nothin'. If they want somethin', make 'em trade."

As the coach rolled up to them, the warriors spread out and engulfed it. Ross noticed that their bows were strung, but none had taken an arrow from a quiver. He pressed his back against the poultry crates and guarded his side of the coach as Cy watched the other.

"I don't know too much about these Utes," Cy said. "But if they're anything like Comanches, I'd say they ain't lookin' for scalps today. They ain't painted much. Their horses, either."

"Maybe they're just curious. We are a strange-lookin' outfit."

The warriors had been circling the coach, speaking freely to one another, and studying the cats. One poked at a cat with the end of his bow. A bunch at the back of the coach burst into a short fit of laughter over some mumbled joke. Ross recognized the rider they had seen earlier in the day, caught his eye, and nodded to him.

The warrior nodded back and said something.

"What?" Ross said, shrugging.

The warrior pointed at the cats, spoke again, made an eating sign, pointed at the men on the coach.

Ross and Cy glanced at each other, grimaced.

The brave smiled, gestured at the cats again, and tossed his head in an inquiring gesture.

"He wants to know what we're gonna do with 'em," Cy said. He handed the reins to Ross and slowly put his shotgun back under the seat. "You watch 'em. I'm gonna try to get along with 'em."

He climbed down from the coach as the Indians gathered on his side. Ross started to complain, but felt more comfortable with all the warriors bunched together, so he let Cy handle it his way.

"Now, there's a big town," Cy said, pointing down the stagecoach road. Some of the braves looked down the road, but none of them understood. Cy used the same finger he had pointed with to make a line in the dust on the side of his coach.

"What are you doin'?" Ross asked.

"Drawin' Virginia City," he said, finishing the roofline and front door of a cabin. Next to it, he drew another cabin, and behind them, more rooftops and chimneys. He pointed again down the road. One of the braves nodded and spoke to the others.

"Now we're gittin' somewhere," Cy said. Beside the town he made a drawing of a rat: a big rump, two small ears, a pointed nose, a long tapering tail. He looked back at the Indians and they grunted, nodding at him.

Cy pointed at the rat drawing, then pointed at the ground, his eyes bulging. He charged the point of ground, began stomping in circles as the Indian ponies withdrew nervously. Finally he ground his heel in the dirt and grinned at the warriors, swelling with pride.

The Indians chuckled at him, spoke loudly to each other.

Cy picked up his invisible dead rat by the tail, flung it over the coach, and dusted his hands against each other. Suddenly he flinched, his eyes locking onto another point of ground. He charged the spot, stomped it to death. Then he spotted another, pointed at it. Another under an Indian pony. Another between the coach wheels. More rats overhead, underfoot, everywhere. He stomped crazily as the Indians laughed. He tore at his hair, threw his hat, and finally gave out in exhaustion.

But his eyes brightened as he conceived an idea. He pointed at a cat in a cage, and with his next breath, became the animal himself, hunching over, prowling. He was hunting—taking several quick steps, then crouching, his eyes riveted to the picture of the rat he had drawn on the side of the coach. When he was close enough, he sprang, flinging himself against the side of the coach. He scuffled for a few seconds, then made out like he was eating something. When he stepped away, the Indians could see that his rat drawing had been wiped out.

"Now I got 'em with me," Cy said, looking up at Ross. He gestured toward his coach loaded with cats and beamed with pride. Now he was a coach driver again, bouncing on the seat, cracking his whip over the team, shaking the reins. He spotted something ahead and pointed. He broke character just long enough to point to his drawing of Virginia City, then he was with the coach again, driving into town.

"Whoa!" he said, pulling back the reins.

The Utes found this hilarious, saying, "Whoa,"

to one another, and mocking Cy's exaggerated motion with the reins.

But Cy was into the next scene, waving at townspeople, shouting voicelessly for them to come out of the houses and stores, showing them his cats. He had to stop somebody who got too close, however, and he held out his hand, pointing at his open palm with a finger of his other hand. He smiled, closed the fist, and stuck it in his pocket. Now he took an invisible crate off the coach and handed it to the customer.

He sold another cat, and another, continued to stuff money into his pocket until his pocket would hold no more. He filled up both front pockets, both hip pockets, and began stuffing money in his shirt.

Finally he sold the last cat, waved at his customers as they left. He breathed a sigh of exhaustion, fanned himself with his hat. He smacked his lips as he surveyed the street. He spotted something, pointed, and smiled wide.

Swaggering, he strode without moving. He pushed open a pair of double doors, nodded, shook hands, talked, laughed. He took some money out of his pocket and slapped it down. His hand cupped and lifted something. He raised it to his friends. It seared his nostrils when he smelled it, but he threw it down his throat, anyway.

The Indians yelped as Cy's eyes widened and his tongue lolled out. He gripped his throat as he gasped for air. He pounded a fist against his chest, placed a palm gingerly upon his stomach. Finally he squinted, shook his face with a growling kind of moan, and grinned glassy-eyed. He snatched another handful of money from his pocket, slapped it against the bar, and held his glass out for a refill.

The Ute raised their bows and ripped the prairie air with a war whoop that shivered Ross's spine and tightened his grip on the reins. Then something came over him and he reverted to battle. The Rebel yell growled somewhere deep, began to come up with a rattle, breaking into a squeal.

The Indians stared up at him as Brother Cy climbed up to the seat. In the silence, Ross looked around and saw the vast grasslands in spring green. Not a tree in sight, save for the vague darkness of the forests on the distant mountains. The wind whipped a feather on top of a warrior's head.

Cy took the reins. "Do it again, Sheriff. You got 'em!"

Ross stood and raised his Henry overhead. He sucked in an intoxicating breath of sage-scented air and let the Rebel yell tear at his windpipe again. He screamed his defiance at the world; at life, fate, and at the whole damned West.

A chorus of Ute squalls rose to join him and he fell back against the cat cages as Cy cracked his whip between the horses. The warriors rode as escort for a mile, then turned for the Park Range and rode away as if mounted on antelopes.

Cy let his worries go on a breath. "Them Indians know firewater," he shouted over the rattle of the cargo.

Ross nodded, his rifle bouncing on his thighs. He felt as if he were driving a hundred miles an hour back into Virginia City. Cy was saying something else to him, but he wasn't listening. What was he going to do about Sage, about Parkhill, about Heck Beauchamp? Oh, what on earth was he going to do about Julia?

Do I remember holding her? Yes, I do, but it means almost nothing now. I remember her skin, her scent, her vital embrace. Remembering isn't enough. A man who holds just a memory holds less than thin air.

THIRTY-THREE

THIS MIGHT BE a good road for you," Ross said. "Virginia City to Butte." They were only a couple of hours from town, passing troops of miners returning on foot to the Alder Gulch diggings.

Cy waved at the men who stopped on the side of the road to stare up at his strange cargo. "I thought the placer mines was playin' out up at Butte."

"Not really," Ross said. "There's still some traffic up that way."

"I've heard good things about Last Chance Gulch," Cy said. "Ain't that the biggest strike in Montana now?"

"The Parkhill Line already runs to Last Chance. Twice a week."

"Then I'll go every three days," Cy said.

Ross shook his head. "You don't want to mess

with Parkhill. He's mean, and he's Old South. He wouldn't take well to you competing with him."

"I don't care," Cy said. "The man can't be no meaner than a Comanche."

Ross rode a quarter mile in silence. He caught himself inspecting the telegraph line as they flanked it, as if he were still a Galvanized Yankee charged with keeping it intact. "It's different up here," he finally said. "Parkhill had a franchise on the Last Chance Road. The government did away with the franchises, but he still treats the Last Chance route as his private toll road. He's trouble and everybody knows it. Folks pretty much stay out of his way."

"Well, Sheriff, Brother Cy don't step out of no-body's way—Old South, Northwest, or in between. If the best diggin's is in Last Chance Gulch, that's where I mean to run my line."

"The diggin's are just as good at Butte. Leave Last Chance alone."

"Say!" Cy shouted to a clot of miners taking a break alongside the road. "Where you gentlemen headin'?"

"Last Chance!" they shouted as the coach passed.

"Good luck!" Cy yelled, then turned to grin at Ross as his whip cracked like a rifle shot. "I ain't the kind to let no Parkhill back me down, Sheriff. You ain't, either. Not the way I saw you stand against the lawman in Denver." He laughed. "You got mad right quick when he come up, Sheriff. Brother Cy got a temper, too. I go after what I want. Damn a man who tries to stop me."

"Even if it gets you killed?"

"I ain't afraid of dyin'. I'm afraid of not livin'."

"Ain't that the same thing?"

"I'm talkin' about not livin' while I'm alive. Ain't no Parkhill or nobody else gonna keep me from goin' after what I want long as I'm breathin'.'"

Ross wasn't big on philosophies, but he found he could grasp this one. What did he want out of life? Julia. She was the only thing he had ever worked or planned for, and now she belonged to somebody else while he rode shotgun for a load of damned cats. He had let Hector Beauchamp stand between him and the only thing that made life worth living. Cy was right. A man could die years before he stopped breathing.

The coach hit a rock in the road and almost lurched Ross over the side. When he clawed back onto the seat he had made up his mind. He was going to do something. He would not let Julia forget him so conveniently. He wasn't afraid of dying. Not now that he had lost everything worth living for. The only thing left in his life was to get Julia back, or die trying.

When they reached town, an instant throng formed behind them and followed, cheering, down Wallace Street. Ross had sent a wire about the cats to Fritz from Salt Lake City. Apparently, Deputy Green had alerted the town.

"Well, Sheriff," Cy said as he pulled the reins in at the jailhouse. "You got us here, and we only lost one head of livestock. I'm obliged to you."

Ross smiled, shook the coachman's hand, and climbed down to the ground.

"Where did they come from?" Johnson asked, having just lumbered up with his notepad. "Did they come all the way from Texas?"

Cyrus began hawking his cats on the spot, but

the sight didn't compare to the show he had put on for the Ute near the Park Range.

"Ask the cat-wrangler," Ross said, turning away. "His name's Cyrus Rose."

"Welcome back, Sheriff!" somebody said.

Ross nodded as he pulled his bag out of the carriage boot. He found Fritz Green standing at the door to the jailhouse. "Howdy, Fritz," he said. "Any trouble?"

"The usual," Fritz said. "A lot of drunks. A few fights. One of 'em was at the Golden Sage."

Ross felt the burden of Sage again. "What happened?"

"One of the girls quit. Said she was movin' to Last Chance. Miss Sage accused her of sneakin' off to meet you in Colorado, and she tore into the poor little thing like a bulldog. I thought I was gonna have to throw her in jail."

Ross entered his office, sighed, and dropped his bag on the floor. He put his rifle on the rack. That did it. This had gone on long enough. He was tired of having his life run by Parkhills and Sages and Beauchamps.

"How'd your trip to Colorado go?" Fritz asked. "I heard you were goin' to check on some mines, then I heard you were goin' to investigate a stage robbery. Now you come back with a load of cats. What happened?"

"Let's just say the trip was a total loss," Ross said. "Except for the cats." He looked through the window, saw Cy exchanging a caged cat for a pouch of gold dust. Then a shadow covered the glass and Parkhill's face appeared.

"Colby!" the big man said, stepping into the jailhouse. "Did you catch the bandit?" Wink stepped in behind him, his afflicted eye under the calming influence of valley tan.

Ross smirked and plopped down on his desk chair. "Damnedest thing. Turned out it wasn't the same bandit. This was a young fella tryin' to copy our hermit. He wore a white beard made of horse-hair. Ain't that the craziest scheme you ever heard tell of?"

Parkhill spit on the floor. "You mean you didn't do me one damn bit of good?"

The way suddenly became clear for Ross, like sunlight bursting through a cloud bank. Sage wasn't going to be happy with him. Hector Beauchamp was likely to murder him. And Julia was either going to hate his guts or love him more than ever. But Ross was ripe for a desperate course. "I wouldn't say the trip was a total loss."

Fritz smirked. Sheriff Colby hadn't made sense to him in months.

"What's that supposed to mean?" Wink said, slurring.

Ross propped his feet on his desk. He could hear laughter outside, and knew Cy had his customers where he wanted them. "Parkhill, I'm at the end of my rope over this Hermit Bandit. What you need to do is hire an expert. You need a detective. And I found one for you down in Denver."

Parkhill angled his eyes to look through the window. He sneered and shook his head. "It's a sorry damn day when a man has to go clean out of the territory to find a decent lawman. Who is this detective you're talkin' about?"

"Name's Hector Beauchamp. He's sheriff there, and a deputy U.S. Marshal. He's the best tracker and investigator in the Rockies. If you really want to catch this Hermit Bandit, I'd try and hire him."

Parkhill looked at Wink. "Ain't it a pity, Wink? Man can't do his own damn job."

Wink belched.

"If I get robbed again, I'll damn sure contact this Beauchamp," Parkhill said. "Hope he's better than you."

"There's just one problem," Ross said. "Beauchamp don't like to leave his wife and baby on any extended trips. So, I suggest you invite the whole family up here. Put 'em up in a nice hotel like a summer vacation. I doubt he'll come without his wife."

Parkhill's indifference showed as he grabbed the door handle. "What the hell are lawmen comin' to, when they won't travel without their wives." He hissed as he opened the door and looked out on the street. "I hope that boy you brought back with them cats ain't plannin' on runnin' that coach to Last Chance Gulch. That's still my road."

"He's been advised of your claim on the road," Ross answered.

"That's all we need is a bunch of free niggras up here runnin' white men out of work. Come on, Wink."

Wink bumped into the edge of the open door on the way out and cussed the carpenter who had hung it there.

When they were gone, Fritz Green went to the door and watched the black man hawk his cats. "Sounds like you had more of a trip than you're lettin' on," he said.

Ross nodded apologetically. "I don't mean to be

mysterious about it, Fritz, but it was mostly personal business."

"Well, it would help if you could keep me a little better informed," the deputy said.

Ross stood and picked up his bag. "I'll try to do that. In the meantime, just stay on your toes." He looked out at the crowd milling around Cy. They were bidding on cats by the head now. "I have a feelin' all hell's gonna break loose around here this spring."

THIRTY-FOUR

H ANDS UP, DRIVER!" Ross waved his double-barrel threateningly, saw the shotgun rider reaching for his weapon behind the seat. "Double-aught comin', less'n you git them hands up, boy!"

Reluctantly, the two Parkhill men raised their hands.

"Throw the box down!"

"Ain't hardly nothin' in it, old-timer," the driver said. "You picked the wrong coach to rob."

"Ain't gonna be hardly nothin' left of your head if'n you don't throw it down!" Ross growled. He could tell the driver was right when he lifted one end of the box with one hand and tipped it over the edge of the coach. It didn't matter. He wasn't after gold this time. He just wanted to goad Parkhill into summoning Hector Beauchamp.

"That's all there is," the shotgun rider said. "Just let us go now, and we'll leave you be with it."

"Pick up them reins!" Ross ordered. "Now, git, and don't look back less'n you want to meet the devil!"

The driver reached for the leather, whistled at the team, and started off down the slope.

When they had gone far enough, Ross dragged the box into the trees and picked up the pry bar he had left there. A twist or two popped the latch off, and he threw the lid back to find a mere half dozen pouches of gold dust and some mail. Not much of a haul, but it had served its purpose. He was putting the first pouch in his pocket when he heard the running gear rattle.

They were coming back! Panic roared through him like a fireball. Where in the hell had they turned around? He grabbed the last two pouches as he sprang to his feet and sprinted across the road. He made it just before the team came into view at the top of the pass. He slid behind a clump of sumac and turned to get a glimpse of the coach.

A large patch of bright red paint glistened through the underbrush. That was no Parkhill coach!

"Whoa, team!" the baritone voice sang. "Which way did he go?"

That was Brother Cy's voice! What the hell was he doing on Parkhill's road?

"He dragged the box over here!" the Parkhill driver shouted.

Cy leaped down from the seat. "See if you can

pick up his trail. I'll take my lead horse loose and try to chase him down."

Ross's breath burned his throat and his heart throbbed against his stomach. He craned his neck to read the yellow scroll lettering through the underbrush. What did it say? The Last something. The Last Chance ...

THE LAST CHANCE EXPRESS

"He left his shotgun!" the Parkhill man yelled.

Ross looked at his empty hands. Damn!

"Son of a bitch! It ain't even loaded!"

A couple of passengers got out of the Last Chance Express and began helping Cy with the lead horse.

"The footprints go across the road!" the Parkhill driver yelled.

Ross turned away and picked a quiet path on the pine needles. He had moments to get to his horse. Then what? He knew Brother Cy. That man would come after him hard. He broke into a sprint as he pulled off the old jacket. He tore the horsehair beard from his face and stuffed it into a sleeve. He could see his horse grazing in the clearing below.

He dropped the suspenders from his shoulders and collapsed as he reached the blanket he had spread on the ground earlier. The boots came off none too quickly and he wriggled out of his oversized pants like a man in an ant bed. He slipped the boots back on and yanked the laces tight, neglecting to tie them, stuffing them into the boot tops. He rolled the blanket sloppily around the fake beard and hermit costume.

He heard Cy's big lead horse coming as he tied the roll on behind the cantle. Glancing across the clearing, he sprang into the saddle, kicked his horse. No time to check for evidence left behind. Brother Cy was almost in sight.

Ross rode recklessly down the slope, weaving among trunks of young pines, bowing his hat brim to whipping branches. His mount would have the advantage in speed over Cy's, but what if Cy could read sign? He had to think of something. And quick.

The glint of water caught his eye below, and Ross remembered the stream. An idea began to form. He charged downward, his mount leaping rocks and dead trees. Yes, it might work. He had maybe two minutes to smooth out the details.

Pulling leather at the stream, he made his horse step in. He rode downstream a few yards. No, better to ride the other way. He turned upstream and flogged the hesitant horse with his boot heels, watching his back trail for signs of Cy.

After charging a hundred yards up the stream, he turned back toward the road. He hadn't ridden thirty seconds when he heard Cy's big draft horse crashing through the forest, and angled across the slope to catch him. His first glimpse revealed Cy riding bareback on the draft horse, reaching for the Colt at his hip as he wheeled.

"Hold it, Brother Cy. It's just me!"

Cy eased up on the hemp reins he had tied. "Sheriff! Where'd you come from?"

"I had him, Cy! Damn it, you came along at the wrong time!"

"What the hell are you talkin' about, Sheriff? How'd you get here so quick?"

"I got a tip on the robbery. Somebody left a note at my cabin. Didn't credit it much, but decided to follow the coach a little ways just in case, and sure 'nough, I saw the whole thing!"

Cy slid forward on the broad bare back of the horse. "Why didn't you stop him, then?"

"Hell, I didn't want him to shoot nobody. I let him rob the coach, then I started slippin' up on him through the trees. That's when you came over the pass in that big red coach and spooked him. I saw him cross the road just before you came over the rise. I angled across to catch him, heard you ridin', and thought you were him."

"He ain't far ahead," Cy answered. "I was on him just before you caught up to me. I heard him crashin' through the trees this way."

"Come on," Ross said, spurring his mount in front of the draft horse. "Maybe it's not too late."

They galloped downhill, Ross leading the way to the stream, stopping at its edge to study the water.

"Looks like he riled the water ridin' in the creek. Cy, you go downstream and look for him. I'll go upstream. If you don't find anything, meet me back at your coach."

"Yes, sir, Sheriff!" He kicked his lead horse and lumbered away down the creek bed.

By the time Ross and Cy got back to the Last Chance Express, Parkhill's men had abandoned it and gone on to Virginia City. Ross sent Cy on to Last Chance Gulch, then lay tracks in the woods to bolster his story. It was dark when he finally got back to town, and he found Parkhill and Wink waiting for him when he rode down Wallace Street.

"Did you get him?" Parkhill asked, turning convulsively to spit over his shoulder.

"No. He gave me the slip somewhere up a creek."

Parkhill stomped his feet like a five-year-old. "Goddamn, Colby! You had him in sight, on foot, and you still let him get away!"

"He got mounted and got away. I would have had him if Cyrus hadn't come along."

"Who the hell is Cyrus? You mean the colored boy? What the hell was he doin' there, anyway? I thought you warned him about my road."

Ross resisted looking back at his bedroll. He wanted to check it to make sure no white horse-hair was sticking out of it, but it was better not to draw attention to it. "It's called competition, Parkhill. You'd better get used to it."

"Used to it, hell. I'll get rid of it. Anyway, don't change the subject. What about this note you got on the robbery?"

"Somebody slipped it under my door."

"Where is it?"

"In a safe place. It's evidence. So's this." He patted the sawed-off shotgun tied to his saddle strings.

"What else did you find?" Parkhill said, his thin eyes searching the horse. "What's in the bedroll?"

"Blankets. Camp gear. What do you think?"

"What did you carry that for?" Wink said, his eyes blinking on every word.

"I was ready to stay on the bandit's trail for days if I had to. But, like I said, he lost me up a creek. I was that close, too." He put this thumb and forefinger almost together in the air.

"Shit," Parkhill muttered. "I doubt you even seen him. If you can't catch the old bastard with somebody tippin' you off, Colby, you're worthless. I'm gonna bring in that Marshal Beauchamp from Colorado."

Ross shrugged. "If he'll come. He might not want to leave his wife and baby."

"Then I'll tell him to bring 'em, damn it. Anybody's better than you."

Ross frowned. "Look, Parkhill, I want this bandit caught just as bad as you do. That's why I recommended Beauchamp. He's a specialist. In fact, I'll tell you what I'll do. I'll contact him for you. He knows me."

"You sure you can handle it?" Wink drawled.

Parkhill smirked. "All right, Colby, you take care of it. It's the least you could do."

Ross nudged his horse up the street. He had to get to his cabin. Sage was waiting for him. He had to hide the gold, manufacture the note he had told everybody about. Then he had to get rid of Sage and compose a dispatch to Hector Beauchamp. What might happen after that was anybody's guess.

Parkhill put his hand on Wink's shoulder when the sheriff had ridden out of earshot. "Wink, how would you like to get stinkin' drunk tonight?"

"Planned on it."

"I want you to hit every saloon in town. Spread

the word that the Vigilance Committee has met
and issued a warning."

"About what?"

"About the Last Chance Express. Anybody
caught ridin' it's liable to get lynched right alongside its black-assed driver."

THIRTY-FIVE

HECK HAD BEEN so considerate on this trip, Julia thought. Stopping a full three days in Salt Lake City for her and Fay to rest. She kept telling him that it wasn't really necessary; that she could travel just as hard as he could and keep going till they got there. She thought of telling him about how she had ridden and marched with the 11th Ohio Cavalry from Leavenworth to Laramie, but talk of her days with Ross always made Heck grind his teeth.

Those memories were hers to cherish in silence. Of course, when Fay got older, she was going to tell her all about her daddy, and Heck would just have to take it. She wasn't going to pretend Ross had never existed.

It was raining and the coach was stuffy with the canvas covers rolled down over the windows.

They flapped a little when the coach rocked, letting in a gust or two of fresh air with the raindrops. The mud had slowed them down some, but they would make it to Virginia City soon. Heck had insisted it was going to be as much of a holiday as a job. Julia couldn't remember the last time she had had a holiday.

She wondered if this would be a regular part of life with Heck. She hoped so. Denver could get dreary at times, and she tended to get mired in memories. She liked seeing new places. In fact, it was she who had talked Heck into coming here.

"I don't really know this R.W. Colby," Heck had said. "Met him one day in town with a load of cats headin' for Virginia City. He was a little testy that day. I'm surprised he wants me in his territory."

"I say we should go," Julia had answered. "It doesn't sound dangerous. The bandit's an old man. Anyway, it's going to get hot here, and I'd rather stay cool in the mountains."

The whip cracked outside, and the driver forced a rattling yell up his throat. Julia nudged Heck, who was snoring on her shoulder. "We're almost there," she said.

Heck pulled himself up on the coach seat, curled his handlebar mustache. "Already?"

Julia rolled the canvas. She didn't care if she got wet, she was going to have a look at this town. The first thing she caught sight of was a collection of ramshackle huts with floodwaters coursing among them. My Lord, she thought, say this isn't the town. But the people looked different, dressed in unfamiliar garb. One wore a hat like a dish. Why, if they weren't Chinese.

A row of log cabins swept by, then a frame

building. Now a brick store. This was more like it. The coach sloshed mud as it rounded a curve and rolled between rows of two-stories. She saw a laundry, a drug emporium, a photographic gallery. The team slowed as it passed the newspaper office, then stopped near the portico of a large hotel.

The driver jumped down and threw a board between the coach and the hotel steps. Heck squeezed past Julia and jumped out into the mud. He steadied her as she climbed out with her child and walked along the board to the shelter of the portico.

"I'll get your bags," the driver said. "You folks can stay dry."

It was chilly here. Crisp and clean-smelling. She had never been this high, and she noticed a peculiar shortness of breath. It made her slightly dizzy.

"You Hector Beauchamp?"

Julia turned with a start. She knew that voice. Looking into the darkness of the hotel lobby, she saw a big man emerging. Camp Marshall came rushing back at her through the months. She retreated a step, felt Heck's strong arm against the small of her back, held Fay closer to her breast. She hoped her daughter wouldn't wake now to see the likes of Sergeant Parkhill.

"I am," Heck said. "Who are you?"

"Name's Parkhill. It's my stage line the old bandit's been robbin'." As he reached for Heck's hand, his eyes angled to Julia and locked on her.

"This is my wife, Julia Beauchamp," Heck said.

"*Your* wife?" He glared at her. "Lady, I know you. Camp Marshall. You was that boy's wife." He snapped his fingers, trying to remember the name. "You washed uniforms."

"That boy's dead," Heck said, sounding perturbed. "The Cheyenne got him. She's Mrs. Beauchamp now."

Julia felt faint. Her mind had long since pushed thoughts of Parkhill aside. But seeing the big conspirator here now made Ross come alive again.

"Howdy, Sheriff Beauchamp."

My God! She was hearing his voice! Blinking as she gaped into the lobby, she saw the familiar cut of his shoulders materialize from the shadows. She was seeing him now, in this bearded lawman! That was his face in the mass of whiskers! His swagger! Her dead husband's hand reached for her live husband's, and they shook.

"Mrs. Beauchamp," he said, looking right at her, glowering, touching his hat brim.

That was him! Her knees trembled. Ross's eyes cut angrily from her, to Heck, to the baby. She felt Heck's arm tighten around her waist as she saw the ghostly-white woman appear at Ross's side. A grin parted the black beard and Ross's arm took in the corseted waistline. He pulled the woman hard against him, and the woman put a familiar hand on his shoulder, smiling eerily for no reason.

"I'd like y'all to meet a lady friend of mine," Ross said. "This is Sage. Sage, this is Heck Beauchamp, and his wife . . . Julia."

She glanced at the red lips against the pale cheeks, the full bosom heaving from the fancy low-cut gown.

"Miss Sage," she heard Heck saying vaguely, as if far down a canyon. Parkhill's suspicious glare rushed by her as if she were back in the coach and rolling past him. She felt Fay squirm, tried to lock her elbows under Ross's daughter. She glimpsed the side of Heck's face, a dark curl against that woman's bare neck, a brown stain at the corner of Parkhill's mouth.

It all began to whirl, and her knees buckled under her. Ross's black beard grew like a powder blast, engulfing everything in its ugly darkness as she felt herself falling.

THIRTY-SIX

T HE SMUG GRIN dropped from Ross's face when he saw Julia's eyes flutter, and he scrambled to catch her as she fell. She reeled back, protecting the baby even as she collapsed, and Ross caught her inches from the floor on one knee, bumping Sage aside.

"Take the baby," he said to Beauchamp, turning Julia's limp body in his arms. He remembered carrying her across the threshold on their honeymoon. It was different then, her body full of life and clinging to him. Now it was all he could do to keep her from slipping through his arms.

He carried her up the stairs and lay her on the bed in her room, though he didn't want to let go of her. Looking over her peaceful face, he felt a wonderful moment of hope. Then Sage pressed herself against him.

"Miss Sage," Heck said, shoving Fay into Sage's arms. The baby had slept through it all, but was opening her eyes now, shedding nameless dreams.

Sage held the child awkwardly as Heck sat on the bed and patted Julia's face.

"Here," Sage said, abruptly handing the little girl to Ross. "I'll get some water."

Fay looked at Ross and began to cry, trying to push herself away from him. Somehow, he knew to cradle her upright, to give her arms and legs freedom, to let her see her mother lying on the bed. He pulled the soft white blanket back from Fay's face, bounced her in his arms, felt her tiny hand grasp his finger.

"There, now, honey," he said, speaking smooth as silk. Her large round eyes looked up at him and he smiled. She had a lot of her mother in her, and he liked her, in spite of who her father was.

Julia gasped and looked at the ceiling. Ross carried Fay around the side of the bed and let her crawl to her mother. Julia looked at him, astonished.

"You all right, honey?" Heck said, patting her hand.

"We better go," Ross said. "We can talk in my office later, Beauchamp."

Sage put a glass of water on the table beside the bed and followed Ross from the room. At the door, he stopped and looked back, and he stared at Julia for a moment, suddenly consumed with guilt. Then Sage closed the door in his face.

"Who is she?" Sage said, starting down the stairs.

Ross stopped, looked down on Parkhill in the lobby. "What do you mean?"

"She fainted dead away when she saw you."

"Well, it ain't my fault. Maybe it was Parkhill. He's a damn sight uglier than me. She said she knew him from Camp Marshall."

"She was looking at you," Sage insisted, her eyes contradicting the perpetual smile.

"For God's sake," Ross said, taking her by the arm and leading her down the stairs. "If you ain't jealous of your own shadow. Now, I've got business to take care of over at the jailhouse, so I'll see you later."

"You'd better," Sage warned.

Parkhill joined Ross at the front door of the hotel, where Sage turned for her side of town.

"Is he comin' down?" Parkhill asked.

"As soon as she's feelin' better." He stepped into the rain and ran across the street, feeling the muddy water in his boots. As he reached the opposite boardwalk and turned for the jailhouse, he heard Parkhill splashing behind him.

"I knew this was a bad idea," Parkhill said, "him packin' women and babies with him."

"Once they're settled in, they won't slow him down any." He stomped his feet a couple of times and entered the jailhouse.

"You don't know that woman," Parkhill said, coming in behind the sheriff. "If I'd have known he was married to her, I'd have never hired him."

"What difference does it make," Ross said, feeling irritated, "as long as he gets the job done?"

"She got me thrown in the stockade back at Camp Marshall. Her and the damn Georgia cracker son of a bitch she was married to then. They was spyin' on us old Rebels for the camp commander. Little Yankee-lovin' slut."

Ross's fist clenched quick as a snakebite. He saw Parkhill's square jaw as a target, the big man turning toward him now from the door. His arm was coming around before he could think, the knuckles landing solid against the bulge of tobacco.

The thick neck wrenched to the right, the well-packed quid flying out and bouncing off the jailhouse wall. Parkhill fell against the door he had just shut. His eyes bulged with surprise and reflex anger as his fists came up.

Ross felt the burst of realization, but it was too late now. He tried to follow his first punch with a left. But Parkhill stopped the amateurish roundhouse blow with his right forearm and buried his left fist in the sheriff's stomach. Lunging, he rammed Ross with a shoulder, staggering him back to his desk.

Ross rolled, gasping for breath as he got the desk between himself and Parkhill. He read the warning in Parkhill's eyes as he scrambled around the desk to keep out of the big man's reach.

"What the hell did you hit me for?" Parkhill growled, grabbing across the piece of furniture.

"You shouldn't talk about ladies with that kind of language," he groaned, putting his hand over his stomach.

Parkhill put one knee on the desk. "And you shouldn't try stoppin' me." He sprang onto the desk and leaped like a panther, scattering paperwork.

Ross grabbed the bill of Parkhill's Confederate cavalry cap and pulled down with everything he had, rolling the big man headlong to the floor.

Then he backed off, his mind racing. He could run, but Parkhill was mad enough now to shoot him in the back. He could shoot, but he hadn't resorted to murder yet. Or he could stand up and take a whipping.

As Parkhill found his footing, he came after the sheriff, who he found waiting, fists up, in the middle of the office. Parkhill stepped right into a punch that made his ears ring a little, but otherwise failed to phase him. He snapped a meaty row of knuckles into Ross's eye and felt the instant satisfaction as the sheriff backpedaled into a jail cell door.

Ross kept from falling by holding on to the iron grating. When Parkhill approached, he grabbed the iron bars with both hands, lifted his feet from the floor, and kicked, two-footed, like a mule. One boot heel missed, but the other landed squarely on Parkhill's nose.

Ross saw the blood gushing as the Alabaman staggered back, and knew he'd better follow with something quick. He rushed Parkhill, threw a punch. But the big man blocked it, and Ross found himself stumbling senselessly back again. He felt the grating hit him in the head and the floor hit him in the rear.

The next thing he knew, he was rising, his shirt cutting into his armpits. He felt the blow to his stomach take his wind. He bit his tongue when the fist caught him under the jaw. He tried to fight back, but could see only blurs.

Panic surged through his limbs. He brought a knee up violently and heard a muffled groan. The floor jolted him again, and he knew he was in for it now. He blinked and saw Parkhill doubled over, just a few feet away. He heard a growl like that of a surly grizzly bear and saw Parkhill's glare appear under the bill of his cavalry cap.

A line of gray light appeared behind Parkhill as the big man took one step and kicked hard. Ross moved his head fast, and the boot only clipped his ear. The line of light widened, and Ross focused on it long enough to make out Heck Beauchamp reaching for a side arm.

"Hold it, Parkhill!" the deputy marshal yelled, cocking his revolver. "Back up, or I'll shoot."

"This ain't got nothin' to do with you, Beauchamp."

"I said back up!" Heck ordered.

Ross rolled to all fours and pulled himself up on the grating.

"What's this all about, Colby? You want to make an arrest?"

"Like the man said," Ross answered, his tongue swelling in his mouth, "it ain't none of your business."

Heck looked the two men over and glanced around the office. "Somethin's goin' on here," he said. "I don't like this. You don't act much like a lawman to me, Colby, brawlin' like this."

Ross staggered toward the door. "Don't you Colorado boys ever enjoy a good ol' fight?" He opened the door, stepped outside, and stuck his head under the eave of the jailhouse roof, letting the cold rainwater pour onto his head.

"Not to the point of stovin' each other's heads in." Heck put his revolver in the holster. "Parkhill, do you have an office in town?"

"Over the Break o' Day Saloon."

"Wait for me there, and we'll talk about this

bandit you've had trouble with. I want to talk to Colby first."

Ross heard Parkhill's big boots scuffing the floor as he left for his saloon.

"You up to some detective talk?" Beauchamp asked.

Ross shook the water from his hair and squinted at the deputy marshal through his one open eye. "Yeah, I guess so. How's . . ." He knew better than to call her by her first name, but he couldn't bear to call her Mrs. Beauchamp again. "How's the lady?"

"Well enough to run me out of the room. And a damn sight better off than you."

Ross raked his wet hair back over his head and took a good look at Beauchamp. His knuckles were still throbbing where they had connected with Parkhill's jaw. He had waited a long time to take a jab at the big man, and it had felt good. He almost wanted to laugh.

He caught himself smiling as something peculiar occurred to him. He was beginning to like Heck Beauchamp. The man had a way about him. Ross might have wanted to kill him, but damned if he didn't see things he admired in Julia's new husband.

"I hope we'll all be a damn sight better off when this thing is over," Ross said. "But I'm afraid it may not come that easy. Somebody's liable to get hurt."

THIRTY-SEVEN

D EPUTY GREEN WILL show you," Ross said. "I've got things to do in town today."

Fritz looked up from the shotgun he was cleaning. This was the first he had heard of it. What had happened to Sheriff Colby's promise to keep him better informed?

"Well, let's get goin'," Heck replied. "I want to see where every robbery happened." He jammed his hat down and walked outside.

"Go borrow a horse at the livery, Fritz," Ross ordered.

Fritz put his tools down and grabbed his hat on the way out. Parkhill followed. Ross stood in the jailhouse door and waited for them to mount.

Stepping down from the boardwalk, Heck walked around the back of Parkhill's mount and paused to pull a long stroke down the horse's tail with both hands. He got two long hairs for his trouble and wound them around three fingers as he moved to his own horse. As he passed between the two horses, he noticed a brown streak of something, glistening in the sunlight on the rump of Parkhill's mount.

Turning away, he put the hairs in his pocket and began tightening his cinch. He didn't hold much respect for a man who would spit on his own horse. The horse didn't know better, but the man ought to.

Ross stood at the door until they had mounted and ridden away. He saw Fritz come out of the livery on a little black. He watched them ride down Wallace Street and drop from sight on the road out of town. He waited a minute, then crossed the street and walked down to the Virginia City Hotel. He breezed through the lobby without speaking to the desk clerk, went upstairs, and knocked on Julia's door.

The door opened and Julia's face peered out. She looked so beautiful that he could hardly breathe. Finally she opened the door wider and let him come in.

When he heard the door click, he turned, and blinked in reflex to the open palm rushing at his cheek. He drew a startled breath when he felt the sting, and started to speak.

Julia put her finger over her lips and glanced at the child on the bed. "Shh! Fay's asleep."

"Then what the hell did you slap me for?" he whispered hoarsely.

She gasped. "I don't believe your gall! I know all about you, Ross Caldwell, alias R.W. Colby. I had a long talk with the newspaper reporter, Miss Mary Johnson. She told me all about your scandalous affair with that woman!"

Ross nodded for a moment and shuffled his feet. "Well, I'll tell you one thing. I dang sure ain't *married* to her!" he hissed.

Her eyes sparkled. "If you hadn't deserted me, I wouldn't have gotten married. I thought you were dead!"

"I never deserted you."

"You certain never came back!"

"I did!" he said, taking her arm. "But it was too late."

She yanked her arm away. "I thought I knew you."

He took a deep breath. "Listen. Give me a chance, and I'll explain. That's all I ask."

She crossed her arms and tapped her foot. "Oh, I wouldn't miss hearing it for the world."

He paused to group his thoughts. He wasn't sure he could explain it all to himself anymore, much less to Julia. Start at the beginning, he told himself. One step at a time. "We were at the mouth of the Crazy Woman. Parkhill's men were gonna kill me, and Captain Jones found out about it, so he ordered me to desert and wait in Virginia City. He was gonna tell you where to find me, but the Indians got him."

"Why didn't you come back?" she said, sneering, her hands propped on her hips.

"There was no telegraph here then. By the time I heard about the massacre and got to a telegraph station, you had already left Fort Marshall. I wired back home, but they hadn't heard a thing from you." He paused, narrowed his eyes, and came to something that had nagged him through the seasons without her. "Why didn't you bother to tell the folks back home what had happened? Didn't you care?"

"Oh, hush!" she gasped. "I cared so much I couldn't bear to think of you dead. I refused to admit it, and I refused to write home until I had proof."

Ross glanced around the room in frustration. "What proof? I'm not dead, damn it. What proof did you have?"

"I hired Heck to search for you, and he found some Indians who said they had killed you. They had your weapons."

"What weapons?"

"The Spencer carbine, and the Remington revolver with your initials on it."

Ross's eyes shifted. "Why, that sorry liar. He never found diddly, Julia. I never lost my weapons." He pulled his old Remington from his holster. "Here's my pistol, right here, and there's my initials. I bet you described my guns to him before he went lookin', didn't you?"

Julia stared at the gun grip as if it were a lost memory come alive. "Yes," she said. "But I never thought he'd ... I mean, I never dreamed."

"He lied through his teeth. He wanted you for his own. That explains everything."

She was confused now, angry at them both. They were liars. All men were liars. "It doesn't explain your relationship with that woman."

Ross dropped the Remington into his holster and raised his hands. "She tricked me," he said.

"She trapped me just as sure as Beauchamp trapped you."

"How?"

"She's blackmailin' me. She won't hardly let me out of her sight. She gets jealous enough to fight every time some other woman speaks to me. She's off her rocker, Julia."

"She's blackmailing you?" Julia said. This had the smell of another lie, and her face showed her suspicion. "What's she going to do? Tell everybody who you really are? Turn you in to the army as a deserter?"

"No, she doesn't even know my real name."

"What, then? What has she got to blackmail you with?"

Ross's mouth moved, but he couldn't find words to spit out. "I can't tell you that," he finally said.

"Why not?" she blurted.

"I can't tell you why not, either." He stood in front of her, gesturing uncertainly, knowing she didn't believe him.

She reached for the doorknob. "Then get out. I don't want to look at you anymore."

"But you don't understand."

"That's the honest truth." She opened the door and stood glaring at him. "I don't understand how I could have been so wrong about you."

"But what are we gonna do?" he whispered.

"About what?"

"About us. About Beauchamp. Are you just gonna forget we ever married?"

"I don't know, Ross. God help me, I don't know what to do. Just get out!"

A stranger passed by the open door and glanced at the couple. Ross stepped out, turned back, started to say something. But the door closed in his face. He stood there for some time, considered bursting back in. Then he heard her sobbing through the door, and he turned toward the stairs.

Thirty-Eight

Hᴇᴄᴋ ꜱʜɪꜰᴛᴇᴅ ɪɴ the chair, making it squeak something awful. He looked over his shoulder to see if he had wakened Julia or Fay. They both slept like angels. He turned back to the window overlooking Wallace Street and stared down at the town.

"Don't make a damn bit of sense," he muttered to himself, wrapping three white horsehairs around his fingers.

The light of early dawn revealed three drunken miners staggering arm in arm down the street, singing. Heck turned his ear to the thin pane of glass, trying to make out the words. Ah, yes, "Gypsy Davy." He found their place in the song and sang along under his breath.

"Yes, I've forsaken my house and home
To go with the Gypsy Davy,

And I'll forsake my husband dear
But not my blue-eyed baby,
Not my blue-eyed babe."

"Why are you singing that?" Julia said.

Heck flinched so hard that the horsehairs cut into his tough fingers. "Dang, woman," he said. She had a way of sneaking silently up on a body. "You give me a start."

"Why were you singing that song?" She stood at his shoulder and looked down on the street.

"Just singin' along with the boys," he said, pointing at the trio winding its way down the street. "Didn't mean to wake you up." She had been downright cantankerous ever since he brought her to this town, and he was trying not to rile her.

"You've been muttering to yourself for an hour," Julia said. "What's wrong?"

Maybe this would help, he thought. She liked to talk about investigations. "Oh, it's this Hermit Bandit case. It don't make no sense." He turned his chair toward her.

"What doesn't make sense?" she said, sitting on the edge of the bed.

"For starters, this Sheriff R.W. Colby. He's the one called me in on this investigation for Parkhill, right? Well, you'd think he'd want to help me solve it, but so far he hasn't lifted a finger. Every time I go to talkin' about the bandit, he changes the subject around to Parkhill. Keeps tellin' me Parkhill is a vigilante boss in these parts, suspected of killin' the last sheriff and lynchin' a boy who was tryin' to compete with him on the road to Last Chance."

"Knowing Parkhill, I wouldn't doubt it," Julia said. "He was jailed at Camp Marshall for conspiring to lead the Knights of the Golden Circle in a mutiny."

Heck grunted and nodded. "Him and Colby don't get on good at all. I caught 'em in the jailhouse the other day tryin' to break each other's necks. Parkhill says at first he suspected Colby of bein' in on the stagecoach robberies."

"What?" Julia said. "Why?"

"Because on the days of the first three robberies, Colby was either fishin', huntin', or prospectin', but he never brought back no fish, game, or gold. Then Parkhill found out he'd been carryin' on with this woman, Sage, over at that hurdy-gurdy house. Parkhill figures that's a good enough alibi, but I ain't so sure."

"Why not?"

Heck rubbed the stubble on his chin. "During the first four robberies, the only person who could place Colby was this Miss Sage. So I went to talk to her. Well, she got to carryin' on about how much of a good fella Sheriff Colby is and how her and him have been collectin' money for charity since last year. She showed me the books she keeps for the relief fund, and I'll tell you, Julia, either this is the biggest gold strike since forty-nine or this town is made up of the most generous people God ever put on earth."

"Why do you say that?"

"Sage's books says they've spread thousands of dollars of gold dust around this town to poor folks. I asked a few saloons how much they give to the relief fund a month, and they told me, and I sort of averaged it out and multiplied by the number of saloons and other places in town, and it don't even come close!"

"What does that prove?"

"Could mean Sheriff Colby and Miss Sage have got another source of gold somewhere."

Julia began to see Heck's logic. "You think he's in on the robberies?"

Heck shrugged innocently. "He hates Park-hill's guts. Wouldn't surprise me to find out he's been playin' Robin Hood. And there's somethin' else, too. What was Colby doin' in Denver when I met him the first time? He says he went there to escort that load of cats to Virginia City. But the colored fella, Cyrus Rose, says that ain't so, that he just happened to meet Colby there by accident. Deputy Green says Colby went to Denver to check on some mines he owns down there. Parkhill says Colby went to Denver to investigate a stagecoach robbery by the Hermit Bandit."

"I don't remember any such robbery," Julia said.

"That's because there wasn't one. But Colby told Parkhill they caught that bandit in Colorado and he was a young fella tryin' to pin it on the Hermit Bandit by wearin' a fake beard made out of white horsehairs."

Julia was worried, but she had to smile. Ross could come up with some wild notions. "That's preposterous."

"I ain't so sure," Heck said. "I went out to all the robbery sites. Studied 'em pretty good. I found these in three different places." He unwound the long white hairs from his fingers and gave them to Julia.

She studied them in the light a few seconds. "From the hermit's beard?"

"Them ain't human hairs, Julia. I reckon I ought to know a horsehair when I see one. I've pulled enough of 'em between my fingers."

Julia's heart broke into a gallop. What had that damn fool husband of hers done? "But if Sheriff Colby's the Hermit Bandit, why would he invite an investigator to come up here and catch him?"

"That's the thing that don't make sense." Heck got up and paced the floor in his stocking feet. "He had some other reason for wantin' me here, and I can't figure it out. It must be right in front of my nose, but I can't smell it."

Julia squirmed on the edge of the bed. She knew that look in Heck's eye. He was close. He would figure it out in a day or two if not sooner. "Are you going to arrest him?"

"Not yet. All I have is a lot of talk and three horsehairs. Juries like solid proof."

Julia winced at the mention of juries. "What are you going to do?"

"I've got two angles left. The first is this scattergun Parkhill's men found after the last robbery. If I can link that scattergun someway to Colby, I'll have him."

"What's the other angle?"

"If I can't get anything on the scattergun, I'm gonna go ahead and search Colby's cabin. If he's the bandit, or if he's in with the bandit, I'll find somethin' there. I got a gut feelin' about this Colby, Julia. When a man starts spreadin' a bunch of different stories around, that means you can't believe any of 'em. I think he's lawman and outlaw rolled into one. And he's something else, too, but dang it . . ." He scuffed his foot across an elkskin throw rug. "I just can't quite figure out what it is."

THIRTY-NINE

JULIA DIDN'T KNOW what she would say when she got to Ross's cabin. There was no clear way ahead of her; no obviously right thing to do. Everything had been twisted. Her first husband was a stagecoach robber. Her second husband was a liar. She, herself, was a fool. Maybe it wasn't her fault that she had been made a fool, but she was a fool nonetheless.

She tried to behave as if she were out for a stroll as she passed the prospectors and townspeople on Cover Street. She just vaguely knew where Ross's cabin stood, from Mary Johnson's offhand descriptions and from seeing Ross walk that way from the jailhouse.

When she found a likely cabin near the gulch, she stopped across the street from it, looked both ways, pretended to scrape mud from her shoes as she waited for the street to clear. She walked calmly to the cabin, trying not to attract attention.

She rapped on the door. Ross opened it. He gasped with surprise to see her there, coughing on a cloud of cigar smoke.

"May I come in?" she said, trying to sound civil.

"Of course." He stepped aside and held the door open for her.

"When did you start smoking cigars?" she asked, fanning the sharp odor away from her nose. She felt very awkward here.

"A couple of winters back, in Boulder," he replied, snuffing the ember from the end of his stogie.

They stood in silence for a moment, looking at each other.

"Where's the baby?" Ross said.

"I left her with Mary Johnson."

Ross nodded and shuffled his feet. "Do you want to sit down?" he said, gesturing toward his finest chair.

"No."

"What did you come here for? A couple of days ago you said you never wanted to look at me again."

Julia held her tears back. She had changed her mind about that. She had wanted only to look at him ever since she figured out how Sage had blackmailed him, and how Heck had tricked her into marriage. They had both been played for fools. It still made her sick to her stomach to think of Ross with that other woman, but she knew he had to feel the same way about her and Heck.

"I came to warn you," she said.

"About what?"

"Heck traced the hermit's sawed-off shotgun back to Sheriff Jackson. He knows it had to come from the jailhouse or this cabin. He knows you're the bandit, Ross."

"What? That's the craziest nonsense I ever heard," Ross said. "I'm the law here. I couldn't have ..."

"Oh, hush, Ross. Heck found white horsehairs from your fake beard at the robbery sites. He's going to search your cabin for more evidence in the morning."

Ross stared at her, put his palms on his face, and rubbed his eyes.

"Why, Ross? Why did you steal all that gold?"

He let his arms fall to his sides. "I didn't keep any of it. I spread it around to the poor folks. That damned Parkhill was runnin' things around here with his secret societies just like he did back at Camp Marshall. I had to do somethin'. I couldn't let him get away with it again. If it hadn't been for him and his Knights of the Golden Circle, I'd have stayed at the Crazy Woman, and I'd be dead and happy right now."

"It's not that bad," Julia said, taking a step toward him.

"It's worse. Every minute I've spent away from you, I've just been diggin' a deeper hole for myself. Now you're married to another man who's gonna arrest me tomorrow. How could it possibly be worse?"

Julia bowed her head to hide a tear she felt

on the verge of escape. "There's only one thing to do," she said. It had just come to her, like a reflex.

"Run like a scalded cat?"

"Yes." When she nodded, the tear came rolling down her cheek. "We'll leave tonight. No, we'll leave immediately." The tears came like a flood current, and she stepped closer to Ross. "I'll get Fay and we'll leave right now."

Ross was stunned, and he wanted badly to go along with her plan, but it wasn't that simple. "I didn't mean you and Fay," he said, taking her uncertainly by the arms. "I meant me. If you and Fay come, Beauchamp will come after us."

"We'll cross the border into Canada," she said, sobbing.

"That won't stop him. He'll go anywhere to get his wife and daughter back."

Julia inhaled a tear, tasted it on her tongue, held her breath as if her windpipe had closed. She wiped the blur of tears away from her eyes and gawked at Ross. "*His* daughter? My God, don't you know?"

Ross glanced around the cabin. "Know what?"

"Fay is *your* child. I didn't even meet Heck until after she was born." She saw wonder and astonishment sweep his face. He might have been a boy looking at a pony or a sinner finding salvation. His eyes moistened. His mouth dropped open, then grinned.

"Mine?" he said. He could see it now. Yes, she did look like him. Or at least like he used to look before the beard and the hard living.

"I thought you knew," Julia said.

Ross wrapped his arms around her, almost

crushing the breath from her in his excitement.
His whole body crawled with fire. "All right,
then," he said. "We'll all go together. The three of
us." He released her, took her shoulders in his
hands, slipped one rough palm behind her neck.
He kissed her, and everything that had happened
since Camp Marshall sank into oblivion.

Suddenly Julia wrenched free and pushed herself away. "I hate you for sleeping with that
woman, Ross Caldwell."

"I couldn't help that," he said, dazed by the sudden turn. "She would have turned me in if I
hadn't done it."

"I hate it."

He remembered Denver. "Well, I'm not real
happy about you marryin' another man, either."

She rushed at him again, wrapping her arms
around him. "I swear I never loved Hector
Beauchamp. I'm sorry, Ross. I've made mis-
takes."

Ross felt his anger subsiding, an avalanche of
cares falling away. "If you've made one mistake,
God knows I've made a hundred." He closed his
eyes and held her, only now remembering how
good it felt.

"How will we get away?" she said, her voice
muffled against his vest. "We'll have to leave right
now. But . . . How?"

"It's Tuesday, ain't it?"

"Yes," she said, looking up at him. "What has
that got to do with it?"

"The Last Chance Express runs today. We can
head north and keep goin' to Canada."

"Can we get a seat this late?"

He chuckled. "On the Last Chance Express? We'll get a seat. Cy hasn't had a single passenger since Parkhill started spreadin' rumors about lynchin' anybody who rode his stage. It's the best chance we've got to get out of town unnoticed and get a jump on Beauchamp."

Julia stepped away from him and pulled her shawl back up around her shoulders. "I'll get Fay and meet you on the coach," she said. She grabbed him by the face and placed a quick kiss on his lips before she turned to the door. Cracking it, she looked out to see if the way was clear. She stepped out, but before she closed him inside, she turned back to him. "If we can get through this, Ross, we can get through anything." She saw him smile, and she closed the door.

She wanted to sprint back to Mary Johnson's boardinghouse room to get Fay, but she restricted herself to a brisk walk. Everything was all right, she insisted. Heck wouldn't miss her till after dark. He wouldn't figure out what had happened until morning. By then it would be too late for him to catch up. It would serve him right. He had been only slightly less devious than that woman—that Sage.

As she approached the corner of Wallace Street, an arm reached from an alley and pulled her in. She gasped, stumbled between the buildings off balance, and caught herself against a wall. Wheeling, she found the emotionless stare of the infamous Miss Sage piercing her.

"What were you doing in there with my man?" Sage said.

Julia felt her heart throb fear. Mary Johnson had mentioned the beating Sage had dealt her for dancing with Ross. She steeled herself, refusing to look intimidated. "None of your business. Get out of my way."

She started out of the alley, thinking how odd it was that this strange woman should smile so serenely at her as she left. She looked toward the street, but saw the sky rush down, felt the hair pulling at the back of her head. She hit the ground, saw a swirl of Sage's skirt over her, and felt the pointed shoe kick her ribs.

Fury flooded into her and she scrambled like a wild animal, lashing out as she found her footing. But Sage somehow reached through her flailing arms, grabbed another handful of hair, and pulled Julia off her feet. She had done this before. She knew tricks. Julia kicked at Sage's shins and caught a glimpse of the doll-like face still smiling eerily down at her.

Suddenly her hand bumped something cool on the ground. As she kicked, her fingers groped for it, wrapped around it. She hurled it, and saw it—a green bottle—bounce off the pale brow.

Julia found a split second to leap, rising to face the dance hall mistress. She stomped on a toe, slapped away a hand reaching for her hair, and punched Sage hard in the ribs. She heard herself growling as she leaned into the woman and shoved, sending Sage tripping backward. She pursued, feeling an advantage, sensing time slipping away. When Sage stopped, she was there, ready, balanced, and certain. She aimed her hard fist at a painted eye and saw Sage buckle under the blow.

Sage sat against the wall, stunned. She put her hand over her eye. Looking up, she saw Julia dusting herself off, walking toward the street. Then Julia stopped, turned toward her, and glared down at her with hatred.

"He never was your man, you *dog*," Julia said. Then she was gone.

FORTY

Cy DRAGGED OPEN the sagging double doors of the barn he had rented and let the evening sunlight swell inside. He was determined to stay on schedule, even if he didn't have any passengers. He had managed to keep running by charging low rates for freight, but even that trade had dwindled since Parkhill began spreading rumors.

He turned back into the barn to inspect his coach, and the sight made him hold a breath. What a vehicle. He cleaned it thoroughly after every run, and it gleamed now in the rays of sunlight slanting through the open doors. Behind six strong horses, it all but came to life.

Reality clouded the bright paint a little as he went about his inspection of wheels and running gear. If he didn't start attracting some passengers soon, he would be out of business in Virginia City.

He had stretched the cat profits about as far as they would go. He hated to let Parkhill get the better of him, but what could he do? He was thinking now of moving his operation to Idaho before it was too late.

He walked around the back of the coach and inspected the luggage boot. The leather was getting a little cracked around the edges. It would have to be replaced before too long. He sighed as he ran his fingers over a pitted iron wagon tire. They were expensive up here. He had never planned on it being easy, but making a living in Montana Territory had proved harder than he had thought.

As he walked past the right-hand passenger door, something unfamiliar caught his eye, leaping from the intricate paint job like a wounded squirrel or something. There, scrawled across his beautiful yellow lettering, painted sloppily in bloodred paint, were three numbers obliterating the word "Chance" on the side of his coach:

$$3-7-77$$

"What in the hell," he groaned. He stood back, put his hands on his hips, and stared at the eyesore. "Don't even make no damn sense."

"Brother Cyrus!" The voice rang clearly through the barn.

Cy walked to the front of the coach to find Sheriff Colby standing across the tongue. "Howdy, Sheriff. Say, what do you know about arithmetic?" He gestured toward the right side of the coach.

"Enough to know I'm gonna make it worth your while to run me to Last Chance Gulch." He tossed a pouch of gold dust to the stage driver. "I'll take every seat if we can leave as soon as you get the horses hitched."

Cyrus caught the heavy leather pouch and forgot all about the nonsensical formula on the side of his coach. "You got yourself a deal, Sheriff."

"Bring your wheelhorses, and I'll start hitchin' 'em while you get the others."

Cyrus left at a trot for his corral, and Ross pulled the doors halfway shut for some privacy. As he lay out the rigging, he kept a watch for Julia and Fay between the weathered boards of the barn doors.

His family came into view finally as Cy was fixing the blinders on his lead horse. Ross felt a current of joy mix with his desperation, and he glanced both ways for trouble through the cracks in the doors. He saw a few people in the street, but nobody seemed to notice anything out of the ordinary.

When she walked in front of the barn doors, Ross pulled Julia in and took Fay from her arms. He couldn't keep himself from chuckling as he bounced his daughter in his arms and grinned at his wife. "How come you named her Fay?" he asked.

Julia shrugged. "I liked the way it sounded with Caldwell. Her middle name's Alice."

"My mother's name," Ross said.

Julia nodded, smiling.

It suddenly occurred to Ross that Julia had a few hairs out of place, and a lot of dirt ground into her clothing. "What happened to you? Did you fall down somewhere?"

"With a little help from your Miss Sage." Her

face hardened as she brushed a wispy hair back from Fay's eyes.

Ross looked up to find Cy staring back at him from the front of the team. He handed his daughter back to Julia and coughed a warning. "Tell me about it later," he said to his wife. "Right now I think you better get in the coach."

"Afternoon, Mrs. Beauchamp," Cy said, catching Julia's eye. "What brings you around this side of town?"

"She's coming with me," Ross said.

Cy watched Ross as he helped the mother and child in through the left-hand door of the coach. "Is Heck comin', too?"

"No," Ross said. "Trust me, Cy. It's best that you don't ask a whole lot of questions on this one."

The stage driver shrugged, and checked the reins running through the rings in the horse collars. "All right. We'll be headin' out directly, Sheriff. Better git yourself in."

Ross climbed in with Julia and sat across from her so he could look at his wife and child. "Where do you reckon we'll end up?" he said. He heard Cy climbing up to the driver's seat.

"It doesn't matter," Julia answered. She felt the team take the slack out of the rigging.

"We don't have much of a choice, do we?"

Julia smiled. "No, we don't. Like the sign says. This is the Last Chance Express."

Light began to fill the coach as it pulled out of the barn.

"We'd better let the shades down till we get out of town," Ross said.

Julia untied the straps around the rolls of canvas on the right side of the coach and let them fall over the windows. Ross turned to the left side and watched the open barn door pass by him as he yanked the slipknot out of the strap holding the canvas up. The roll fell, unwinding, covering the window to the outside world.

Only a glimpse of the street made it to Ross's eyes as the coach cleared the barn door, but with it came the face of Sage. The perfect curls had burst into wads of fluff. The paint had been smeared around one swollen eye. But the born smile, still hinting false serenity, passed by the window just as the canvas darkened the interior of the coach.

Ross slid away from the window, as if from a nightmare, and heard the whip crack as the coach made the turn into the street.

"Did she see us?" Julia asked.

"I don't know."

"What if she followed me here?"

Cyrus was putting on his usual show outside, cracking pistol shots with the whip, hollering at the team.

"Don't worry," Ross said. "She won't tell Heck. She's in it too deep herself now." He moved to Julia's seat, sat beside her, and peeked through the gap between the canvas and the edge of the window. He saw Sage standing in the street, watching the coach pull out of town. He chuckled.

"What could you possibly find amusing?" Julia said.

"You must have used her head for a mop," Ross replied. "She looks like somethin' Brother Cy's cats dragged in."

FORTY-ONE

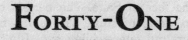

SHE COULDN'T THINK of a way to hurt him enough. This was nothing. This would probably just get him kicked out of the territory. Even if he got sent to prison, he would get out someday. She thought about telling Parkhill, but then it would be over too quick, and R.W. would just be dead. She needed to think of something that would torture him through the years.

"Well," she said. "Aren't you going to do something?"

Heck looked down on Wallace Street from his hotel window. "You're sure you saw 'em both in the coach?"

"Yes, I've told you, I'm sure. It was them. They were together. They had the baby with them. Are you going after them or not?"

Heck nodded, looked at the sky. "I'll catch 'em

before dusk." He took his gun belt from the bed-post and strapped it around his hips.

"Who is she to him, anyway?" Sage said, leaning casually back against the dresser.

Heck jammed his hat down on his head. "She used to be married to him, till he ran out on her."

Sage nodded vaguely. Now he's running out on me, too, she thought, but he won't get far. She wasn't going to let him have that woman, or the baby, or his freedom. That would hurt him, but it was still not enough. She had to think of something more.

"Here's what I want you to do," Heck said, putting his hand on the doorknob. "Go to the sheriff's cabin and pull up the floorboards where he's been hidin' the fake beard and the gold and all. I'll have Deputy Green meet you there to collect the evidence. He'll arrest you and put you in your own custody, then he'll follow me on the road to Last Chance and help me bring Colby in."

Sage nodded and left through the door Heck held open for her. She walked with him down the stairs and through the hotel lobby, quite aware that they were being stared at.

Heck stopped her before he turned for the livery stable. "You're lucky you turned yourself in, Miss Sage. I was plannin' on arrestin' you and Colby both tomorrow. I'll put in a good word for you with the judge."

She walked away unimpressed. All she could think of was hitting R.W. Colby where it hurt. She would have done anything for him. She would have fought off every woman in town, catered to his every desire, lied for him with her dying breath. But he had proven no more worthy than any other man she had ever made the mistake of claiming.

Still, it was different with R.W. He had been kind to her. He had never hit her, or cussed her, or ridiculed her. In a strange way, it made her hate him more than she had hated all the others put together. After that woman came to town, he had brushed her aside like an insect.

Oh, that woman's words had echoed around her since the moment they were spoken: "He never was your man, you *dog*."

She knew how to hurt most men. If they were gamblers, you traded some ruffian a few pleasures for breaking a few fingers. If they were swindlers, you went for the face. Nobody trusted a scar or a broken nose. But how did you hurt a gentleman sheriff? How could you make it stay with him as long as he lived?

She found herself at the cabin, opening the door, walking in. She could smell him. She remembered every moment they had shared here. Looking back, she realized that he had been one step from bolting the whole time. She had been a fool to think she could hold on to him, though she had tried every way she knew.

"He never was your man . . ."

She lifted one end of the heavy table and swung it aside. Kneeling, she caught the edge of the loose board with her fingernails and flipped it over, revealing the bedroll below the floor. She picked it up, dropped it on the table.

She was getting ready to untie the rope around the bedroll when a glint in the light from the window caught her eye. He had left his lawman's trappings in a pile on the chair. Leg irons, handcuffs, jailhouse keys, and his shiny sheriff's badge. She remembered fogging the badge with her breath, polishing it with a lacy cuff.

"... you *dog* ..."

The hemp rope around the bedroll was a new one, and its stiff bristles pricked at her tender fingers like thorns. She unwound it from the blanket, slipped the noose off, and spread the blanket roll across the table, revealing the evidence. She leaned over the hermit costume, clutched it in her hands. She settled facedown on the table, her cheek against the fake beard, her breast upon a half dozen pouches of gold. She had made him put the outfit on one night, almost laughing at the way he looked in it.

And where was he now? She pushed herself away from the table, taking the rope in her hand as she stepped back. How did you hurt a man who risked his life to rob money for poor people? What was his weakness?

She slipped the noose of the rope around her wrist and drew it tight. Something he had said one night spoke to her, as if he were floating above her.

"I never wanted to drag you into this. I don't want anybody gettin' hurt on account of me. I couldn't live with that."

She looked up for the voice, saw the log rafters overhead. Now, that might work. She saw his soft spot now: his conscience. Poor tortured soul. It would destroy him. She would have to do it right, though. No backing out. No second thoughts. And she would have to do it now, before Fritz Green got here.

She stepped over the hole in the floor to snatch

the handcuffs from the chair. Glancing through
the small window, she saw no sign of Deputy
Green coming, but knew she might have no more
than a minute to pull it off. She snapped the cuffs
around one wrist and climbed onto the table.

She took the noose from her wrist, pulled one
end of the rope over a rafter spanning the hole in
the cabin floor. She tied a knot and left the noose
dangling six feet above the floor. She climbed
down from the table to move it a foot away from
the hole in the floor. She wasn't going to leave
herself a way out. She might change her mind, try
to step back up on the table. But now it would be
too far away.

"He never was your man, you *dog*."

She hissed at the echo. "Go to hell," she said,
wishing she had said it when Julia was standing
over her.

Glancing through the window one last time, she
still saw no sign of Deputy Green. She put her
knee on the table, climbed back on. She was glad
it was built sturdy. She pulled the noose toward
her, stepped to the very corner of the table. She
had to lean out over thin air to get the loop
around her neck.

Groping blindly behind her back, she closed the
open ring of the cuffs around her free wrist. Now
everything was set. She looked at the sheriff's
star gleaming in the sunlight.

"I'm so sorry," she said aloud. "But you deserve
it." Closing her eyes, she stepped off of the table
and felt the stiff bristles rake her tender skin.

FORTY-TWO

"WE'RE COMIN' UP on Bear Pass," Ross said,
looking ahead through the window as the coach
slowed. "This is where I robbed Parkhill the first
time."

"Hush," Julia said, covering Fay's ears. "Don't
talk about it anymore. You don't know what your
daughter will remember."

"Sorry," he said. "I won't bring it up again. We
can put it all behind us now."

They stared at each other as the team fell to a
walk up the steep grade. Fay reached for Ross's
hat and he handed it to her, chuckling as she bit
the brim.

Suddenly Cyrus shouted something from the
driver's seat and cracked his whip. Ross sensed a
shadow filling the window and turned to see a

man opening the right-hand door of the coach as
it jerked to a stop.

"Colby!" Wink shouted, waving his revolver as
he stepped into the coach. "What in the hell are
you doin' here?"

"What is this?" Ross demanded.

"Is Colby in there?" Parkhill said, riding up
next to the coach to look inside.

"And a woman!" Wink said. "That marshal's
wife. Her baby, too."

Ross ignored the gun and backed Wink out of
the coach. He found three Parkhill men holding
guns on Cyrus, Cyrus with his hands in the air.

"What are you doin' in there with Beauchamp's
wife?" Parkhill said.

"What are you doin' here wavin' guns at this
coach?" Ross demanded.

"Park, you didn't say nothin' about no passengers," one of the men complained. "Especially not
no women and babies."

"Shut up!" Parkhill shouted. "If they can't read
the sign, that's their own damn fault."

"What sign?" Ross said.

"The numbers," Wink replied, closing the coach
door to show Ross. "Painted 'em on there myself."

Ross turned to see the bloodred numerals mar-
ring Cy's fine paint job.

"You the dumb-ass who wrote that?" Cy said
from the driver's seat. "Hell, boy, don't you know
you can't take away seven from three? That's
less'n zero."

"Don't you call me boy," Wink said.

He angled his pistol toward Cy, and Ross
lunged, punching Wink hard in the jaw. As he
reached for his own revolver, he heard Cy shout at

the team, saw Parkhill groping for a weapon. One
of the Parkhill men fired, spooking the team and
the saddle horses. The coach jerked forward.

"Ross!" Julia shouted. "Get in!"

Ross swung his Remington up as he heard a
whip whistling. The leather cut Parkhill's horse
behind the ears and the animal twisted in terror,
wrenching the big man from the saddle. Ross
jumped onto the iron step as the coach began to
roll over the pass.

Cy screamed bloody murder and shook the
reins. Splinters flew from new bullet holes. Ross
fired at one of the gunmen as he passed, saw a
shoulder take the impact. The whip cracked again
and the coach rocked dizzily down the grade.

"Git 'em!" Parkhill yelled, springing from the
ground as his horse bolted back toward Virginia
City. "Mount up, Wink!" His voice grew weaker as
the Last Chance Express rattled away.

Ross looked back and saw Parkhill pulling the
wounded man from his saddle as Wink led a horse
from the trees. "Stay low!" he said to Julia, and
began scrambling to the driver's seat as the coach
bucked over a rock. He heard Fay start to wail.

The team hit the bottom of the grade at a full
gallop, slamming the coach down on its running
gear as it started up the next slope.

"Why didn't you tell me about the numbers?"
Ross shouted at Cy, clawing his way to the seat.

"Didn't know they meant nothin'." Cy cracked
the whip at the team and looked over his shoulder.

"You want me to explain it to you now?"

"I saw the rope."

Ross looked up the road, trying to wish the

coach faster. "What are the chances of us out-runnin' 'em?"

"Up this mountain? We better plan on out-shootin' 'em." He whistled through his teeth. "That baby sure got some good lungs."

Looking back, Ross saw the four riders coming. He had four rounds left in his Remington, and no time to pack new loads or fix percussion caps. His Henry rifle was in his office at the jailhouse. A lot of good it did there. Cy had six loads in his revolver and two in the shotgun. That made twelve rounds. Every third shot would have to count, and from the top of a teetering stagecoach.

Ross waited for them to pull within range, but when he raised his revolver, they split into pairs and took to the trees. He could only catch glimpses of them between the pines. "They're gonna try to get in front of us!" he yelled.

The coach lumbered out of the coulee and began to pick up speed through a level park. The way was flat, but it snaked around big trees, throwing the vehicle onto two wheels as Cy lashed the team harder.

"They're gonna catch us!" Cy shouted. "Just don't let 'em get their hands on the team!"

Ross hunkered down on the seat, catching flashes of horseflesh among the trees over his pistol sights. One of Parkhill's gunmen made a dodge for the team, but swerved back off the road when Ross fired. A blast from behind glanced off an iron strap and sang over Cy's shoulder. Ross wheeled and fired back, but Wink was already angling for cover. Another man burst from the timber for the right side of the coach. Ross missed with his first shot, saw the man's hat fly away with the second, and watched him ride blindly into a low tree limb.

Cy's revolver pealed, and Ross turned to see him fire a second shot under his left arm, the puff of black smoke falling instantly behind.

"Save your loads!" Ross ordered, but he wasted his last in driving Wink away from the team.

As he reached for the shotgun, Ross felt a heavy thud against the coach and saw Parkhill's horse pass the team with an empty saddle.

"Ross!"

It was Julia's voice, a muffled scream from inside the coach. He looked over the right edge to see Parkhill riding the iron step, aiming a pistol into the coach.

"Give it up!" the big man ordered.

Ross saw the hammer drawn back on the Colt, like an ear of an angry outlaw horse, and knew he would risk his wife and child if he tried something. "Whoa, Cy!" he shouted. "They got us. Parkhill's got Julia!"

"Damn!" Cy said, his lips twisting in frustration, his eyes cutting desperately back and forth. Fay's voice fell off with the speed of the coach and faded as Cy drew rein on the team and stopped between two towering pines.

Parkhill's laughter roared. "It hit me about the time I hit the ground back there!" he shouted, looking up at the driver's seat as he jumped down from the step. "She called you Ross. You're Ross Caldwell, you son of a bitch!"

"So I am," Ross said. "What of it?" Nervously he watched Wink move in on the left side of the coach, the third gunman taking a position in front of the team.

"Wink, what we got here is a couple of Yankee-lovers."

"Two white niggers and a black one," Wink said, his eye flickering like a moth's wing.

Parkhill waved his Colt. "Get out, Mrs. Caldwell, or Mrs. Beauchamp, or whoever the hell you are."

Julia stepped to the door. "Don't you hurt my baby," she warned.

"Wait a minute, Parkhill," Ross said, climbing down from the seat. He hit the ground and raised his hands. "I'll make you a deal if you'll let everybody go but me."

Parkhill bellowed with laughter. "You ain't got much left to deal with!"

"Yes, I do," Ross said, glancing at Julia. "You let Cy drive Julia and the baby out of here alive, give 'em a good head start, and I'll tell you who the Hermit Bandit is."

Parkhill's tobacco-stained teeth disappeared as the smile changed to a frown. "You know?"

"Yes," Ross said. "And I'll tell you, if you'll let the coach go on to Last Chance. It'll never come back, and you can have your road to yourself again."

Parkhill chuckled. "Wink, get that niggra's guns and keep him guarded. Charlie, give me your rope and watch these two."

Ross put his arm around Julia and felt her trembling. "What about my deal?" he said.

Parkhill put his pistol in his holster, took the rope from Charlie, and looked up. He searched beyond the top of the coach, beyond Cy, and spotted a good tree limb over the stage, jutting from a huge trunk. "Caldwell, you sorry Yankee-lovin'

Georgia cracker. You can take your deal and go to
hell. When this coach pulls out from under that
black buck and leaves him kickin', you'll tell me
who the bandit is."

"Like hell I will," Ross said. "You hurt anybody
here and I won't tell you a damn thing." He had
felt this way before. The day he was ordered to
march into his first battle. The day he stepped
into the prison yard at Camp Douglas. The day he
saw Heck Beauchamp embrace Julia. But today it
was worse. The rotten dread in his stomach just
kept growing, pushing out all the hope he had
taken north from Virginia City.

"You'll tell me anything I want to know,"
Parkhill said, stepping up on the wheel of the
stage, the coiled rope in his hand. "I don't think
you want to see me hang any white people."

FORTY-THREE

HECK SAW THE riderless horse trotting toward him and reined his mount back to a lope. The loose animal tried to get around him, but he cut in front of it and caught a rein.

"Somebody's madder'n hell at you," he said, habitually looking the animal over for evidence. It took him only seconds to find the streak of brown tobacco juice on the horse's right hip. "And his name is Parkhill." He pulled the new Winchester Yellow Boy rifle from the boot of the empty saddle. "Don't mind if I borrow this, do you?"

Ross Caldwell's wild claims came back to Heck as he spurred his horse to a full gallop northward. If Parkhill really was a vigilante bent on keeping control of this road, the Last Chance Express would be a tempting target, Cy Rose would be a likely victim, and Julia would be in the wrong place at the wrong time right about now.

In a strange way, he felt a small measure of relief. He had been wondering what he would do when he caught up with the stage. Would he shoot Caldwell for resisting arrest? Would Caldwell shoot him? Julia was likely to shoot him, for all he knew. But now he suddenly had a new viewpoint. He was coming to rescue Julia, instead of riding to catch her and her felonious husband.

When he came over Bear Pass, his horse almost jumped sideways out from under him before he saw the wounded man in the road.

"What happened?" he asked, but the poor bastard didn't have enough life in him to answer. The stream of blood running from the dying man's shoulder was only about four feet long, trickling steadily down the steep grade into the coulee. He had been shot just a few minutes ago.

Charging into the coulee, Heck checked the breech of the Winchester and found a live round ready. He hit the bottom of the grade, slacked his horsehair reins, and spurred his mount up the rough trace carved in the opposite bank. His horse was heaving when he came out of the coulee, traveling slow enough that Heck could read the tracks, the coach skidding with speed around a curve, reeling to the left, riding on two wheels.

He passed a horse standing in the road, saw a dead man lying nearby, shot in the head. Parkhill's men were taking the worst of it so far, Caldwell and Rose shooting to kill.

He came to a straight length of road in a level park and spotted the bright red coach at the other end. "There she is," he said to himself, reining his horse back to a walk. His eyes found Julia first. Then they saw Ross beside her, both of them under guard of a gunman. A second gun barrel pointed up at the coach driver.

Heck reined his horse off the road and continued to approach at a walk along the tree line. His left hand gripped the reins with the forestock of the Winchester, his right filled the steel loop of the lever. Lifting, his eyes made out the chiseled frame of Parkhill standing on top of the coach. Then he saw the rope, hanging slack from a tree limb over the stage. The neck he saw in the noose was Cyrus Rose's, the stage driver's hands tied behind his back.

"Oh, my word," Heck mumbled to himself, turning his mount broadside, cocking the Winchester. He could hear Parkhill's booming voice:

"Come on, boy! Tell 'em to git up!" The big vigilante knocked Cyrus down on the seat with an overhand blow, lifted him back up with the rope. "Start them horses, or I will!"

Over the iron sights of the Winchester, Heck found the gunman guarding Julia and Ross. A long shot, offhand, on a heaving horse. He used a few seconds finding the rhythm of the horse's breathing, then began pulling the trigger as he watched the irons drift from the gunman's hat to his gun belt.

The shot made every man, woman, child, and animal on the road flinch, and spun to the ground the man guarding Ross and Julia. Fay burst out in a squall as the dead man hit the ground.

Through the blur of his own blood, Cy saw Parkhill look south, and seized the moment. He threw himself down on the seat and kicked the big man in the midsection with both feet, bowling him off the stage. He felt the team start and rolled from the seat, groping for the reins with the hands tied behind his back. He felt the leather under one finger, but the rope tightened around his neck, pulled him away.

"Whoa," he started to say, but the noose choked it short. The coach drove under him as he stumbled over it, grasping for a way out. He felt the rear luggage rail under his heels, knew the next step would be on air. He leaned back on the rope, tried vainly to draw a breath. The last thing he saw before the whirling fogginess covered him was Heck Beauchamp charging down the road.

FORTY-FOUR

——✦——

Ross had shoved Julia toward the trees and was about to make a dodge for the dead man's revolver when he saw Cyrus swing like a pendulum from the back of the moving coach. Wink was lifting Parkhill to his feet, firing wildly. A bullet cut through the fleshy part of Ross's thigh, feeling as though a fisherman had set a big hook there with a hard jerk. He hobbled, holding his breath for some reason, and braced himself to catch Cy.

He had to dodge the black man's flailing knees as he caught him around the thighs and lifted. It wasn't enough. He could hear Cy choking. Gunshots and hoofbeats were coming from down the road, and still Ross had not looked to see who the rescuer was. He hooked an arm under one of Cy's legs, lifted Cy to his shoulders. He made stirrups of his hands and felt Cy standing in them. He heard a gasp and knew the stage driver was getting air.

He looked for Julia, saw her shielding the baby behind a tree, Fay still screaming with terror. He watched the stagecoach roll down the road, Parkhill and Wink retreating behind it. For the first time, he felt the cross fire. The muzzle blasts appeared in front of him like raindrops splattering in dust. Directly behind him, he heard the rapid fire of a rifle, the growing rumble of hooves.

He felt a bullet slap the leather of Cy's boot top between his arm and Cy's leg. Dirt flew around him as the horse planted and slid. The animal came around, protecting him. He looked up and saw Heck Beauchamp holding the brass-bellied Winchester and the horsehair reins in his left hand. The right hand held a long, tarnished blade.

Heck drew the knife back for a swipe at the lynch rope, but a horrible flinch shook him and blood erupted from his vest. He dropped the rifle and reins, but as he fell, he made the swipe at the rope over Cy's head.

The three men fell in a pile, and Ross kicked his way out from under Cyrus and Heck. He grabbed each man by the collar as he stood, and dragged them toward the trees. Cy helped by pushing himself along with his legs, but Heck Beauchamp was limp.

"Oh, my God," Julia said, taking the blanket from Fay and pressing it against Heck's chest wound.

Ross drew the revolver from Beauchamp's holster, pulled his legs in behind the tree, and looked up the road. He saw the Last Chance Express disappear around a bend, but caught no glimpse of Parkhill or Wink.

"You gonna make it, Cy?" he said, looking back at the stage driver.

"Yeah," Cy groaned, nodding, his back against the tree.

He looked at Julia and found her ear over Beauchamp's mouth, trying to listen over the baby's yelling.

"He says to hold out," Julia said. "Hold out because Fritz will be coming."

Ross looked at the revolver in his hand. "Julia, untie Cy's hands for him. Then watch the road south. Let me know when you see Fritz."

A bullet splintered tree bark, and Ross fired back at a puff of smoke across the road. He saw Wink dive behind a tree and wasted another round. He had four shots left in Heck's revolver, then he would have to use time reloading. He looked at the road to see the Winchester lying on the ground. No telling how many rounds it had, the way Beauchamp had been firing as he charged. The dead man in the road still held a pistol, but Ross didn't know how many live rounds it contained, either.

"Sheriff," Cy said hoarsely, rubbing his swollen neck. "If Fritz don't get here in time, I just want to thank you for keepin' me from hangin'."

"Don't mention it," Ross said, scooting to the other side of the tree to watch for an attack.

Cy started chuckling, his laughter coming out like a wheeze.

Ross looked back at the sorry-looking group he was protecting. Sorry-looking except for Fay and Julia. The two of them were beautiful, and Fay had stopped crying now that the gunfire had let up. He saw Beauchamp's eyes looking alertly from side to side. "Cy, what the hell is so damned funny?"

"The things that cross a man's mind," Cy whispered. "All the time I was hangin' there, sittin' on your shoulders, I just kept hopin' nobody was gonna shoot you in the head. Then I thought, it don't matter, 'cause if they do, I'll hang, anyway."

"That's interesting, Brother Cy, but shut up and keep your eyes open, will you?"

"Can't shut 'em," Cy said. "Thought they was gonna pop out of my head."

Ross heard Heck muttering.

"What's he sayin', Julia?"

"He said to stall them. Give Deputy Green more time to get here."

"How?"

"Talk to them."

"What am I supposed to say to 'em?"

"I don't know," Julia snapped. "Think of something."

Ross sighed. He heard someone scampering, caught a glimpse of Wink, and fired a wild shot. Three rounds left. Julia was right. He had to stall. "Parkhill!" he shouted.

Silence held the mountains except for the rattle of Heck Beauchamp's breathing.

"Parkhill, what about our deal?" Ross yelled. "I can still tell you who the bandit is." He looked back and saw Beauchamp smiling.

"Who?" Parkhill yelled from up the road.

Ross had them both located now. "You ain't gonna believe it when I tell you."

"You're probably right, Caldwell. Try me, anyway."

"It's your right-hand man."

Some aspen leaves rustled faintly on a breeze that came through the park.

"Wink?" Parkhill said.

"That's right," Ross answered.

Parkhill's laughter came bounding down the road like a boulder. "Wink, I'd kill a son of a bitch for talkin' about me like that!"

Ross saw Wink's shadow on the road alongside the shadow of a tree trunk.

"Ross," Julia whispered, "I see Fritz."

"Where?"

"Around the bend in the road. He's already off his horse and sneaking up through the trees."

Ross sensed Wink getting ready to cross the road. "Well, I can't stall any longer," he said. "They keep movin' in. I'm gonna try somethin' else." He held the hammer of Heck's Colt back and rotated the cylinder two chambers, to the last live cartridge, leaving the hammer cocked.

The moment he saw Wink spring out into the road, he leaped from cover and fired. He missed, as he had figured he would. He never had been much good with a handgun. Wink was firing back, but Russ stood his ground and pulled the trigger again and again, letting the firing pin fall on the spent rounds. He stood stupidly for a second, as if he couldn't figure out what had happened. Wink slid to a stop in the road. Ross made a dodge for the Winchester rifle, but the cross fire drove him back to cover.

Fay started crying again when Ross slid to safety.

"What are you doing?" Julia growled. "You almost got killed!"

Ross shushed her and glanced down the road. "Come on, Fritz," he muttered, spinning the cylinder to a live round.

"Park!" Wink's voice said. "I think they're out of shells!"

"Like hell we are," Ross shouted. "We've got plenty of damn shells."

The cruel laughter rolled down the stagecoach road again. "He's lyin'," Parkhill yelled. "Go ahead and move in, Wink. Take 'em alive."

Ross put the barrel of the revolver in his hand and held the butt toward Cyrus. "Brother Cy, how would you like to have the honor of blowin' Parkhill's head off?"

"I'm a little stiff in the neck," Cy said.

"You're still a better shot than I am."

Cy came alive like a miracle cure in a medicine show. He took the pistol, pulled his feet under him, and got ready to spring from his crouch.

"What are you going to do?" Julia asked. "Who's going to get the other one?"

"Fritz, I hope," Ross said. He cupped his hands around his mouth. "Parkhill!" he shouted. "I'm comin' out in the road. Don't shoot. I want to make a deal."

"What are you doing?" Julia hissed.

"Relax, honey," Ross said. "We've got 'em hoodwinked."

"Honey?" Cy said to himself. He hoped he would live to hear an explanation to all of this.

"All right, step out where we can see you," Parkhill said.

Ross looked at Cy. "Don't shoot until somebody else does."

Cy nodded.

"Ross," Julia whispered. She was bouncing Fay on her shoulder, crouching over Heck. "Be careful."

He saw the fear in her eyes and smiled. "Comin' out!" he shouted, raising his hands. He ambled toward the Winchester, looking both ways down the road. For a moment, he seemed to be alone. Then Wink stepped from cover, aiming a revolver at Ross from the hip. Ross looked the other way, saw Parkhill approaching along the tree line. When he glanced back at Wink, he caught a glimpse of Fritz taking position behind a fallen log.

"You don't have much to deal with," Parkhill said, grinning.

"We've still got our knives," Ross said, "and it'll get dark pretty quick. We'll fight to the last man unless you meet our conditions."

Parkhill laughed, and Wink echoed.

"Just out of curiosity, Caldwell, what conditions are you talkin' about?"

Damn it, Fritz, shoot, Ross thought. What are you waiting for? "Let the woman and baby go. Give 'em a horse and a good start north. Then the rest of us will surrender."

"So she can tell everybody what happened here?" Parkhill said. "I don't give a damn about the baby. I'll leave it in the coach. But that little Yankee-lovin' bitch is gonna disappear with the rest of you." Parkhill raised his pistol, looked over its sights. "I'm gonna enjoy the hell out of this."

Ross stuck his hands higher in the air. Fritz needed something. A signal. "For God's sake!" he yelled out of the side of his mouth, trying to make his voice carry in Fritz's direction. "Don't shoot me in cold blood! I'm unarmed!"

He heard the cadence of the slug slamming into Wink's back, followed by the powder blast that had sent it, followed by the first of a dying line of echoes. He was lunging toward the Winchester when Parkhill's shot shattered his shin, wrenching him to the ground. As he crawled on his stomach toward the rifle, he saw Cy jump from cover and fire, catching Parkhill high in the chest.

The big man dropped his pistol and staggered backward three steps before regaining his balance. "Goddamn you, boy," he said, pressing his palm over the wound. He walked deliberately to his Colt and stooped to pick it up.

"Don't, Parkhill," Ross said, levering a live round into the chamber of the Winchester. "You're whipped." He twisted his body a little getting the rifle to his shoulder, sending a streak of pain down his wounded leg.

"Kiss my ass," Parkhill said, rising to his full height, the Colt in his hand. "I've been shot worse than this." He cocked the pistol, angling it upward.

As Ross pulled the Winchester's trigger, he could see the pistol bucking in Cy's hand, and almost felt Fritz's bullet hurling over his shoulder. Parkhill fired a shot into the dirt as the triple load of lead picked him up and slammed him lifeless to the ground.

Julia released a belated scream and sprinted into the road with Fay to fall sobbing on Ross.

"I'm all right," Ross said. "Just a busted leg is all." He rolled over and embraced his wife, her tears joining Fay's in a cascade onto his chest. "Hush, Julia," he said, smearing a tear across her cheek. "You're upsetting my daughter." He looked beyond them to see Cy Rose and Fritz Green looking down on him.

"You gonna live?" Cy said.

"Yeah," Ross answered. "Drag me out of this road before somethin' runs me over. I want to see how Beauchamp is doin'."

Fritz took the Winchester and set it aside. The deputy and the stage driver pulled Ross behind the tree and lay him beside Beauchamp.

"You've got a lot of explainin' to do," Fritz said.

"I know, Fritz," Ross answered. He rolled to his side to look over Beauchamp's face. "I didn't want it to turn out like this, Beauchamp. I'll admit I didn't know how it was gonna turn out, but I never wanted this."

Heck nodded feebly and looked up at Fritz. "Deputy Green," he said, mustering all the strength he had to speak. The mountains were quiet now, except for the baby sobbing, and they could hear him. "Did you speak to Miss Sage?"

Fritz sighed. "Didn't get a chance to. She hung herself in Sheriff Colby's cabin."

Ross stared up at Fritz, then looked at Julia and Cy. When he turned his eyes back to Heck, he saw the deputy marshal give him a curious grin.

"But I found the disguise," Fritz continued. "I'm afraid I'm gonna have to put you under arrest for robbin' stagecoaches, R.W."

Heck laughed, bringing on a weak cough. "You already killed the Hermit Bandit, Fritz. It was Wink. He was stealin' from his own boss. Ain't that a hoot?"

"How do you know?" Fritz said, stooping over the dying man.

He was in it with Sage. It was Sage's job to keep Sheriff Colby busy so Wink could rob the stage. But she wanted all the gold herself, and double-crossed Wink. Tipped the sheriff off, and the sheriff got a glimpse of Wink on that last robbery. We searched Wink's place a couple of days ago. Found the disguise and the gold and hid the evidence in the sheriff's cabin."

"Why didn't you just arrest Wink?" Fritz said to Ross.

Ross stumbled for a moment. "You tell him, Heck."

"I talked Sheriff Colby—Caldwell, I mean—into waitin'. We both wanted to catch Parkhill in one of these vigilante raids, and figured he might not pull one if we distracted him by arrestin' Wink."

"Well, why was R.W. on the coach with your wife?" Fritz asked.

"That's another story," Heck said. "I'll let him explain that one to you."

"Fritz, I've left you in the dark a long time, but you've never let me down. If you and Cy will go find the stagecoach and drive it back here, I'll explain the whole thing to you on the way back to town."

Fritz sighed. "Well, I guess you're still the boss. Come on, Cy, let's catch the horses."

Heck had no strength left to open his eyes, but he could hear the two men shuffle away. "They gone?" he asked.

"Yeah," Ross replied.

"I've always been a hell of a good liar," Heck said. "Used it to my advantage plenty of times.

The mistake I made was I had you figured all wrong, Caldwell. Thought you was some no-'count backslider run out on a good woman. But them lies . . . They catch up to you. Lordy, they catch up in the damnedest way."

"Yeah," Ross repeated.

"I know you don't owe me nothin', but I'd like to ask you a favor."

"What?"

"I want to have a word with . . . your wife. I want to speak to Julia."

"She's right here," Ross said. "Go ahead."

Heck grunted. "Julia."

"Yes, Heck."

"You almost got widowed twice in one day."

Julia just looked at Ross, then out across the park, rocking Fay as she watched the shadows creep into the meadow.

"Come closer, Julia." His voice grew weaker with every word. "I want to whisper somethin' in your ear."

Julia looked at Ross. He nodded. She handed Fay to Ross and leaned over Heck's face, her hair brushing his closed eyelids. Ross let Fay stand on his stomach and held on to her hands. She smiled, her eyes sparkled, and she jumped with excitement, almost squeezing the breath out of her father's innards.

Julia was pulling away from Heck, relief and sorrow mingled on her face.

"What did he say?" Ross asked.

"He didn't say anything," she replied. "He just died."

FORTY-FIVE

"GOOD MORNING, SHERIFF Green," Mary Johnson said. She stepped up behind Fritz and hooked her arm around his.

"Morning, Mary," Fritz replied, lifting the hat from his head. "You come to see the Caldwells off?"

"Yes," Mary said. "Where are they?"

"Getting their pictures made in the photographic gallery." He heard the jingle of trace chains and looked down the street to see Cyrus Rose's bright red coach rounding the corner onto Wallace Street. "Here comes the Last Chance now."

Cy stood on the footboard for show, bracing his legs against the seat. "Whoa," he said, reining the team in at the Virginia City *Post*. "Right on time,

Sheriff," he shouted. "Special charter to Idaho, Utah, and Salt Lake City!"

"Decent of you to make the special run," Fritz said. "Mrs. Caldwell wouldn't want to ride all that way with a bunch of stinkin' miners."

Cy bounded to the street, stepped up on the boardwalk, and greeted Mary Johnson with a bow. "I been needin' to make a run for supplies, anyway. You know how much them freighters charge for haulin' from Salt Lake?"

"High, ain't it?" Fritz said.

"Yes, sir." He turned to Mary Johnson. "Miss Mary, I heard you took over the relief fund."

"That's right," Mary said. "Do you wish to donate something?"

"Well, I'll make you a deal. Passenger service has sure picked up. I got a full coach almost every run. How 'bout if I donate every tenth fare to the fund?"

"That would be wonderful! I need every penny I can get. I don't know how Ross Caldwell did it. I haven't been able to collect half as much as he used to."

"I'll be glad to throw in my share," Cy said, "but you have to do somethin' for me in return."

"What is it?"

"Find a home for a mammy and her seven little young'ns."

"My word," Mary said. "Where are they?"

Cyrus reached for the door handle of the stagecoach. "Right here." He opened the door to reveal a languid cat nursing a row of tiny fur balls no bigger than their mothers' feet.

Mary Johnson gasped with delight and pushed

Fritz aside to get at the kittens. "Fritz, go get a crate or something to put them in," she ordered.

"Put 'em in here," Fritz said, taking his hat off, "and we'll find a place for 'em together."

Cy was beaming. "She thought that would be a nice quiet place to have some babies," he said.

"She don't know the Last Chance Express," Fritz replied.

As Mary carefully lifted the mother cat from the coach, Ross stepped out of the photographic studio and, in spite of the cumbersome crutches under his arms, insisted on holding the door open for Julia and Fay.

Before the family could reach the coach, Johnson burst out of his newspaper office with his pad in his hand, a pencil behind his ear. "Any idea where you'll be going?" the editor asked.

Ross paused to grin into the hat full of kittens. "There's a vacant sheriff's job in Denver," he said to the editor, "and I thought I might . . ."

Julia hit him with her handbag. "We're going to find a town that needs a hardware store," she said.

"You'll write us, won't you?" Fritz asked. "Let us know where you've settled?"

"Sure," Ross said. "It'll be someplace on about a five percent grade."

A look of intrigue crossed Cy's face. "What do you mean by that, Brother Ross?"

"The doc says this wounded leg'll heal a half inch shorter than the other one, and by my calculations, it'll take a five percent grade to keep me from limpin'."

"Till you have to turn around and walk back," Cy said. "Then you're liable to fall all over yourself. You better find some level ground and just limp."

Ross chuckled. "They can have that flatland down below," he said. "I couldn't leave the mountains now. I'll just hitch one stirrup shorter than the other and make do."

The group stood in a circle for a few seconds. Then Mary hugged Julia, the cat in her arm tickling Fay, making her laugh. Ross shook hands all around, then slid his crutches into the coach. He helped Julia step in, hopped one-footed up on the step, and sat opposite his wife in the coach. Cy climbed up to his seat and filled his hands with the slick leather of his whip and reins.

"Good luck, R.W.," Fritz said, holding the hat full of kittens in one hand, shutting the door with the other.

"Same to you, Fritz." He was going to advise his former deputy to watch his back, or sleep with one eye open, or something like that, but decided it would only upset Mary.

The whip cracked and Cy's jubilant voice turned heads, up and down the street. The horses sprang against their collars and started the long pull. Up on the high seat—his feet braced against the footboard, reins between his fingers, momentum already gathering his coattails behind him—Cyrus Rose descended on a clot of miners blocking the street.

"Watch it, gentlemen!" he shouted. With a sure sweep of his arm, he flicked the whip over the team and split the thin mountain air. "Make room!" The vital roll of the coach under him was almost like that of a practiced woman, but longer-lasting and less dangerous. "Last Chance Express comin' through!"

The miners came back together in the dust after the coach had passed.

"That ain't the way to Last Chance," one of them said, watching the coach roll by the turn to Parkhill's former toll road.

Another pulled a fallen suspender over his shoulder. "Hell, they don't know where they're goin'."

But Cyrus Rose knew. Ross knew; and Julia. Even little Fay could sense it. It had no place name, no flat label on a map. It drifted unseen on thin mountain air, eluding every mortal sense. None of them could speak of it, but each felt the Last Chance Express carrying them ever closer.

"Mary and Fritz make a nice couple, don't they?" Julia said, waving to the vanishing group of well-wishers.

"I guess," Ross said. He took Fay from his wife. "They would have made good friends for us."

"Oh, hush. Don't start. That's not the kind of life I want for my family—wondering from day to day if you'll come home alive or in a pine box. We were perfectly happy with our hardware store in Athens, remember?"

Ross sighed. "Barely. Seems like a hundred years ago."

Julia watched the buildings pass outside, the faces of strangers staring up at her. She turned to look at Ross, his face lit handsomely by a slanting ray of sun. He didn't look like a hardware man anymore. Back then he went clean-shaven, his skin smooth and pale. He would never be that innocent again. She moved gracefully across the coach and sat beside him, putting her arm over his shoulders.

"Honey," he said, trying to keep Fay from crawling through the window, "I hope I never have to spend another day out of your sight. Trouble seems to cloud up and rain all over me when you're not around."

"Oh, you're just saying that now," she replied. "A week from today you'll be chewing your leash in two."

"You know I can't tell what I'll be thinkin' a week from now. I'm talkin' about this minute. But if I do go to chewin' at my leash next week, you just put a stouter one on me."

She smiled and stroked the hair at the back of his neck.

"You really think Mary and Fritz make a nice couple?" he said.

"Yes, don't you?"

He shrugged. "They've got nothin' on us. I'm just a free-millin' ore, Julia. I'm not worth a nickel on my own. But you get around me like quicksilver and draw pure gold."

She smiled and clutched a handful of hair on the back of his head. "Except for that silver tongue." She turned his face toward hers and risked a kiss, struggling to keep her lips on his as the Last Chance Express pitched wildly down the road.

Meet your favorite authors at the

WESTERN WRITERS OF AMERICA CONVENTION

JUNE 10–14, 2008
CHAPARRAL SUITES HOTEL
SCOTTSDALE, ARIZONA

Founded in 1953, the Western Writers of America promotes literature, both fiction and non-fiction, pertaining to the American West.

Some bestselling authors who have attended the convention are:

C. J. Box ★ Don Coldsmith ★ Loren D. Estleman
W. Michael Gear and Kathleen O'Neal Gear
Tony Hillerman ★ Elmer Kelton ★ Larry McMurtry

And many, many more!

EVERYONE IS WELCOME!

For more information please visit www.westernwriters.org
and click on "Convention."